HAUNTED WATERS

HAUNTED WATERS

The Phantom Series Book 3

LAURA C. REDEN

CONTENTS

HAUNTED
WATERS
3
LAURA C.
REDEN

HAUNTED WATERS

by Laura C. Reden

The path through the woods was narrow and twisted. The sun had set long ago, and the chill was starting to settle in. So was the mist. It hovered in the treetops like a blanket over the forest, shielding the outside world from what lay within. I'd once thought of this realm as a prison, but I no longer felt that way. If this was a prison, and Walker was here, then I would voluntarily offer my wrists and stay shackled for eternity.

The gravel settled beneath my feet as my pace quickened. I needed to tell my gran about my revelation. I wouldn't be returning home. I knew I could find her ghost in the depths of the haunted forest. It was where the mist collected and stirred in the air, bringing her world and mine together. Unfortunately, it also brought other things, like malevolent, skinless creatures; hauntings of the unseen; and lush, beautiful poison. The unseen was the worst.

I'd thought about it long and hard, ever since the Fourth of July fireworks show. Walker and I had been encapsulated by the glowing embers of falling fireworks. The lake had been illuminated by an aqua light and was no longer a scary place. I didn't have control over this realm yet, but I thought maybe one day I could. I had every intention of learning how to hone my skill and make Baylor the place of my dreams.

Beautiful poison would just be beautiful. Skinless creatures would only be forest critters. And the unseen . . . That would be a feeling of wonder, and nothing else. I'd swim in Baylor Lake again, and instead of manifesting nightmares of people who'd passed, I'd visit with their spirits. It would be a magical place where I could have cupcakes with my gran, and she'd read me her latest novel. I'd swim with the fish all afternoon. And when it was time for dinner, Walker would be waiting for me at the dock with a towel. It wasn't a place that existed yet, but it was a world that I belonged to. All that was left to do was create it.

If I created this magnificent world here in Baylor, under the blanket of mist, then why would I ever want to go back? Sure, I'd miss my parents and my brother, but who's to say I couldn't visit? After all, I could see my gran, and we weren't in the same realm. Perhaps I could go to my family in a dream. And as for my friends, they were here with me; well, most of them. And then there was Walker—the love I'd never known existed. Now that I'd found him, I didn't think I could let him go. What kind of life would that be?

I searched the treetops when I heard crows calling above. They dove, piercing through the mist and swooping back up again, disappearing into the gray blanket of fog. I hurried along the trail, walking even faster than before. The forest at night was not the place for me to be alone. I needed to find my gran, tell her the news, and then get back to bed. I pushed my hands deep into my pockets and pulled my coat across my chest. The temperature continued to drop as the fog slithered closer to the ground. I wondered how much longer it would be before my gran appeared, and I could only hope that it was before the mist settled at my feet—that's when the bad things happened. I checked over my shoulder for the umpteenth time. She was nowhere to be found.

I wasn't sure how to tell her I wouldn't be going home. She'd known it was a possibility when we'd spoken at the hospital. I hadn't known what she'd meant at the time, when she'd said that I would *hopefully* return home, but I did now. This was a tempting world to live in. I wondered if Gran would be happy that I'd decided to stay. After all, I'd get to stay in touch with her. Going home would mean that I'd have to say goodbye to her, and I wasn't ready for that. I doubted I ever would be.

A crow called a long and gravelly warning that sent my eyes searching once again. There was a flash of movement in the distance, but it was only a dense shadow. I fixed my eyes on the path and scurried through the pines. Even though this world was still new to me, and much of it spawned from a nightmare, I felt the power deep in my belly that could grow into something magical. I wanted to see it come to fruition, and I couldn't bear the thought of leaving without having my wildest dreams come true. What lay before me was an opportunity.

Walker and I were going to train every day. Train like we were headed for combat. Like a war was on the horizon. He was working on developing training sessions for me to build what he called muscle memory, but for my brain. I'd learn how to control the dream using a multitude of techniques, and eventually it would become natural to me. I'd train myself regardless, because this was a war I couldn't afford to lose, but if practicing meant I'd be spending countless hours under Walker's instruction, I'd willingly be there all summer. And maybe I'd even fake it a little, so that I could get extra help . . .

A twig snapped behind me. I whipped my head around to see who was there, fully expecting it to be my gran, but it wasn't. A figure stood in the distance, draped in a red cloak. I froze, then took a few steps backward, watching intently and looking for signs that I should run. The crows swooped down again, and my eyes jumped toward one of the massive black birds. In that brief moment of inattention, the stranger had disappeared. I looked all around me but saw nothing. The crows called out in warning, and goosebumps prickled my arms. I started walking as fast as I could, eager to see my gran.

"Going to grandmother's house . . ." the wind whispered.

I wanted to share my news, tell her I was in love, and that my love was a double-edged sword because I would not be returning home. The heavy fog settled into the trees, and with it came a cool breeze that ruffled a loose strand of my hair. The mist curled around my ankles, and I knew that if I didn't see my gran soon, this could very quickly turn into a nightmare.

"Gran?" I called out.

No answer.

I scanned the trees, checking for her one last time before closing my eyes and wishing that I was back in the cabin. I didn't think it would work, but I was getting desperate. As soon as my eyes closed, I again heard the whisper in the wind, "Going to grandmother's house . . ."

My eyes sprang open, and I started to take off toward the cabin. Checking over my shoulder one more time, I saw the cloaked figure hiding behind a thin tree trunk. I stopped, trying to get a better look. A dark crimson cloak poked out from both sides of the tree, and the large hood bowed in my direction. Two piercing eyes glinting in the moonlight were all that could be seen in the blackness beneath the hood. The figure ran from tree to tree, pausing momentarily behind each one and checking to see if it had been noticed. I glanced down the path. Maybe I should investigate. It couldn't have been *that* dangerous if it was hiding from *me*. I'd come into the forest intending to find someone, and someone had appeared. I suppose it was my job to find out who. And why.

I took a slow, measured step off the path, followed by another, venturing into the thick forest. The further I got from the path, the colder it grew, and the fog became denser. The red-cloaked figure took notice of me and scampered more quickly, stopping to peek at me frequently. I hurried after it.

"Wait!"

Laughter wafted through the air and swirled all around me. It reminded me of a time before. A time when I'd almost caught Layla Barns. *Layla.* It was just like a witch's cackle. Was I chasing Layla? I slowed my pace, uncertain. The trail was so far away. My stomach twisted uncomfortably. I shouldn't be this far off the path. Could it be a trap? I could hear her laughter growing. It was all around me. The fog pooled at my feet and began climbing up my shins. I *really* shouldn't be out this far alone. The red cloak appeared behind me, only two trees back, and I saw Layla's face peeking out beneath the crimson velvet.

"Layla?" I asked.

A slow, sly smile appeared on her face. And with a twinkle in her eye, she turned and ran. I darted after her.

"Layla! I just want to talk. I'm not trying to hurt you!" But no matter how fast I ran, she was faster.

I jumped over fallen trees and weaved through the pines. "Wait!"

The crows screamed overhead, and twigs snapped under my weight. My lungs burned. I couldn't keep up. She led me deeper and deeper into the forest—to the deepest parts of my mind. This wasn't a place I wanted to be, a place I ever wanted to know.

"Layla?"

As the woods closed in around me, I realized I was not getting closer to finding my answers, but in fact getting further from them. She was leading me into a trap. I slowed to a steady walk, pinching a cramp in my side, and finally stopped completely. I panted as I looked around, uncertain of where I stood. All the trees looked similar in the darkness. I'd run far enough that I couldn't see what direction the trail was, and I had no way of getting back. My chest rose and fell quickly, as I looked up toward the stars. But there was no midnight map sparkling above; there was only fog.

"Don't stray from the path . . ." the wind whispered.

I swallowed hard, knowing I'd made a deadly mistake. There was something about this girl that seemed familiar. Not just that she was the mysterious Layla Barns, or even the cackle that filled the air around me. It was something that I couldn't quite put my finger on. It was almost as if it was a story I'd heard once before . . .

A massive crow dove at me, swooping in front of my face and missing my cheek by mere inches. I stumbled backward, half stunned, then changed directions. The crow screeched, and I had an odd feeling that it was trying to tell me something. Something I should have known. Something that should have been obvious. In the blinding fog bank, I took a few steps, but halted when the crow swooped again.

I flinched and spun in an entirely new direction. Had it been telling me which way the path was? A single black feather cut a path through the mist as it fell from the sky. Before it hit the ground, I thought of Levi. I wasn't sure how he passed; all I knew was that the crows had taken him away. In the storm's wake that night, millions of pitch-black feathers had fluttered to the ground. *Levi.* I tilted my head toward the treetops, and several shadows flew overhead. There was one shadow unlike the rest. It was magnificent, really. Its wingspan was twice that of the others, and its eyes were so yellow they pierced through the fog. It was the one who had moved into my path when I had lost my sense of direction.

"Thank you, Levi," I whispered into the sky.

I hurried through the pines toward safety. The sinister cackle came at me from all directions. A flash of red here, a flash of red there. She was all around me. And yet, never really there at all.

I didn't know why she hid from me. And truth be told, I wasn't sure I wanted to find her anymore. If I wanted to stay under the Baylor phenomenon spell, then why should I pursue her? I felt obligated to do right by Walker, and help him find his happily ever after, but maybe the best thing for him was not a girl who had run away, but rather a girl who was willing to give up everything just to be with him.

I had been looking for Layla all summer, but aside from the sighting at the Fourth of July parade, she'd kept herself hidden well. And tonight, she had steered me in the wrong direction. If I didn't know any better, I'd say she was dangerous. Perhaps I should be the one running from her.

All I'd wanted to do tonight was tell my gran I'd fallen in love and that I was here to stay. Instead, I was led deep into the woods, chasing a red cloak of ill will and mystery. And then it hit me all at once. The red figure was a symbol, and I was in another fairy tale. That was the *something* I'd remembered about her. Something that was familiar. It wasn't déjà vu. It was a story my gran had read to me, time and time again, when I was a child.

The fairy tales my gran had read to me had always

been the key to finding Layla. But maybe I didn't want to find her anymore—in fact, maybe I wanted to hide from her. She was out here in the woods with me, and I wanted nothing to do with her. The fairy tale wasn't a key to finding answers; it was a warning sign. Gran was reading the stories so I would know how to prepare myself for what lurked around the corner. Poisonous apples, witches, and warlocks hidden in stone towers. I looked over my shoulder, because the only thing missing now was a wolf.

As soon as the thought entered my head, I felt the presence. It had been stalking my every step. Watching and waiting for the moment I grew weak and frightened. Because the moment I let my guard down was the moment it would pounce on me. My heart galloped in my chest. My skin broke out in tiny goosebumps. I trembled, because that moment was right *now*.

A deep, wet growl ripped through the fog, piercing my ears as I gasped and spun around. I shut my eyes tight and held my breath—one that would surely be my last. But the attack never came. Instead, I found myself tangled in my gran's crocheted blanket. My heart was nearly leaping out of my chest, and my skin was covered in a thin sheen of sweat. My wide eyes searched my surroundings. The dark bedroom. The cabin. Again. *Always.*

I closed my eyes, rolled onto my belly, pressed my face deep into my pillow, and I screamed.

CHAPTER 2

I was standing on the back deck waiting for Walker. The morning dew had evaporated, and the air was warm and dry. The daisies were sunbathing and the bees were buzzing. Gunner played on the shore with a stick, and the guys were down by the dock practicing their golf swing using my dad's old clubs. Most of them had probably never played, but that hadn't stopped them from entering the Baylor Celebrity Golf Tournament.

Baylor was a small, hokey town around the base of a Great Lake. Needless to say, we didn't have celebrities. The golf tournament celebrities were usually B-list TV anchors or a basketball player who nobody had ever heard of, and of course there was always a lot of alcohol. The alcohol was for two reasons: to keep the cash flowing freely, and so nobody called attention to the missing celebrities. I could never understand why they hadn't just changed the

name of the tournament. The Water's Edge Golf
Tournament sounded just as good to me.

"Hey, Kins, why don't you give it a shot?" Noah called
out. I'd been in the tournament several summers ago, but I
wouldn't be attending this year.

"Maybe later," I yelled back.

"There's not going to be a later. We're leaving soon."
Noah rested the golf club across the back of his neck and
lazily draped his wrist over the other end of it. It sent my
eyes traveling down the length of his body.

"Sorry!" I held up my coffee mug as if I were too busy.
The truth was, that ship had sailed long ago.

"Well, you're at least going to come watch us, right?"

I opened my mouth to reply, and then clamped it shut
when Emma stepped out onto the deck. "Are you ready for
the library?" she asked.

"Yeah, I'm just waiting for Walker." I checked the
time. "He should be here any minute."

Noah jogged up the hill, and I hid my face behind my
mug. I didn't want to do this song and dance with him any
longer. But having *the talk* with him was even more
daunting. I had been trying to convey my feelings toward
him through bodily cues, and I'd thought it was working—
but it apparently wasn't enough. I could tell from the look
in his eyes that he knew our time had come and gone, but it
didn't stop him from trying, and I respected that, though I
didn't have to like it.

"Hey, Kins, you're coming to the tournament, right?" he asked, a little winded.

Emma scoffed. "Golf? We have research to do."

Noah looked at me, and I sighed. "Sorry, we have plans for the library today." I spotted Walker out on the lake. He was only a tiny dot on the water. Noah must have noticed my change of expression, and he looked over his shoulder. He stared at Walker for a moment, and then glanced down to the ground, defeated.

"What's more important than the golf tournament? They have alcohol . . . and Sampson says he knows a girl who works the cart. We can buy beer from her. And Mason is going to bring some mixed drinks in his thermos."

"I'm sure you guys will have a blast, but—"

"There are celebrities there!" Noah continued, as he checked over his shoulder again.

"Oh my god, do you mean Parker Shallon?" Emma asked.

"Who's Parker Shallon?" I should have known by her expression that it didn't matter who Parker Shallon was. I'd probably never heard of the guy.

"He's the childhood actor from that show with the fence. You know, they were always meeting in the backyard? And the fence covered that guy's face?" Emma covered her face with her coffee mug, and I laughed.

"Oh yeah, that guy. He's the celebrity this year?" I asked.

Noah clenched his jaw. He'd lost the argument, and he appeared ready to concede defeat. He looked over his shoulder again, and I followed his gaze. Walker was paddling into the cove. A swarm of butterflies erupted in my stomach, but I tried not to let it show on my face.

"They have golf carts. You can be our caddie, and I'll let you drive," Noah said.

Emma looked between us and tapped her foot. "You realize she has a golf cart in the garage, right?" Noah glanced behind him again, and I widened my eyes at Emma.

He was trying awfully hard to get me to join him today, and I was starting to feel bad. "Look, we need to figure out this whole dream thing. If we can understand it, we can control it. And then we can do whatever we want." I shrugged, making it sound simpler than it was.

Noah took some practice swings as Walker climbed the hill to the cabin. "Like what?" he asked.

"I don't know, Noah, like win a golf tournament. Wouldn't you like that?" He glared at me, silently reminding me that there was something else he wanted. If only he had a choice. My eyes flickered to Walker, and I smiled.

"Morning," Walker said. Noah took a swing—a warning shot. "Nice swing you've got there. Try twisting at the hips, you'll get a better follow through." Walker swiveled his hips in demonstration, and my brows shot sky high. Noah's face turned red with fury. Emma's was red for an entirely different reason.

"D-did you used to play?" Emma stuttered.

"A little when I was a kid. My uncle used to take me to lessons." Walker smiled up at me, and his dimples cast shadows on his cheeks. A small hum escaped my throat, and Noah shot me a deadly glare.

The air thickened with enough tension to attract a curious bee. It buzzed by, taking multiple passes. Noah swatted at it mindlessly as he tried to talk up Parker Shallon. The rest of the guys climbed the hill to join us. My back stiffened when I saw the bee fly toward Walker, but before I could say anything at all, it flew straight through him. My breath hitched in my chest. The bee had flown *through* him, as if he was made of air . . . Maybe he was?

I watched Walker's expression closely. He hadn't noticed the bee penetrate his chest and pierce through the other side, and neither had anyone else. It reminded me just how different Walker was than the rest of us, and I wondered if he was invincible here in Baylor.

"Kins?" Kai asked.

"Huh?" Everybody was looking at me. Waiting for something.

"She was the weather girl on channel five. She was the celebrity in the tournament a few years back . . ." I looked at Kai blankly as his words trailed off. "Her name.

Do you remember her name?" Kai laughed, shaking his head.

"Oh! Um, Shelly Trot," I said. Kai snapped his fingers, and everybody agreed.

"I wish Trot was going to be there instead of Parker Shallon." Mason suddenly recoiled, swatting at the bee.

"Oh, shit!" Asher jumped sideways. We laughed at him as he ran, belly first, across the lawn. He waved his hands aimlessly through the air, making us laugh even harder.

The kitchen window slid open, and Kimber yelled out, "Run!" without an ounce of humor in her tone.

"Oh, yeah, isn't he allergic?" Mason asked.

Asher tripped and rolled down the hill, causing the laughter to stop. "Like how allergic?" Noah asked.

"*Deathly* allergic!" Kimber yelled from the window. I froze in place, unable to think of a way to help. Asher scrambled to his feet, kicking up tufts of grass in his wake, and charged for the cabin.

"Hurry!" Emma waved him on.

Asher took the steps three at a time; the bee was mere inches from his back. I swatted at the air, trying to fight the beast off, but it was no good. At the exact moment that Asher reached for the door, Kimber barged through from the other side brandishing an EpiPen. The door slammed into Asher, pushing him backward into the bee.

We held our breaths and watched helplessly as Asher

gathered his wits. At first, we didn't know if he'd been stung or if he was simply stunned from the blow to his head. He stood, eyes wide and blinking rapidly. I couldn't see or hear the bee any longer.

Everyone looked at one another uncertainly until Asher made a small, scratchy sound in his throat. Kimber pulled the cap off the EpiPen and dropped to her knees. She raised her arm and thrust the needle into Asher's thigh. I gasped. Emma dropped her coffee, splashing it on everybody near her and shattering one of my homemade ceramic mugs. Gunner barked with excitement.

Mason and Kai grabbed Asher and carried him inside. Kimber dropped the pen, fell to her butt, and started to cry. I kneeled down next to her and stroked her shoulder. "You were so brave, Kimber. How did you know how to do that?"

"His mom taught me. She tells me all the time where he keeps the pen. We practiced together one night when she was drunk. She accidentally injected her sofa," she sobbed.

Walker squeezed my shoulder as he passed by. He went into the cabin to check on Asher, and Emma busied herself picking up broken pieces of ceramic from the deck. "I don't want him to die. Kinsley, I don't want him to die!"

"Nobody is going to die." It wasn't until the words left my mouth that I realized just how foolish a statement that was. Somewhere inside, there was a calendar that showed precisely how many more of us would die this summer. Eight. Eight of us would. And the probability that one of those eight was Asher was pretty high.

"That's not true. You know that's not true," she said.

I ran my hands through my hair, trying to think of something else I could say to help calm her, but there was nothing.

"Look, maybe we can learn how to bring him back?" Emma said, hopefully.

"What?" I shot Emma a look. Not only was that doubtful, but it wasn't something I wanted to try. I'd seen movies before about raising the dead—it never ended well.

"Can you do that, Kinsley? Can you bring him back? Because I can't live without him." Kimber's eyes glistened a pale, sky-blue.

I opened my mouth, but nothing came out.

"Can you?" she asked again, dipping her chin and giving me doe eyes.

I was about to lie when Walker opened the patio door, bumping into my back. "Sorry," he said, looking down at me. My stomach dropped in preparation for the news.

Walker lifted his gaze to Kimber. "He's okay. We couldn't find the stinger, and no sign of swelling—" Kimber scrambled to her feet and blew past Walker mid-sentence.

"He wasn't even stung?" Emma asked.

"Looks like it was a false alarm," Walker said, shrugging. Emma looked at me in surprise, my labor of love broken in her hand. She went inside to see for herself, and I sat on the floor, deep in thought.

Had *I* saved him? Just by thinking about it? There was no way of telling if it was luck or magic, but if I had a choice, I'd say magic.

"What are you thinking?" Walker asked, no longer hiding his concern. His face reflected the same confusion and worry I felt.

"I don't know. I think, I think maybe I reversed it."

"Do you think he was stung?" Walker asked.

"Yes, and then because I was worried for him, I changed the outcome so that he wasn't allergic?" It was a stretch. Walker's lips twitched. I could tell he didn't think I was ready to pull off that kind of magic. And truthfully, he was probably right.

"Well, whatever it was, we need to work on it. If you had full capability and total control of your dreamwork, you could have extinguished that bee the second it came around. Hell, you could make bees extinct, if you wanted." Walker scratched the back of his head, and I could tell he was imagining the possibilities.

"Do you really think so?" I asked. A world without stingers sounded like a nice touch.

"I really do, Wilde. I really do." Walker's eyes burrowed into mine, and I could feel that he was being honest with me. He believed in me.

I smiled, feeling the heat across my cheeks. "Then let's

get to it," I said, reaching my hands out. Walker grabbed my hands and pulled me to my feet. While standing, our bodies touched, and we were closer than *just* friends should be, but he didn't seem to mind. It felt natural. We were more than friends, after all. No, we weren't boyfriend and girlfriend, but we weren't just simple friends either. There was something between us. Something bigger than life, and even he couldn't deny it. I planned to whittle it away until there was nothing left except the bare truth.

Walker pushed open the door to the cabin, and I followed him inside. Asher looked perfectly fine. His face was red, but I imagined that was because of embarrassment more than anything else. "Are you feeling okay?" I asked.

"Yeah, I'm fine. Everything except my thigh," Asher said, glaring at Kimber and rubbing his leg.

"What? I was trying to save your life!" Kimber argued.

"You stabbed me! I wasn't even stung!" he said in a high-pitched voice.

"How was I supposed to know that?" Kimber raised her hands and turned away, shoulders hunched.

"Listen, we'd better get going or we're going to be late for the tournament. Kins, you're coming with us, right?" Noah asked, nodding as if it was a done deal.

I jutted my head back; did he really think I was going with them? I had already told him I wasn't. Walker looked at me questioningly, and I frowned. "No. I said we were going to the library. We're doing research." My tone was quick and cutting, and Noah's cheeks flushed under my scorn.

"Okay, okay. Sorry. I thought you told me you were going to go." He shook his head and looked at the floor. I knew what he was trying to do, but I wasn't giving in. It aggravated me that he was being so pushy. He didn't like Walker one bit. And that was going to be a problem.

Kimber and Asher stayed back in the cabin. As much as Asher would deny it, I think he was more rattled than he let on. His hands were shaky, and he looked sick to his stomach. The others headed off to the golf tournament, and I knew they would have fun. A piece of me was jealous. I wanted to go, but I knew my work at the library was far more important. When all this was over, and I was the master of my destiny, I could make everyday Celebrity Golf Tournament day if I wanted. For today, Emma, Walker, and I headed out to the library. It was a nice day, so we walked the mile and a half into town.

CHAPTER 3

While our walk had started out pleasant enough, it had warmed significantly by the time we were halfway to the library. The nape of my neck was hot and sticky, so I pulled my hair back into a bun with the elastic I carried on my wrist. We talked about how bizarre it was that Asher hadn't been stung and all the ways it could have ended, but hadn't. Emma was convinced that he was going into shock from the trauma, and I thought I'd seen signs of that too. But Walker said that it was just the Baylor phenomenon. That I wouldn't have been able to reverse a moment in time without proper training.

"Do you think she will be able to time travel?" Emma asked, using one hand to shade her eyes from the sun.

"I think that's just the tip of the iceberg. I think this thing is massive. We have no idea what she is capable of, or how quickly she'll learn. From blowing out candles with her mind, to bringing back the dead . . ." Walker's words sent a chill down my hot spine. Goosebumps prickled my arms despite the heat of the day.

He looked up at the sky and frowned. I followed his gaze to see an enormous black crow circling above. *Levi.* By the look on Walker's face, he'd known there was something peculiar about the bird, but he didn't say anything. It made me wonder about all the times we had shared before. How much had I missed? And how much had he hidden from me?

"Bring back . . . the dead? As in, Lainey?" Emma asked. It was a nice idea, of course, but it only reminded us she wasn't here to begin with, and the sadness seemed to hit both of us again.

"Maybe," Walker said.

Emma glanced at the bird and her breathing deepened. "And Levi?" she asked, in a small, faraway voice.

"Maybe."

The crow cawed above, and I wondered how long he'd been following us. I wondered if was possible for me to bring Lainey back? And Levi? But what kind of person would that make me? Would I be dark? Would I be evil? Or would that make me a goddess?

"And what about *you*? Could she bring *you* back?" Emma asked.

My heart froze in my chest. It stopped beating

completely and then sputtered, kicking back into rhythm. I bent at the waist, coughing, and Walker patted my back.

What about him? I wondered. Could I bring him back? Was it possible? He'd been a ghost for so long. Was there an expiration on this type of magic? I cocked my head to see Walker's expression, and it alarmed me. He wasn't in shock like I was—he'd thought about this before. His jaw was set firm and square, and his eyes narrowed into tiny slants. Had this been his plan all along?

"Are you okay?"

"Yeah," I said, slapping my chest. But Emma's question went unanswered as we reached the library.

"After you," Walker said, holding the door open.

Emma smiled and dipped under his arm, seeming to forget all about her question. But my thoughts were a jumbled mess. I couldn't stop thinking about that bird stalking us and the idea of raising the dead. I paused, passing Walker, staring him in the eyes. It seemed he'd had big plans all along. Ideas that he'd never shared. He'd said he wanted to train me, but what for? I wasn't sure. His golden eyes told no secrets. I bit my bottom lip and entered the library. Walker's gaze was hotter than the sun could ever be, and passing him in the doorway was like jumping through a ring of fire. I was thankful for the cool air conditioning.

The library was small but rich in literature. What it lacked in size was made up for by the cozy ambiance. It was an old historical library, and it had been here for as long as I could remember—apart from the fact that it had recently moved itself down the street. Regardless, it had all the classics. But perhaps the best part was the smell. The smell of the books, worn thin and well loved. I'd never been a reader, but that didn't stop me from wishing I were. I'd always wanted to lose myself in a good story, the way my gran did—the way Emma does. Instead, I lost myself in the depths of my twisted subconscious. Oh how I wished I could dog-ear the page and close the book on my mind when I grew weary and tired.

Emma's eyes beamed, all but forgetting the crow in the sky and how somber she'd felt just moments ago. "Do you mind if I—"

"No. Go for it." It's not like Emma would be able to concentrate until she checked out whatever book was on her mind, anyway. She'd been trying to get through the library's fantasy section over the summer, and she had made a sizable dent already. Emma scampered off to the back of the library, disappearing into the aisles of books. Walker took my hand and led me to the small section of personal development books. I picked through them, frowning at the titles and feeling like I was broken and in need of self-help. I turned to glare at Walker, but he was oblivious to my concerns.

"I've heard of this book; it teaches you how to become lucid in your dreams. There's technique involved, stuff I don't know yet. Probably stuff I can't find online. These books are ancient, and there is information here that you can't find anywhere else. Trust me, I've tried." Walker glanced at me and flinched. "What's wrong?"

"The self-help section. Really?"

"No, it's not like that . . ."

"Oh, yeah?" I held up a book titled *How to Be Everything You're Not.*

Walker rolled his eyes and turned his attention back to the shelf, running his fingers down the spines of the books. "It's not here. That can't be right."

"Are you sure they had it?" I asked, stuffing the book I probably should have checked out back on the shelf.

"Positive. I called before we came." Walker looked frantically through the bookshelf.

"Well, maybe we can just start with another one?"

"We can't start with another one. That is the *only* one. It's called *Waking Dreams,* and it is the only book here about dreams and the first one ever written on the topic." Walker crouched down, checking the books at knee level.

"I'll go check with the librarian. Maybe she pulled it, expecting you to come?" I asked.

"Okay. Good thinking. I'm just going to poke around here. In case it was put back out of place."

I turned around slowly and went in search of the librarian. But when I got to the checkout counter, she wasn't there. As I waited, idly drumming my fingers on the counter, I let my eyes wander around the little library until they landed on a girl drawn into a book at a small desk against the back wall. I hadn't seen her when we'd come in. She had lush dark hair that draped in front of her face as she read. Nobody has hair that pretty . . . except . . .

"Can I help you, dear?" a rickety old voice asked.

I spun around to find the librarian standing behind the counter as if she'd appeared out of thin air. She was an elderly lady, probably not more than four feet tall. Her nose was bulbous and red, and she had short, gray scraggly hair. Her eyes were beady behind her thin-rimmed glasses, and for reasons I couldn't understand, it felt like her eyes could see right through me.

"Hi. My friend called earlier this morning about a book. I think he said it was called *Waking Dreams*. We're having trouble finding it. Do you know where it is?" I asked, averting my eyes.

"Oh . . ." The librarian patted her pockets and then reached up to the top of her head, searching for something. She only stopped looking once she pinched the silver metal rim of the glasses that were resting on her nose.

"I thought maybe you pulled it earlier. Could it be up here with you?"

"I remember a young man calling about that book, but I didn't take it off the shelf. A young lady came in asking for it just moments ago. It must be a popular book today."

"Really?" My stomach tumbled. I knew there was something going on with that girl in the back.

"Sorry dear." The librarian gave me a smile. "Is there anything else I can help you find?"

"No, thank you."

I peeked again at the girl in the back, and I found Emma nose deep in fantasy, one aisle away. She was so entranced in what she was reading, she didn't see me coming, and I spooked her. She let out a squeak, drawing attention to herself. The librarian scowled, and I smirked.

"Dear god, never do that again," she hissed.

"Sorry. Hey, did you grab the *Waking Dreams* book already?" I asked. I pointed to the book she was reading.

"No. Sorry. This is all dragons and castles."

"Do you mean dragons and castles with big barbarian shirtless men with oil-slicked, tan bodies?" I asked, with a tilt of my head. It was like confronting an addict.

Emma's face turned a swarthy red as she lifted the book to hide her face. The cover was exactly what I'd imagined it would be. Bronzed pecs and an eight-pack of abs. I shoved Emma, and she stifled a giggle.

"I think you'll find that in the philosophy section, right? Or maybe personal development?" She pointed in Walker's general direction, dismissing me to anywhere in the library but here. I grabbed hold of her book and lowered it from her face. Her pupils were dilated, and I briefly wondered what exactly she was reading.

"Look, you have all night to read this book, but right now, we're in search of the dream book. The librarian said that a girl already checked it out, and I hoped it was you."

"Yeah, no. I'll help you look. Just let me finish this page real quick."

"Okay. Come find us when you're done."

I headed back to Walker but stopped when I saw the girl in the back corner. She was the only other girl in the library, and she had to be the one reading that book. I peered at her through the bookshelves, trying to get a clear view of her face. She absently brushed her hair back, revealing her profile. "Well, I'll be damned," I whispered. It was Layla after all. I knew I'd recognized her hair.

From the moment I'd decided I didn't want to find her, she'd started finding me.

I strolled down the aisle, peering over the tops of the books, trying to get a better glimpse of the mysterious Layla Barns. My heart pounded in my chest like I was about to enter a battle. With Layla being here, so close, this could all end for me in a matter of minutes. I could go back to my real life—wake up in the hospital bed in Decord City, just outside of Clover. I could deal with my wounds and properly mourn my grandmother. Or should I pretend I'd never seen her? I could stay here in Baylor for the rest of my life, learning magic and figuring out how to get Walker to fall in love with me.

Layla tucked her hair behind her ear, exposing the

bridge of her nose, the curves of her lips, and the line of her chin. It was the first time I had taken in her beauty, and in that moment she reminded me of the beautifully poisonous red apple in the haunted forest. She seemed perfect on the outside, but what lay within?

Layla had what I wanted. She had Walker's heart. But now that I wanted a life here, she had so much more than that. Layla symbolized a great threat to me. That girl had the power to take my love, take my manifestations, and take my dreams straight out from under me. And I didn't like it one bit. I felt utterly powerless compared to her, and that made my skin crawl.

And now, of all things, Layla wanted to learn about lucid dreaming. Why? Somehow, she knew I needed that book. Somehow, she'd known that Walker and I would look for it today. There was something in *Waking Dreams* that she needed to get to before I did. I had to get that book.

Without realizing it, I had taken several tiny steps, inching myself toward Layla. I found myself standing directly behind her, so close I could reach out and run my hands through her silky brown locks. I froze in place and tried to swallow through my suddenly dry throat. All I wanted to do was run away, but instead, I found myself drawn to her like a magnet.

I worried Walker would find her sitting in the back of the library and realize she had no desire to close the distance between them. She must not love Walker the way I did, and it broke my heart. She didn't deserve him.

"Hey, I'm done reading. I made myself close the book for you. Do you even know how hard it is to close a book once you've read the first line of the next chapter?" Emma whispered from behind me, startling me from my trance.

I wanted nothing more than to hide Layla's presence from Emma and Walker, but she was right here, inches away, and hiding in plain sight. In slow motion, I saw Walker heading in our direction.

"*No. No. No. No.*" I whispered maniacally.

"What? What's wrong?" Emma asked. I whipped my head back toward Layla, and she was looking directly at me. Our eyes locked, and her lips curved in a small, impish smile.

"Can I help you?" Layla asked, her tone like a full-bodied dark chocolate—rich and savory.

Only it wasn't Layla by the time she was done speaking. The curves of her lips had spread wider and flatter. Her long brown hair turned ashy before my very eyes. And by the time Emma laid eyes on her, the girl looked three years younger, and her cheeks were dusted in freckles.

"Oh my god, I'm so sorry. We'll be quiet." Emma placed her finger in front of her lips and motioned for us to find a new place to talk.

The young girl's eyes bounced from Emma to me to

Walker. Her chair screeched on the floor as she jolted backward, apparently stunned to see him. She slammed all her books shut and scrambled to collect her papers into a messy heap in her arms. She jumped to her feet, causing her chair to tip over behind her and land on the floor with a thud. She took off running, nearly bumping into Walker on her way out of the little library.

"Miss! You need to check those out! You can't take those books without checking them out!" the librarian called out after her. She waved her fist in the air, but by the time she had gotten out from behind the desk, the girl was gone. And so was the book.

"Doggone it. Kids these days. No respect. No respect at all," the librarian grumbled beneath her breath.

"What was all that about?" Walker asked, approaching us.

"Shhhh!" the librarian hissed. Emma stifled a giggle with her hand.

"She had our book," I said.

"*Waking Dreams?*"

"Yup."

"Dammit. And she just stole it, too." Walker said.

"I doubt she's going to come back here and return it after that debacle," Emma said.

"Well, Wilde, I guess it's just you and me. I've got some things that we can start working on. It won't be as advanced as I'd hoped, but in the meantime, I'll try to keep looking for that book." Walker forced an apologetic smile.

"Don't worry about it, we've got this," I said, nudging his shoulder.

"Hey, maybe we can find that girl?" Emma asked.

"No, I don't think that's necessary—"

"That's a great idea!" Walker said.

"Yeah, she's probably just sitting at the coffee shop two doors down. It's not like this is a big town. We'll just ask her to borrow the book," Emma said.

"Yeah."

"Nooo, I don't think we really need it . . ."

"Come on Kinsley, find the girl, find the book, master your dreams. It will be fun. Plus, what else do we have to do today? Go to the golf tournament?" Emma said with a laugh.

"Shhhh!" the librarian spat at us, still fuming from the stolen books. Emma rolled her eyes and linked her arm with mine. With a slight tug, we were moving through the library and toward the exit.

The last thing I wanted to do was go on another hunt for Layla Barns. It didn't matter if it really was Layla or just a young girl with ashy hair and sweet freckles; whoever she was, she had something we desperately needed. I tried to convince myself that I could do this on my own. And with just a little bit of luck, or perhaps a manifestation, we would find the book and not the girl.

We did, however, see a middle-aged man holding a heap of papers and a stack of books in the coffee shop's window as we passed by. He glared at me through the glass with distrustful eyes. Nobody recognized her but me, and I kept my mouth shut.

CHAPTER 4

Walker stayed over for dinner that night, and we talked about all the different ways we could start my training. He thought that channeling my energy seemed like a good place to start, and it would give us something to build on. We were going to start after dinner, and I was eager to see how creative I could get under his direction. I remembered the time he'd coached me to find the lost tower, and how it had felt like make-believe. This time, I would know it was real, and the possibilities were endless. With Layla and I having somewhat of an understanding that she would not interfere and I would keep my distance, I could very well have this whole thing in the bag.

Kimber, Emma, and I made spaghetti while the rest of the group was still at the tournament with their one B-list celebrity. Asher and Walker were talking at the table, and it was nice to see him integrate into the group.

"My leg is a little sore, but it could be worse," Asher said.

"Oh my god, he is such a baby," Kimber muttered.

We dished everything up and brought our dinners to the living room. I sat cross-legged on the carpet, and the TV played faintly in the background. We talked about the fun things we could do if we gained control over the Baylor phenomenon. Mostly funny things, sometimes outrageous —we laughed all the same.

"I don't know about you guys, but I'd start my own football team. I'd be the starting quarterback, and I'd win every single game I ever played. I'd be famous and make loads of money. I'd even be on commercials, and I'd sponsor sports drinks and protein powders," Asher said with stars in his eyes.

Kimber slapped his arm. "Are you serious? That's what you're going to wish for?"

"Yeah, why?"

"You wouldn't take away your bee allergy? Or do something good with your power? You'd just play football?" her voice hitched.

"Well, I mean, it's my dream, right? Why wouldn't I be rich and famous?" Asher scoffed.

"God, you're so pig-headed sometimes, I swear."

Kimber shook her head. We all laughed. They sounded like an old married couple.

"Why? What would you do with all the power in the world?" he asked Kimber.

"Well, for starters, I'd pray for you!"

We laughed even harder.

"I think I might open up a library," Emma said. "Maybe I could be a book critic? I don't know, something where I had to read all day, and I would get paid for it."

"Why don't you write a book?" Walker asked.

"Write a book? I don't want to *write* a book. I want to live in one. I want to step into a different world and marvel at every twist and turn. Make one up myself? What's the fun in that? There wouldn't be any surprises . . . That's actually so sad. *Write* a book . . ." Emma had a horrified look on her face. I nodded, thinking she'd already gotten some part of her wish. She was living in a fantasy that she had no control over, and there were certainly twists at every turn. If only I could find a way to get her a paycheck.

I took a bite of spaghetti and then wiped my chin with the back of my hand, wondering what I would do when my powers rolled in. Perhaps I would start to read books. Maybe I'd enjoy them? I could take away my dyslexia, and then I could transport Emma and me into different worlds for the day. We could call them "book trips." Hell, I could even take away Asher's bee allergy. I'd leave the bees but take away their stingers. There would be no venom left in my world. And certainly no poisonous apples.

"What would you do Walker?" Asher asked.

The air shifted, and the room turned quiet. Walker licked his lips and then brushed off the question with some generic lie, but I could tell that whatever he would choose for the world of his making, it absolutely wasn't possible.

We spent some time cleaning the kitchen, and when the dishes were done, Asher and Kimber put on a movie. Emma popped popcorn and joined them on the couch. Walker motioned for the porch, and I nodded, following him outside.

"Aren't you guys going to watch the movie?" Emma asked.

"You start without us. Maybe we'll join later," I said.

Night had fallen and blanketed the cove. The waves lapped gently on the shore below. I stared into the night, knowing the mysterious lake was just beyond the grassy knoll.

"So, I think we need to start out small. Here, take my hands," Walker said, holding out his hands. He didn't need to ask me twice. I slipped my hands into his, eager for his touch.

"Now, see if you can feel the energy." It was hard to concentrate with his golden eyes staring into mine. I felt the energy all right, but it wasn't in my hands.

"What *kind* of energy?"

"The kind that passes through you. Your whole body is made of energy. Try to channel it and draw it into your hands. Once you do that, try to send it through mine."

My hands grew clammy in his, but I blamed it on the energy. I chewed on my lip as I stared up at him, and I began to breathe in quick, shallow breaths. It was late and dark, so I couldn't quite tell, but I thought I caught a blush on Walker's cheeks. If I was right, he was good at hiding his feelings. He kept his stare locked on mine, and I blew out a long heavy breath through puckered lips.

"Here, try to breathe with me. Sync your breath to mine." Walker drew in a deep breath, and I did too. "Wilde?" he asked, tilting his head.

"Yeah?"

"Close your eyes."

Heat spread across my cheeks. "Oh. Yeah, right."

I squeezed my eyes shut and found it much easier to focus without Walker's dimples to distract me. I concentrated on all the energy I had swirling inside of me, and I channeled it into my hands. It must've been working, because my hands grew hot and slick with sweat. A few moments later I felt a tingling in my fingertips. I tried to merge my energy with his, sending little waves of electricity through our touch.

"I think I feel it. It's like tingling all over my hands," he said. I smiled, feeling prouder of myself than I had in a long time. If this was working, and he could feel the tingling of my excitement, I wondered how he would react if I sent my feelings for him through. I dug deep, drumming up all the emotion I had in my heart for him, and I started to push it down my arms, past my elbows, and into the palms of my hands.

"Do you feel that?" he asked with a shiver.

My smile grew, but I kept my eyes shut, and I continued to push and push until he felt the full force of my feelings for him. But just when things started getting interesting, the door behind us was flung open, and a very drunk Mason and Noah stumbled outside onto the deck with us. I pulled my hands out of Walker's, dropping all the energy I'd collected.

I couldn't read the expression on Walker's face. It had almost looked like he knew what I was trying to do. As if it had actually worked, or was about to. Either way, he looked like he knew a secret but didn't know what to do with it. I could feel the heat rising in my cheeks, and I was so afraid of being rejected, again, that I darted to the bathroom to hide.

"I'll be right back," I said, as I pushed between Noah and Mason. I felt Noah's eyes heavy on my back, but I couldn't think about him right now. I wished I could send my feelings for Noah through a glare; then I'd never have to say it aloud. Regardless, he was drunk now, and anything I said or did wouldn't be remembered come morning.

"Whoa, easy there," Scarlett May said, as I burst through the bathroom door.

"Sorry."

"What's got your panties in a bunch?" She puckered her lips in the mirror as she retouched her lipstick.

"I-I'm falling for a guy who doesn't feel the same about me," I said, shutting the door behind me, trapping Scarlett May inside. She patted her lips with her middle finger and glanced at me through the reflection.

"Oh, you mean Noah?" she asked with a nonchalant tone. I scoffed. Apparently, falling for the wrong person was a thing I did. It was on par for me, and everybody knew it. I sighed, pressing the back of my head against the door.

"That was so last month," I said with a small laugh. Scarlett May smiled and turned to me in a moment of understanding that I hardly recognized in her.

"Oh, is it that new guy? That ruggedly handsome one that you've been hanging out with? Walter or whatever? Yeah, he is kind of out of your league." She winced, as if it brought her discomfort. That was the Scarlett May I knew. I could always count on her for the painful truth.

"Walker. And you have no idea . . ."

"Why don't you just tell him how you feel about him and get it out of the way? Sometimes, confidence is the sexiest thing about a person. And the best part about that is, you can fake it." Something shifted in Scarlett May's face, and I could tell that this was a candid moment for her. A moment where she was letting her guard down and showing her true self. She was never like that with me, although I imagined she had been with Trinity.

"I've done it before, and it works like a charm. Almost every time. And if he doesn't like you, then you just keep on acting. Act like you couldn't care less and it's his loss. Usually, if it doesn't work the first time, it'll work the second time." Scarlett May placed a hand on my shoulder with a tender touch. Maybe there was a caring side to her after all. I smiled at her in a split second of gratitude before her tender touch turned icy and she pushed me out of the way. She was just trying to leave the bathroom. I sidestepped, feeling slightly stupid.

"Thank you," I said. She winked at me before disappearing.

Scarlett May was right. I had nothing to lose. I was on my deathbed somewhere out there, and either I fell in love with this world that I'd created, or I'd go back home, to all the problems I never wanted to see again. I'd never told Walker that he should be with me instead of Layla. I'd never told him I was falling for him. But that was going to change. I was going to march right out there, and I was going to tell him. Tonight. Right now. I might not look him in the eye while doing it, but the words were going to come out. And when he turned me down, like he always did, I was going to pretend that it was his loss.

I opened the door and strode down the hall, through the kitchen, and out to the back patio. But when all I saw was Mason and Noah, my plan came crumbling down in a heap of failure. "Where's Walker?" I asked.

"You didn't even ask how our game was," Noah said, slurring his words. I looked around, aggravated.

"Where is Walker?" I crossed my arms.

Mason laughed. "I told him that Noah was basically your boyfriend, and that he was breaking code by hanging around. I told him he better leave you alone, or else . . ."

"You what!"

I turned to scan the lake for Walker, but the night was too dark, and I couldn't see past the halo of the patio lights. I pushed past Noah and Mason as they continued to make fun of Walker. I ran down the hill, nearly slipping on the dew-slick grass on my way down. I ran to the end of the dock, and I could just see the tail end of a canoe disappearing into the night. I threw my head back, panting, as I looked up toward the stars. Would I ever catch a break? I listened to the quiet trickle of his paddle long after the canoe was out of sight. I stood staring at the twinkling stars until I couldn't hear him any longer. He was gone, and so were my hopes of faking confidence.

Noah had been a problem for me since the incident with Trinity, but I didn't know where Mason had gotten the idea to ruin things for me too. I intended to find out. I marched up the hill with the same determination I'd originally had for faking my confidence. I marched right up to Mason, chest to chest, and I put my finger in his face. "What the hell did you do that for?" I said, seething.

"Whoa. Calm down, Kinsley. It was just a joke." Mason held his hands up in the air.

"Does it look like I'm laughing Mason? Why did you do that to him?" I asked, pointing toward the lake.

"Honestly? Because Noah can't get you on his own. He needs help from his wing man—"

"Nooo . . ." Noah said.

"That's me. I'm the wingman. I told him I could do it. And I did. Right?" Mason held his knuckles out to Noah and they fist bumped.

"Walker was my guest. And I don't appreciate you telling him to leave my cabin. How would you like it if I told *you* to leave?"

"Whoa, whoa, whoa. You can't tell me to leave! We're trapped here, remember? We're trapped here because you and your twisted little mind got us caught here. You're like a black widow and we're just stuck in your web." Mason flailed around, pretending to be caught in a web. He barely managed to lift one leg without falling to the ground.

"Yeah, Kinsley. You don't need that guy. You should be with me."

It was Noah's turn to feel my wrath. "Look. I didn't want to do this right now, when you only have half a mind, but you leave me no choice. *I. Don't. Like. You.*" I said, poking his chest with every word.

"Whoa there, you don't need to be such a b—"

"Hey! Hey, don't talk to her like that!" Noah said, shoving Mason. I took a cautious step backward.

"I'm just saying . . ."

"Well don't say!" Noah snapped.

Noah got in Mason's face, and I pushed them apart, squeezing myself in the middle. Out came my finger one more time. "Mason. If you don't go to bed right now and leave me be, you will see the full wrath of my *twisted little mind.*"

I was acting, of course—something I'd just learned from Scarlett May—but it worked. Mason clamped his mouth shut and turned around. He stumbled into the cabin, never turning back. I had fire in my eyes by the time the door slammed shut.

"Noah, I don't know how much of this you are going to remember in the morning, but I want you to understand right now that I don't have feelings for you. And if you continue to get in the way of Walker and me, we're going to lose our friendship as well."

Noah's face took on a swarthy hue, and he looked like he had sobered up considerably.

"But you used to have feelings for me, right? Or did I make that up?"

"Yes, Noah. I liked you. I liked you a lot. But the

moment you chose Trinity over me, that changed. You're a great guy, and we've been friends for a long time. There *was* a chance for something more. But what we had, all the flirting, it's over now. It's nothing. And you have to let me go." It was difficult being angry with someone who looked so sad.

Noah's blue eyes were flanked red with broken blood vessels. I could tell that his last shred of hope had finally died. He opened his mouth to say something and then ultimately shut it again and nodded. He turned to walk away but stopped when his hand reached the doorknob. "Just tell me one thing. Why him?" he asked.

"I don't know, Noah. I guess I'm a sucker." It was the only thing the two guys had in common. They both had eyes for another girl. And I deserved more than that.

"I'm sorry about Trinity. Nothing happened. *Not really.* I mean, a little bit . . . but—"

"I know!" I pinched the bridge of my nose. "It's okay. It's over."

Noah's head dropped, and he opened the door. It slammed shut behind him with a bang, causing me to jump. I took a long, cleansing breath and ran my hands through my hair. It was over. The long-awaited talk was over. I only hoped I wouldn't have to repeat myself in the morning.

If I'd learned one thing tonight, it was how to fake my own competence. I looked toward the invisible horizon, and I wondered if that was the key to manifestation, too. If I pretended I believed in myself, would it be enough? I wrinkled my nose, a bit giddy with the thought, and turned when I heard the sound of a shovel digging into dirt.

It was dark enough that I could only make out the shadow of a man digging a hole, but I knew who it was. And I also knew that he and his wife had moved, or were attempting to. That house wasn't being lived in, yet Mr. Vandal was gardening late in the night? Why?

I rested my chin in the palm of my hand as I watched him dig the hole, wondering how deep it had to be to hide a body. What the hell was going on over there? The boys had broken in before to rescue Gunner, but I wanted to see it for myself. Something weird was going on with the neighbors, and I wouldn't be able to rest until I knew what. I had a weird feeling in my chest, a whispering in my ear, that he might just be the wolf.

CHAPTER 5

I was still exhausted when I woke the next morning. We had to do something different today. I was starting to resent this cabin, this bed, and these sheets. The only thing that changed here was the dwindling number of roommates I had. I didn't want to go downstairs and face Noah and Mason. The thought of having to tell Noah I no longer had feelings for him all over again was excruciating. I squeezed my eyes shut, hoping that when I opened them again I'd be somewhere else. Anywhere else. I lay in bed like that for an hour, maybe more. And I didn't get up until I'd convinced myself that I could at least change something today. Something small. Today, I'd leave Baylor.

I got out of bed, and shouted down the hall, "Emma, Scarlett May, Kimber, get ready! We're going out!" I yelled.

I went back to my bedroom, excited for something new. On the opposite side of the lake, there was a train station. We were going to ride it as far as it would take us. We wouldn't get far, of course, and at the end of the day, we'd be back here eating leftover pizza. But at least I would feel free momentarily, like a dog with its head out the window of a car and its jowls flapping in the wind. I needed this for me. And the girls? They probably needed it just as much.

"Where are we going, Kins?" Emma asked.

"We're getting train tickets. We can eat lunch on the train. It will be fun."

"But, I mean . . . where are we going?"

"Well, I figured we'll get tickets to San Pearson, and we'll see how far we can get," I said.

Emma shrugged. "I don't mean to be rude, but what's the point of that?"

"Emma, it's not the destination, it's the journey. You know that." I smirked.

"Okay. You're right. Let's go explore."

Scarlett May never asked where we were going. She was just happy to get out of the cabin. She'd been spending a lot of time with Sampson and his friends, but he was busy today. And after spending the previous day with Asher berating her about the EpiPen stabbing, Kimber was also eager to get out. I wanted to talk to Walker about what Mason had told him last night, but he wasn't answering my texts, and I figured it would be best to give him a little space as well. If he didn't answer me by tomorrow, I'd march over there myself and bang on his door.

The taxi dropped us at the train station. It was busy for a Wednesday, but most days were buzzing like this during summer. It was always easy to tell who was coming, who was going, and who the locals were. Some families were sunburned; the ones who were heading back home from a stay at the lake. The newly arriving families had a polished look, like they'd just stepped out of air conditioning. The humidity hadn't frizzed their hair yet, and their skin wasn't yet scorched by long hours in the sun. The ones in flip-flops with brightly colored bathing suit straps peeking out from under their tank tops were the ones who lived here or had been here for at least a couple of days.

The four of us sat down on a bench and waited for the train while I profiled every person who walked through the station. I liked to imagine who they were and who they strove to be. Sometimes I wondered what their love life was like. Were they lonely? Were they happy? Creative? Disciplined? A secret genius? Were they even human . . . ?

I watched a girl dig through her backpack looking for something. She was most likely a student. Studious and high-strung. I wondered what she was trying to find. A snack? ChapStick? Or perhaps she had lost her cell phone? She pulled out a book, and the title stunned me. *Waking Dreams.* I sucked in a quick breath as the stranger's hair grew long and lustrous, bounding over her shoulders and stretching to her waist. Her button nose morphed in her sunlit profile, and the shadows shifted on her cheeks, making her jawline sharp and angular. Before I knew it, I was sitting one row over from Layla Barns. I couldn't help but stare, wondering if she knew I sat before her. Or had she bought a ticket for the train today because she knew I'd be here?

I glanced over at Emma, trying not to cause alarm, but it was clear she hadn't seen Layla yet. Kimber and Scarlett May had no idea who she was because they'd never seen her before, but if Emma spotted her, all of this would be over. If I could somehow hide her, there was a possibility that Layla wouldn't show herself to them. Just like she'd hidden in plain sight at the coffee shop as we'd passed by searching for her. She opened the book to a dog-eared page and began reading.

"Kinsley? Are you listening?" Kimber asked. I tried my best to engage, but all I could do was worry that my name had been called out loud.

"What? What? What did you say?" I peeked back at Layla, who was still reading her book.

"Are you feeling okay? You look a little pale." Emma said.

"Yeah, I'm fine." I swallowed a lump in my throat.

"So? When do you think we'll get back home?" Kimber asked.

"Oh, Kai said that he made it as far as Pacer Bay, and I

figured we would probably do the same. I'm not really sure, but there's no harm in trying, right? Plus, it's probably best to know our boundaries."

"I can make a map," Emma said in a rush. She seemed really excited about the geography project, and I didn't see anyone else fighting for the job.

"Yeah, that's a great idea. You should do that," I said, peeking back at Layla, who was now staring directly at me. I froze. My breath stalled and my chest tightened. I couldn't pry my eyes away. Staring into Layla's eyes did weird, unexplainable things to my insides. The seconds stretched by until somebody walked between us, breaking the eye contact. I looked down at my hands in my lap and fidgeted with my fingers. Had my nails always been this shape? They seemed more square than normal.

"All boarding, San Pearson, Monroe, and Yearsgold. You may now take your seats," a voice called out over the speaker.

"Is that us?" Kimber asked.

"Yes!" Emma said, jumping to her feet. She scooped up her backpack and tucked her book under her arm. "Pacer Bay is about halfway to San Pearson, but we'll just ride it as far as we can."

I fell into step behind the girls, and I didn't dare lift my head. I didn't want to meet Layla's brown, piercing eyes again. It felt like she was looking into my soul, like she could see things in there that nobody else could.

Things I didn't want to look at myself. Things . . . I didn't even know existed. I guess being dead did that to you. It was like that with Walker, too. He saw me like nobody else did. And I liked the way he looked at me—really looked at me. But when Layla did it, it was intrusive. *Rude.*

"Where should we sit?" Kimber asked Scarlett May.

"Try to get one of those little cubbies where the two benches face each other. That way we can all fit together. I think they're in the back," Scarlett May said, pointing to the rear of the train.

I shuffled my feet behind Emma, and once we stepped into the train, I lifted my gaze. The carriage was long, and the aisle seemed to go on forever. Some sort of optical illusion. I squinted to see if it would help and then recoiled when I saw Layla. She was sitting in the first row, and she was staring up at me.

I let out a shutter and jolted back, stepping on the stranger's toes behind me. I whirled around to apologize, but stopped cold as I met her soul-piercing eyes. Standing behind me with a scowl was another Layla. I looked down at my feet and muttered something like an apology.

When I turned around again, the line had moved forward, and Layla was back in the first row. Still staring. My head pounded. I couldn't take the tricks she was playing on me. I felt weak, incapable of defending myself against her power. As I scurried to catch up to my friends, I passed a third Layla sitting on the opposite side of the train.

I winced at the throbbing in my head. I searched row after row. More Laylas. There must have been dozens. And each of them was staring at me with those god-awful eyes. I hooked my gaze over my shoulder, and all the Layla's had turned around, watching my every move. I was the entertainment, center stage in a sea of brown eyes.

Emma, Kimber, and Scarlett May hadn't noticed that all the passengers had looked like a clone of one another. They chatted easily among themselves.

"There! There's one in the back. Hurry, grab it!" Scarlett May said. Emma slid into the seat, tossing her backpack to the ground.

"This is perfect," Kimber said.

Had the illusion been curated for my eyes only? Could they not see her? *Them?*

"They have food on these things, right?" Emma asked.

"You've never been on a train?" Scarlett May asked.

I sat down slowly on the open bench, my gaze fixed on the Layla to my left and the book at which she held. She must be the real one, if she has the book . . .

"When would I have gone on a train? We live in Clover," Emma said.

I leaned into Emma, nudging her with my elbow. When I had her full attention, I discreetly tilted my head toward the Layla on my left. Emma pretended to need something in her backpack. She kicked it to her feet and leaned forward, looking discreetly. Layla's eyes never left mine in a menacing glare. Emma grabbed a ChapStick and put it up to her lips, smearing on a sweet summer watermelon scent, as she whispered in my ear. "What about him?"

Him? I looked back at Layla, and a slow, lazy smile crossed her eyes.

"Well, don't look at him!" Emma hissed in my ear.

"Yeah. You're right. I thought I knew her. *Him.* But I was mistaken." I glanced over one more time, unable to stop. I was drawn to her, like an endangered specimen that might only be seen once in a lifetime. She was rare, and as equally ethereal as she was terrifying. She scribbled something frantically inside the book.

"Seriously, you gotta stop staring at him. You're going to make him anxious," Emma said. "Either that, or he's going to think you like him."

"Oh my god, Kinsley, do you have the hots for that old man?" Scarlett May asked. They were all looking at Layla now. My cheeks flushed and I felt faint.

"No. I thought I knew him from somewhere. That's all."

"Did you ever tell Walter that you liked him?" Scarlett May asked, absentmindedly.

"Who's Walter?" asked Kimber.

"*Walker* . . . And no," I said.

"Did you chicken out? You're such a chicken-shit!" Scarlett May threw her hands in the air.

"No, I was going to, honestly. But when I got outside to tell him, he was gone. Mason told him not to come around anymore. They told him that Noah was my boyfriend," I said.

"Nooo!" Emma gasped.

"Boys will be boys," Kimber said with a shrug.

"More like assholes will be assholes," Scarlett May said.

"Whatever. I just needed a day away from it all. I didn't want to see them after last night. I was glad they were still sleeping off their hangovers this morning when we left. Um, thanks for coming out with me today. I'm glad we're doing this." I kept my voice quiet, conscious of listening ears. I knew Layla would have my head if she knew I was after her man—but what sat next to me wasn't Layla, it was just my fear. An apparition of self-judgment, tucked in the deepest parts of my mind. I tried to ignore it.

"Oh yeah, anytime. We should do it more often. I mean, we are stuck here after all, right? Better make the best of it," Emma said.

"Hey, I've got an idea. How about you figure out how we can win the lottery, and then every day we'll win," Scarlett May said. I raised my brows, pretending to entertain the thought, but I couldn't help myself from glancing over at Layla. I watched as she tore a page out of *Waking Dreams*.

"No, how about you figure out how to reverse time? And then we can reset the day every twenty-four hours like a loop," Kimber said.

"Why? Why would we want to do that?" Emma asked.

The sound of the page being folded in half and creased between running fingertips was louder than the train barreling down the tracks.

"Well, because then we could rob the bank every day, or do whatever the hell we wanted, and there would be no consequences. They'd simply never catch up to us," Kimber said.

I liked the idea of no consequences, but if I were ever to reverse time, it wouldn't be to rob a bank. It would be to get Lainey back.

Layla placed the folded note on her table and stood. When she walked away, it fluttered down to the aisle. She didn't look back as she disappeared down the seemingly infinitely long carriage. My eyes fixed on the piece of paper she'd left behind.

"I'm headed to the restroom," I said, pushing to my feet. I swiped the note from the ground and hurried down the aisle. I could hardly wait to open it. It felt like the note was burning a hole in my hand as I passed row after row of Laylas. When I reached the narrow bathroom door, I hurried inside and slid the lock into place. I took my first full breath since first seeing Layla at the train station. The cabin was tiny, but within these four tight walls, I was free from judgment. I opened the note with trembling hands.

Layla's handwriting was a scribble between paragraphs: *you don't belong here.* I closed my eyes to the throbbing pain at the top of my head.

I know. That was the first thought that came into my head. I knew this wasn't my world, just a temporary holding cell. I couldn't stay here long. But Walker's world was the afterlife, and that belonged to everybody at some point or another. That would be my new home once my transition had completed.

I opened my eyes and faced myself in the mirror. I didn't like the girl staring back at me. *You don't belong here.* I belonged with Walker, though. Our souls were intertwined. How else could he have saved me? How could he have come from an entirely different realm and met me between the living and the dead if we weren't meant to be?

Layla just felt threatened. That's all. She was jealous of me, in the same way I was jealous of her. We were both fighting for Walker's attention. The only difference between us, was that she'd had the chance to be with him all this time, and she'd never taken it. I would not let that happen to me. I would not let her scare me away from Baylor with her stolen books and her red cloaks. I looked away from my reflection. I wouldn't let her deter me either.

I flipped the ripped page over and skimmed through

the labyrinth of words. It spoke of dreamwork and how our minds use symbols. This was the exact kind of thing that Walker wanted to read up on. The thing he couldn't find on the internet. I wondered if she'd ripped out this particular page for a reason. I folded it back up and stuffed it in my back pocket. I'd show Walker the next time I saw him. Right after I apologized for Mason and Noah's prank.

When I left the bathroom, I was relieved to see that all the Laylas had reverted to the unique individuals they once were. I smiled at the old man sitting next to us. He looked nothing like Layla, and I was embarrassed to think he may have heard me and the girls talking about him.

"Where did Scarlett May go?" I asked.

"She's getting a snack from the bar. I told her to grab something for you, too," Emma said.

"Thanks."

"Honestly, though, what are we going to do all summer? Are our lives going to be one long endless summer in Baylor Lake? Will I have a perpetual tan, year-round?" Kimber rambled.

"Yeah, Kinsley, we gotta find a way out of here. I mean, I need to go home at some point. My mom's going to start to worry. And I have college in the fall," Emma said.

"I know. I know. I'm working on it," I said, feeling the full weight of the message burning a hole in my back pocket. *You don't belong here.*

I'd made my choice. I wanted to stay. But it was they

who didn't belong here. Emma shouldn't have to miss college, and Kimber could have a year-round tan anywhere she lived—even if she had to pay for it. But she didn't have to be trapped in Baylor for that. And Asher, he may never become a famous athlete, but he was going to play football in college. And he had many years ahead of him to do whatever he pleased. It was my responsibility to get my friends home. The ones who survived, anyway.

The train jerked violently, and the passenger car seemed to jump beneath us. Scarlett May came crashing into our cubby, and a variety of snacks flew to the floor as she fell on her hands and knees.

"Whoa, what was that?" Kimber asked, hands pressed against the walls.

The train continued to jerk and jump, as we slid helplessly on the benches, unable to catch ourselves. The horizon jumped by in a zig-zagged motion. A sapling tree slapped the window and scraped alongside the car making a screeching sound like nails on a chalkboard.

"We're off the tracks!" Emma yelled.

I leaned over, trying to get a good look out the window, but everything was moving too fast for me to focus. It was a blur of bushes and trees, and it was clear we were off the rails and still traveling at alarming speeds. The train's whistle sounded, two long cries for help.

Scarlett May climbed onto the seat, and we tried to hold on to anything we could. My hands were spread wide across the bench, and I had one foot pressed against the adjacent seat, pinning me in place. Emma tried to hold on to the walls, but her hands continued to slip.

"No, no, no. Not again," Kimber cried.

"Holy shit! We're going to go off the cliff if we don't stop!" Scarlett May yelled, her face as white as a ghost.

"We have to jump. We have to jump!" Emma screamed, scrambling to her feet, and looking for an exit.

Panic ensued. Screams sounded throughout the passenger car, and the man sitting beside me was frazzled and pale. He looked like he may be having a heart attack. His lips were gray, and the collar of his shirt was ripped open. I wished they were all Laylas now, but they weren't. They were families. *Children.*

"We can't jump; it will kill us!" Kimber screamed.

"What do you think is going to happen when we plunge off that cliff?" Emma yelled back, trying to open the emergency door.

Scarlett May slipped and was knocked down to her knees again. She scraped my legs trying to pull herself up.

I leaned back in my seat and let it all happen the way it wanted to. I knew we'd be home soon, and this was just the way to get there. It wasn't nice. It wasn't neat. Or pretty. It certainly wasn't fair. But the sooner everybody accepted it, the sooner we could move on.

I'd be lying if I said I wasn't scared to plunge off the side of the cliff. I was terrified. And I had an incredible fear of heights. But just like watching a scary movie, I told myself it wasn't real. If I could just close my eyes, it would all be over soon.

I knew how to fake confidence now, and it was a trick I tried while everyone else panicked. My jaw was clenched tight, and my back went rigid, but I would not run this time.

Emma got the door open, and a small handful of passengers jumped. Their screams lingered briefly in the air like tiny wisps in the wind. Emma leapt, and her scream snuffed like a candle as the train barreled forward. She didn't even look back.

Kimber wanted to jump, but she stalled for one second too long, and then it was too late.

The bumpy ride stopped as quickly as it started. We glided through the air. The ground beneath us was just a cloud now, and we soared like Levi had. My stomach leapt into my throat.

The ground was getting closer and closer. Bile filled my mouth. I closed my eyes to the chaos. I tried to ignore the screams as I waited for the crash.

But that wasn't the worst part. The worst part was when I woke up, tangled in my bed sheets, feeling like a prisoner of my own making.

CHAPTER 6

The night was long. The girls kept me awake, too frazzled to sleep after crashing to the bottom of the canyon. Emma was the only one who'd made it out in time, and even she was struggling. I couldn't help but feel like they were blaming me for their terror. I knew their fate rested in the palms of my hands, and it wasn't something I was happy about.

I assured them I was heading to Walker's house first thing in the morning, and we were going to get to work on my training. I told them things would be different in no time. And I may have even bribed them a little. It was all I could do when I grew tired and they were still angry with me. Nothing like year-round tans for everyone.

Walker hadn't been answering my texts, but I knew he was staying at the Williams' cabin across the lake. The drive would have taken too long in the golf cart, so I took a cab. By the time I got there, I had checked Layla's note about three times. Each time I expected her handwriting to have disappeared, but it was still there, and it was bolder than ever. As if somehow the indentation from the pen had deepened and the ink spread. I grew anxious about Walker's reaction to her message. Would he take her side? Would he agree with her? Would he forgo my training?

I'd never been to the Williams' cabin before, but I admired the unique cove. The dock was wide and adorned with a fire pit and outdoor lounge chairs. It was a far cry from the rest of the rickety old docks that barely stood on their pilings. Most of the cabins were half dilapidated, and the docks were worse. The Williams' cabin was one of the nicer ones on our end of the lake.

The north side of the lake was something entirely different. It was covered in tiny townhomes, hotels, and summer camps. The coves on the south side of Baylor Lake were privately owned lots and were usually passed down from generation to generation. That's how we'd gotten our cabin. It had belonged to my uncle Tanner, who got it when his parents passed.

I knocked on the door, surprised by my own strength. I was excited to see him, and it showed in the way my knuckles met the wooden door. I shifted my weight from foot to foot as I waited eagerly. When Walker opened the door, shirtless, I lost the words I'd prepared during the cab ride.

"Kinsley?" he said, looking me up and down. The scar on his brow wasn't bleeding, but it was bruised badly.

"Are you okay?" I reached out to touch his brow, and he pulled back. My hand lingered by his cheek before dropping to my waist. "I'm really sorry about Noah and Mason. They were just being idiots."

"Yeah, I'm not worried about it. You don't have to apologize for them," he said, beckoning me inside. This cabin was more spacious than ours and had an expansive open floor plan. I could see the kitchen, dining room, den, and living room, all at the same time. The view of the lake was breathtakingly beautiful through every window.

"So, this is where you've been hiding out all summer?" I asked, admiring the art on the wall. A buffalo painting hung at eye level. The artist had used thick and textured strokes. I wanted to run my hand over the canvas, but that's not what art was made for. *Look with your eyes, not with your hands,* Mom's voice chimed in my memory.

"More like for a couple decades, but yeah." I pulled my eyes from the painting and watched as Walker's expression turned heavy and solemn.

"It must be lonely," I said, thinking of Mason's threat. "The last thing you probably want to hear is somebody telling you to stay away . . . god, they're such assholes."

Walker scoffed, "Nah, don't worry about it. Walker grabbed the shirt draped over the back of the sofa and slipped it on. I soaked up the sight of his obliques before his white shirt draped lazily over his torso. He was better than the art on the wall. *Look with your eyes, not with your hands . . .*

"What are you doing over here Kinsley? You've never come here."

Kinsley? It felt like a demotion. I liked it better when he called me by my last name. "You weren't answering my texts, and I thought maybe you were going to listen to Mason and stay away."

"No. I wouldn't do that."

"Are you sure?" I asked. I could see that he was mulling something over in his head, and since he'd just called me by my first name, it seemed like there was a lot more going on than he wanted to admit.

"Yeah, I'm sure."

I didn't believe him. I trailed my finger across the back of the sofa, taking slow steps in his direction. "You know Noah isn't really my boyfriend, right?" I asked.

"I mean, whatever. Right?" Walker frowned and turned his back to me.

"Well, no. Not whatever. He's not my boyfriend." I needed him to understand.

"Okay?" Walker said with an aloof shrug.

"Okay. He's *not*. And I'm one hundred percent single." *Did I just say that?* I was so taken aback with my ability to humiliate myself, I forgot to close my mouth, blink, and whatever else it was humans did.

Walker turned around slowly, and I was both mortified to find that he was holding back laughter and relieved to see that he was his old warm self again. I'd somehow managed to single-handedly take all the awkwardness between us and wrap it into one sentence I could never take back. Still, I needed him to know. I couldn't have him walking around thinking I belonged to somebody else. I knew from experience that was a painful burden to carry.

"I . . . I . . . Um, I bet you wish all these things were yours. But this stuff belongs to the Williamses, huh?" I asked looking around, hiding the heat in my cheeks by pretending to look at more artwork.

"Yeah, I don't have that much."

"What do you do when the Williamses come into town?" I asked.

"I mean, I'm not really here, right? I'm only here because you're here, and we want to see each other. I don't exist for the Williams family." Walker sat on the sofa facing the picturesque lake-view window. I sat next to him, my foot tucked beneath me.

"But what about my friends? And everybody in town? They see you?" I studied his bruised brow. It was mostly yellow, with bits of green and blue blooming from the center.

"Does everybody see your grandmother?"

"No, but that's different," I said.

"How so?"

I thought about it long and hard, but in the end, I didn't know the difference. I'd always thought my gran lived in a different realm than Walker, but maybe she didn't. Maybe, just maybe, Walker wanted to be a part of my world in a way my gran didn't. Or perhaps she was just busy looking after my grandpa.

"We're all just ghosts. Most of us don't live in the physical form like I have with you. You're my friend Wilde, and I wouldn't be like this if you weren't here."

"Where would you be then?"

"Oh, I don't know. I'd probably be eating grapes and drinking champagne from one of those white puffy clouds up there," Walker said with a wink. His swollen brow stiffened the wink, but he got the job done. I smiled.

"Hey, I have something I wanted to show you," I said reaching for my back pocket. I felt the corner of the note through the denim of my pocket, but hesitated to pull it out. Something inside me seized up. Would he still want to spend his time with me if he knew Layla disapproved of me being here? Would Walker go back to wherever he'd come from, the realm my gran lived in, and the place where Layla lived when she wasn't haunting me?

I fumbled around my back pocket, sliding my hand inside my jeans and pretending I came up empty. The thought of living under the Baylor phenomenon without

Walker was not a pleasant one. And if that were the case, I'd happily return home to the beaten and battered body that lay in the hospital bed. Who knew what awaited me there? Struggle . . . lots and lots of struggle.

"I must have forgotten it," I lied.

"Forgot what?"

"Oh, I heard this thing, it was called a dreamwork. I was going to ask you what you knew about it. I wrote it down . . . just a couple of notes, but I thought you might be interested. It was something about symbols, I can't really remember now," I said, rolling around in the lie I'd just spun.

"That's right. Your mind is a complicated place. A dreamwork is exactly the thing that we need to learn about. That's where your latent mind stores information, and your conscious mind manifests it into a dream like this." Walker waved his hand about. "But your subconscious self doesn't want these dormant thoughts to be out in the open, so it uses dreamwork to manipulate them into signs and symbols to keep them hidden from yourself."

"Dormant thoughts?"

"Yeah. Everything you've ever thought or felt has a home. A place to live, in a dark forgotten corner of your mind."

"That's a scary thought. Are you saying that Baylor Lake might not even be a lake? That it could be a symbol for something that I'm feeling or thinking?" Lainey's ghost pleading to be heard flashed through my head and her voice rang in my ears. *Wake up.*

I jerked my head and shook the thought loose. Walker paused for a moment, studying me. He must think I'm crazy.

"Well, I guess it's possible. Sure, the lake could be a symbol for something you fear. Water can have a lot of meanings. It could mean the thirst for knowledge—"

I laughed. The thought of me dying to learn more was a joke. School had always been slow torture for me.

"—it could mean fear of something you don't have control over. Or new beginnings."

Something I didn't have control over . . . That was more like it.

"Of course, it could be none of those, or several. A body of water in your dream could mean something entirely different from a body of water in mine. That's what's so complicated about dreamwork. Every symbol is unique to its dreamer."

"And just so I'm clear, we can, or we cannot, interpret this dream?" I asked, feeling more exposed than ever. My eyes turned to the expansive window. If that lake were my emotions, we'd have a vat of worries to sort through.

"No, we can't interpret your dream. I mean, we could try?"

"No!" I shook my head, disinterested.

"But it would just be an interpretation. There's no

actual way of knowing what your mind is really trying to tell you or hide from you."

"You think my mind's trying to hide stuff from me?"

"Well, yeah. Everybody's mind does that. I think it tries to protect you from the truth. Sometimes, the truth is what we fear most."

I wondered what my mind was hiding from me. If all the terrible things I'd seen here in Baylor were easier to swallow than the truth, I never wanted to wake up. The real world was a scary place. At least in my dreams I could tell myself it was make-believe.

"What do you think your mind is hiding from you?" I asked, tilting my head to the side, enjoying the tables being turned. Walker laughed and an uncomfortable smile crossed his face.

"Let's just focus on you. Are you ready for training?" he asked.

"Okay. I'll get it out of you someday," I said with a smile.

"We'll see about that. Let's start with the basics. Lucid dreaming. Lucid dreaming is when you are aware and conscious that you are dreaming." Walker jumped to his feet and started pacing back and forth in front of the window. The bright morning rays made his form look like a black silhouette of thought, bouncing from one side of the room to the next. "You're conscious you are dreaming right now, right?"

"Yes." Obviously, this was a dream. Look at how handsome he was . . .

"Most of the time, when somebody is aware that they are currently in a dream, it unlocks a sense of control. But this is where we're running into a problem. You don't have that sense of control."

"No. Not all the time."

"Would it be safe to say that *most* of the time you lack the control?" he asked.

"Yeah. Everything seems to happen to me, or around me. Sometimes I feel like I'm on the outside looking in, and very, very seldom I will feel like I can manipulate what's happening. And even then, when I do, it usually turns out badly. Like I shouldn't have meddled with it in the first place." I hooked my arm over the back of the sofa and watched Walker rummage through notes on the kitchen counter.

"I think the very first thing you need to do is remind yourself that you are in control and that you have the power to change what you see. So, remind yourself of that as often as you can. Sometimes a token can help. Um—" Walker patted his pockets and then looked down at a ring on his finger, twisting it for a split second before pulling it off.

"Here, keep this on you at all times. Every time you reach for it, or notice that it's there, remind yourself that you're dreaming, and you hold the control. Nobody else," Walker said, holding out a gold band.

"Are you sure? I don't want to take this from you," I said, simultaneously reaching out for the ring.

"I want you to have it. It was my dad's. I never really knew him, so it can't mean that much, right? My mom gave it to me when I was a teenager."

"I'm sure it means something to you." I slipped the ring on my finger, but it fell right off. I tried it on my thumb, and it was a perfect fit. I liked the way it looked, and I liked the way it felt even more. Like I had a piece of Walker with me wherever I went. I wanted to give him something of mine as well, but I had nothing to give. "I'll take good care of it," I said, admiring it.

"Just remember to be lucid."

"Every time I look at it, I swear, I'll remember this moment." My heart warmed with his generosity. Walker smiled at me, and I knew the ring meant much more to him than he let on.

When he turned back to his book, his face glowed in a way I had never seen. If I didn't know any better, I'd think he felt honored that I was wearing his ring. Could he possibly have feelings for me? Did he like me back?

"I would say don't get excited, but we don't need to worry about that," Walker mumbled as he ran his finger back and forth across a page of the book.

"What do you mean we don't have to worry about that?" I asked.

"It means, when most people are in a dream state and they realize that they're lucid dreaming, they tend to get excited, and then they wake up. You, you're different. You're stuck here. Unable to wake up because of medications from the hospital. So, you can get excited all you want, but you're stuck here at their mercy." Walker gave me a sympathetic shrug.

I didn't like the thought of getting overly excited and jolting awake in a different realm. What would become of my life here? "What do you think will happen when they try to wake me up?" I asked, feeling vulnerable in an entirely different way.

Walker closed the book and pulled it close to his chest. "I'm not sure. I guess you go home," he said somberly. I chewed on the inside of my lip, wishing and hoping there was another way. Gran said it was my choice, and I only hoped that, when I found my self-control, I could will myself to stay. But fighting against real medications sounded challenging, if not impossible.

"What's next?" I asked, eager to start training.

"I say we kick this into high gear. Let's take it from the top. We'll go hard in your training, and you'll get this in no time, Wilde." Walker placed the book on the kitchen island and came to the back of the sofa.

I nodded my head in agreement; I was ready. I needed

to cram like I was studying for finals. Because I never knew when it was going to be my last day here, and I would need every trick up my sleeve if I wanted to stay and fight.

"I'm ready."

"Then all there is left to do is leap . . . literally," he said, with a wicked gleam in his eyes.

I recoiled. "You know I'm afraid of heights, right?"

CHAPTER 7

Y ou won't be afraid of heights when you learn to
fly," Walker said.

"Fly! I can't *fly!*" I glared at him, hands on
my hips. *Was he crazy?*

"Look, flying is the ultimate dream training.
Everybody knows that if they have control over their
dreams, they can fly. It's the first thing people do when
they turn lucid."

"I don't think that's necessarily true, Walker. Plus, do
you really expect me to fly with no training whatsoever?"
My voice was a sheer squeal.

"You said you wanted to jump into the deep end.
We've got to try this. You can do it. I believe in you," he
said, placing his hands on my shoulders and giving me a
small shake. I stared into his golden eyes, and I trusted he
had my best interests at heart.

"If you say so . . ."

"I know just the place," Walker said with a clap.

The next thing I knew, we were on the forest trails weaving in and out of something that looked to have been a path decades prior. I fell into step behind him and tried not to think of how humiliating this was about to be. "So, what exactly did you have in mind?"

"Do you remember that boulder with the rope swing?" Walker asked, swatting at a bug.

"You mean, the one . . ."

"Yeah. That one."

Silence stretched between us. It was the rope swing that Ethan had jumped from, and he'd never resurfaced. How could I forget? The training had already taken an ominous turn, and we hadn't even started yet.

"I don't know about this," I said, thankful he couldn't see my face. His pace slowed on the trail, but we never stopped walking.

"You have nothing to worry about. I'll be right here the whole time. I won't let you fall," he said. Well, if that were the case, I'd have to make sure I failed. The thought of falling into his arms all day long didn't seem so bad. I even caught a pep in my step.

When we arrived at the boulders, it brought back memories of that dreadful day. I remembered I'd felt disconnected from Walker, and the rejection had been a fresh pinch on my bleeding heart. Ethan's jump played in my head on repeat, and the panic returned to my chest where it had once squeezed like a corset.

"I don't want to jump in the water," I said.

"You don't have to do anything you don't want to. If it makes you uncomfortable, we'll skip it."

The tightness grew as the rope swing came into full sight. The rope hung like a bad omen that only I could see.

"Why don't you crawl up there, and then you can get a feel for how comfortable you are. And if you're up for it, you can jump—"

I stood at the base of the first boulder and took a deep breath, shielding my eyes from the mid-morning sun. I looked warily at Walker. "Noooo . . ."

"Could you jump onto the ground?" He searched my eyes, trying to gage how stubborn I'd be before we came to an agreement. "It's not that far. And if you fall, I'll be here, with my arms out to catch you."

I knew jumping didn't pose any actual risks, other than humiliation. I agreed, begrudgingly, but only because I didn't want to disappoint him.

Walker interlaced his fingers, giving me a step up on the rock. I dug my hands into the crevices of the boulder and pulled myself onto the first landing. Then I made the mistake of looking behind me. I knew it was the worst thing you could do when you're afraid of heights—look back to see how far you've come. It must've been five feet from the ground, but it felt like three times that. I wasn't meant to be this tall.

Walker gave me an encouraging nod and smile, accompanied with a nerdy thumbs-up. I swallowed hard and climbed up the second rock. By the time I was at the top, all I had left to do was stand, but it felt impossible. It must've taken a full minute for me to rise from a crouch to my full height. This was *so* stupid. I had a better chance of passing out and falling off the rock than flying.

"I don't think I can do this!"

"You can do it!"

"No. You're going to have to climb up here and get me down!" I yelled.

"Wilde . . . would you do me a favor?"

I said nothing in return. I just stared down at him through angry eyes.

"Would you look down at your thumb please? What do you see?"

I didn't have to look. I closed my hand over my thumb, and I twisted the ring back and forth. The metal warmed with my touch. He was right. I was in control. I could do this. But I couldn't do it if I thought about it any longer. Without warning, I took one long stride and jumped off the boulder.

"Wait!" Walker yelled.

I didn't think about flying; I didn't even try. I dropped like a brick through thin air. Walker lunged to make good on his promise, but I had given him no warning, and he was only able to barely brush my arm before my feet hit the ground. The shock splintered through my shins, causing me to drop and roll. Walker's hand barely grazed my back.

"Oww . . ." I moaned.

"Are you okay?" Walker dropped to his knees.

I took a moment to count my blessings. Thank god I was back on the ground, and nothing had broken.

"Did I fly?" I asked in a sarcastic tone. Walker laughed.

"Um . . . Almost?" he lied. I slapped his shoulder, and he fell to his butt beside me, pretending it hurt.

"You didn't catch me. What the hell?" I sat up slowly, feeling the sudden onset of a headache.

"You've got to give me a little notice next time, tiger," he said, pulling a twig from the long strands of my hair. There was something about it that seemed intimate. His hand in my hair. *I could get used to this.*

There was a heat in his eyes that was both warm and sultry. I wanted to lean in and kiss him, but that had never turned out well. Instead, I let myself get lost looking into the gold flecks of his eyes. He smudged his thumb over my cheek, and I melted under his touch. My stomach dropped, and if there had been any pain from the fall, I wasn't feeling it now.

"You've got some dirt," he said under his breath.

All of a sudden the heat in his eyes went out, and

exchanged for something I didn't recognize. Hurt? Guilt? It didn't last long; he jumped to his feet. Dusted himself off and held out a hand to help me up. Even his grasp was cold. I picked through the various bits mother nature had deposited in my hair as I tried to make sense of the array of emotions that had flashed through his eyes.

"So . . . what's next?" I was afraid to ask, but I didn't want to think about the pained look I had seen any longer. I'd rather jump from another boulder.

"Maybe we came out too hot. Let's rein it back in. You can jump off something small."

"There's a creek not too far from here that feeds into the lake. It's tiny and has a cute wooden bridge over it. We could start there?" I asked.

"That's perfect."

A short, quiet walk later, I found myself standing on a two-foot-tall bridge. The creek was pretty much nonexistent in the heat of summer. It was only a dry bed of rocks nestled within the trees. I worried about twisting my ankle; if there was a way this could go wrong, I'd find it.

Instead of jumping off the middle of the bridge into the dry bed, I planned to run over the bridge and leap on the descent. It was no more than a jump and skip I might have done on flat ground, but I was trying to appease Walker and his attempt at training me.

I felt stupid even trying, but Walker made it better. After failing to keep his promise earlier, he decided that if either of us were going to do something stupid, it was going to be him first. He ran over the bridge—passing me in the middle with subpar speed—and leapt into the air like a wannabe ballerina. He made a mockery of himself and came tumbling down on the other side. I laughed so hard my knees weakened, and I couldn't hold myself upright.

"I'm going to miss this," he said as he sat up, dried leaves caked to his back.

Something pulled at my heartstrings. "What did you say?"

"I'm going to miss this," he said again, his laughter turning to loneliness.

All I wanted was to watch him laugh. I didn't like it when he was sad. These days, he appeared sad way too often, and it crushed me. "What? This?" I asked, running and jumping off the miniature bridge.

I didn't fly. He was so delusional. We did the only thing we could do now; we joked about it. Walker laughed at my pathetic attempt, and I came to his side with my hands on my hips. Slightly winded and in a more serious tone, I said, "You don't have to."

He took a deep, solemn breath, and reached out to push my hair behind my shoulder. "Let's not talk about that right now." He turned away and started to walk down the path unnaturally fast. I had to jog just to keep up. It was almost like he was running from something, but I imagined, being trapped in this realm, he couldn't get very far. Maybe the lake symbolized the depth of his sorrows.

Was he sad to think that one day I'd leave him? Or was he sad because he wanted me to stay? It felt like our relationship was growing into something more than two peas in a—one-of-a-kind—pod. It was branching out into new avenues, stretching and strengthening. It was hard to trump the way we'd begun, him saving my life and all, but we had never crossed the romantic bridge before, and I had a feeling we were getting close. Walker's eyes had twinkled a little differently in recent weeks, and there was a strong sense of sadness that emanated from him when we talked about me leaving Baylor.

There was a part of me that was riddled with insecurities. That feared he only wanted me to help him find Layla. That he would be sad when I left, because his chances of eternal love would dwindle significantly. That I was his only shard of hope for a life with her, a life of happiness. But there was another part of me, the more rational part, that told me he wouldn't look at me the way he did if he didn't have feelings for me. His eyes wouldn't gleam when they fell upon me. His dimples wouldn't flex. And I wouldn't get that pull in my heart, like two magnets being drawn to each other.

I've been wrong about a lot of things in my life; I'll admit that. I've been incompetent, and I've been blindsided. But I couldn't shake my instincts on this one. I wasn't the only one with feelings here. However deep or shallow? That I didn't know. The reason he'd been denying them? That could be just about anything. There were a hundred reasons why we shouldn't be together, starting with the day he'd died and ending with a curse. None of which I wanted to think about now.

I'd been so entangled in my own web of thoughts, I hadn't realized we'd arrived at our next destination. We were on a small bluff, the lake below us. It was a beautiful lookout point, with a wooden bench in the clearing. Tufts of overgrown grass clumped around the legs of the bench. Walker stood at the edge of the cliff peering over, and I didn't like the feeling that dropped from my chest into my belly. He turned, beckoning to me, and I instinctively took a step backward. There was *no way* I was jumping off that cliff, and there was *no way* I was going to *fly* off it.

"I think this is the perfect blend of height and safety for you to grow your wings."

"No. I'm not doing that. Are you crazy?" I shook my head, taking several more steps backward.

"If all else fails—"

"And it will!" my voice trembled.

"—you'll jump into the water and swim to shore," Walker cautiously approached me, like I was a rabid dog baring its teeth. I took another step back.

"Walker, I can't. I can't." I shook my head maniacally. He managed to grab my wrist in one quick motion and pull me close to him. Tears pricked the corners of my eyes, and he lowered his forehead to mine. He took a deep breath, and I did the same. We were breathing the same air, and it was filled with the forbidden fear of falling. Not falling off the cliff, but falling in love. Falling . . . and not being caught.

When my breath steadied, Walker's grip lightened to a whisper touch across my back, and I blinked my eyes open with conviction. I was going to do it. I wasn't just going to jump off that cliff; I was going to fly. And I prayed he would be the one to catch me. Because that's what happens when you fall in love; you fall without ever hitting the ground. You trust that your person will be there to catch you when the ground approaches. I was ready to take that leap, and the better half of me thought Walker was too.

"Are you ready?" he asked, his voice was like a low vibration I could get lost in. I pulled away from the small bubble we'd made for ourselves and gulped at the ever-thinning air.

"I'll go first. I'll wait for you in the water. That way, if you fall, I'll be right there with you."

"And if I don't?" It had seemed funny before, when we were jumping off the bridge. But there was nothing funny about it now. It felt like life or death. Which was ironic, because that's what we were. I was life, he was death.

"Then I'll swim to the shore, and I'll meet you wherever you land." I nodded, and he wrapped his hand around the base of my head and pulled me in, kissing my forehead.

The tender moment ended before my eyes could open. He dove off the cliff with all the ease of a first-class diver. I heard the splash and started to count. By the time I hit three, it would be my turn. Not another thought about it.

One . . . My heart was pounding with the excitement of new beginnings.

Two . . . My palms were sweating with the fear of failure.

Three . . . I did it anyway.

I ran toward the cliff. No turning back now. I pushed off the edge of the cliff and clumps of dirt gave way under my feet and crumbled into the water below. I clapped my hands together into the fine point of an arrowhead. I felt the air wrap around my body, supporting me as I flew.

But my heart was heavy, and the magnetic pull I had for Walker was fierce. The force was otherworldly, sinking its talons into me like I was its prey and pulling me down into the water to meet him. It was more than gravity; it was something else entirely, something I had no words for. Had I not wanted to fly? Had I not believed in myself? Or was my soul simply diving down because that's where he was?

The needlepoint of my fingertips split the water in two. The lake cracked open and swallowed me whole. The force was so strong, it didn't stop when I broke the surface —I plunged down with all the weight of the universe, cutting through the water like a missile aiming toward the deepest channel of the lake.

I opened my eyes, anticipating the evil darkness I'd grown to expect from Baylor Lake, but instead, I could see everything. It was like another world under the water. Perhaps another realm altogether. The sunlight dappled the water and filtered into a glow of dancing searchlights. It was a fortress of underwater plants and tiny bubbles floating like champagne streamers. The deeper I sank, the darker everything became. The green plants turned a murky dark gray, and the sun-dappled aqua was transformed into a dingy darkness.

When I finally stopped, it was only because I hit the bottom. My feet sank into the mud as I looked up toward the surface. The sunlight was but a tiny dot, so very far away. Walker was nowhere to be seen.

There was no way I could make it back on a single breath. But then I remembered, I didn't technically need to breathe. I closed my hand over my thumb, and Walker's ring. *I'm in control . . .*

I knew I should swim up, because that's where I belonged, but the urgency was lost somewhere in the wonder of the vast lake. Did I belong on the surface? Layla seemed to think I didn't belong in Baylor at all. All I knew was that I didn't belong here at the bottom of the lake, with Lainey and god knows what else.

I saw her then. Like she had come when I called.

Lainey wasn't the double I had first encountered in the lake after she'd disappeared; she was sweet. Angelic. Like a mermaid or some underwater goddess. Her medium-length hair formed sweeping curls around her face. Her freckles glowed like twinkling stars in the night sky. And she was happy.

"Wake up," she said. Her voice cut through the water and surrounded me with its persuasive influence.

I was tempted to stay with her. I wanted to be happy and angelic like my best friend. I wanted to float like an underwater angel and swim forever by her side. But then she said it again. "Wake up."

The water seemed to close in around me, and I stiffened a little. The temptation to stay faded.

"Wake up!" Lainey's words grew louder and more demanding. I took a step backward and stumbled in a bed of rocks.

"Wake up!" The sound waves of her message rippled out and knocked me to the ground. I scrambled to get up, pushing my hands through a sea of silky plants and sharp shells. Something slimy wiggled across my wrist, and I panicked. A strong sense of danger raced through my body, telling me I wasn't where I belonged. That Layla had been right all along.

The lake turned icy as my fear grew. I wasn't alone down here. There were things in this water; secrets of the deep. Secrets I didn't want to know, and probably couldn't handle if I did. Symbols I wanted to keep hidden. Whatever my subconscious was telling me, I wanted to run from it. Because the thought of living two lives at once was a scary thought, and I knew it was unsustainable. I kicked out of the dark silt and started to swim to the surface. I needed to get out of here.

A whisper-like touch tickled my toes and wrapped around my heel, then slinked up my ankle. Lainey had my foot in her grasp. Her hold was soft but strong—gone were the claws of the dead I had known before. She drew my eye to something I hadn't noticed before. She pointed to a door at the bottom of the lake.

It was a red door, bright against the mud and algae. The gold knob gleamed with a warmth that both intrigued and invited me. I stopped fighting for the surface and floated neutrally in the cold water. My arms rose from my sides as I relaxed, staring at the red door. I felt at peace.

Where did it lead? Was it a door to the afterlife? Was it a door to the living? Or maybe it was the door to Walker's heart? It didn't really matter what the answer was, because I was drawn to open it either way. There was something luring me toward it, at the same time that I was pulled to Walker on the surface. Suspended between him above and the door below, I didn't know what to do.

In that moment, I wanted Walker more. But it scared me that it wasn't by much. A decision that important should never be that nebulous. Especially one involving the heart.

Lainey's eyes turned from an ethereal glow to dull and dimensionless. Her starlit freckles turned to craters that ate through her flesh like acid in a rolling boil over her face. Her dancing hair turned to pond scum and drifted to the bottom of the lake in clumps. She deteriorated before my very eyes.

The door was abruptly hidden between rows and rows of headstones that hadn't been there before. Guarded by lurking shadows and leopard-spotted eels. Whatever admission I'd had through that red door was now gone, and so were the warm and fuzzy feelings.

I could suddenly see Walker trying to swim down to get me, but he could only make it so far before having to turn around and go back for air. I kicked my feet and propelled my arms through the heavy water, fighting with all my might. His faint cries pierced through the water, and I knew I had to hurry. I kicked frantically. As soon as I'd made the decision to return to the surface, the need for air had ripped through my chest, and my lungs had tried to expand but couldn't.

My limbs were growing weak with exhaustion when the sun-dappled light finally reappeared. I was getting close. I kicked through the nightmares until Walker met me fifteen feet from the surface. He pulled me to the top where I took a huge, labored gulp of air. He spun me onto my back as I tried to stay conscious, wrapping his arm around my chest and swimming me to shore.

The sky spun, and my head was woozy. There was a piece of me still sunk at the bottom of the lake, lost and scared. I felt like I'd never take a full breath again. I was splintered in two. A chunk of my heart was somewhere beyond that red door, and it left me homesick.

"Are you okay? Wilde, are you okay?" Walker asked, slapping my cheeks as I lay on the sandy shore.

"I'm okay. I'm okay," I said, glaring at the scintillating water.

"I'm so sorry. I'm *so* sorry. We never have to do that again. I never should have pushed you to do that. I'm sorry." Walker held me tight to his chest and rocked me back and forth.

"It's okay. . . I think I was close to flying," I said absentmindedly.

CHAPTER 8

From head to toe, we were all dressed in black to hide within the shadows and camouflage into the darkness. I'd never broken into a house before, but it wasn't the Vandals I was afraid of. It was the wolf.

I pulled on the drawstrings of Emma's hoodie, tightening the hood around her face. Only her petite features poked out through the center. But I didn't need her wrinkled forehead to tell me she was frowning; I could see it in her worried eyes. I loosened the strings, allowing her cheeks to breathe. "What? You can do this," I said.

"I just don't understand. If you think the Vandals are the bad guys, then why are we going over there?" Emma said, as I tugged on her sweatshirt.

"Because we're going to kick some wolf ass!" Scarlett May said.

"But it's not like we can fight. Do you even have

pepper spray? Or something? A prime rib to throw? A net? Do we have a net?" Emma rambled, her eyes fluttering with questions.

"No, but do you think we should grab a hot dog or something?" Kimber asked. I guess it made sense. What dog didn't like meat? It was the perfect distraction.

"Yeah. Grab the whole package."

"Or whatever's left; Mason eats those things like Tic Tacs," Scarlett May said. Kimber ducked into the kitchen.

"So, what do we do when we get inside?" Emma asked.

"Look for anything suspicious. We're just going over there to figure out what's going on. And we don't want to get caught, so don't touch anything. Don't move anything. And don't make any noise," I said.

When Kimber returned with two hot dogs slumped in a dripping wrapper, we were ready to cross the yard. We hadn't told the boys what we were up to, because there was no way they would've let us go alone. We weren't on a mission to trap the wolf and feed it to the fish; we only wanted to know the truth. We wanted to know what we were up against so that we could be better prepared to fight the evil that lurked in the woods. Since it looked like the neighbors were half packed and between moves, we were confident we could get in and out without ever being seen. They probably weren't even in town.

"Ready?" I asked.

"Let's do this," Scarlett May said, slapping a flashlight

against her palm. Emma met my gaze with wary eyes, and I gave her a nod of encouragement.

"Just imagine it's one of your stories. You're the main character, and you're investigating a crime scene," I said. Emma's brows rose into her hoodie and her eyes softened. I could see that she liked the idea.

We set out, huddling together like sheep. Only we didn't know where the herding dog was. We crouched, crossing into the middle of the clearing that stretched between the two cabins. The lawn was wet with dew in the night. The excitement coursed through my veins. It was the liberty to be free and to do what we wanted. We were no longer sitting ducks. We weren't the victims. And we would not sit and wait until the wolf came to us. We were going to find it, and it felt good. Empowering.

Emma let out a shriek when the floodlights turned on. It was the motion-sensor light on the Vandals' house. Perhaps I was the only one who felt empowered. Scarlett May shoved Emma, as she cupped her hands over her mouth. The four of us crouched, frozen in the clearing with the spotlight on us.

"What do we do?"

"Just don't move."

"No. That doesn't make sense. The lights are going to remain on as long as there's motion. We need to get out of the clearing. We need to hurry and cross to the Vandals' house," I whispered.

"Okay. Let's go," Scarlett May said.

We moved forward with the spotlights cascading down on us. Only this time, the air felt cooler and crisper on my side. Our pack felt smaller. Like one had already been plucked off by the unseen dangers of the yard. It was Emma. She was crouching in the middle of the yard all by her lonesome. Frozen in fear.

"Emma what are you doing?" I hissed, beckoning to her.

"I can't do it. I can't do it." She shook her head frantically.

"Yes, you can. Come on."

Scarlett May and Kimber had reached the shadow of the Vandals' cabin. Emma and I were separated in the yard. But I didn't want to go backward, and she didn't want to go forward. She stood to her full height, abruptly abandoning the mission, turned and ran back to the cabin. A small whine escaped her, the sound waning with the growing distance. I threw my hands in the air and watched as she climbed onto the back deck and crouched behind one of the lounge chairs. I sighed heavily and then turned back to the others. They waved me forward and, reluctantly, I left Emma behind.

"We're better off without her," Scarlett May hissed.

"Yeah. She probably would have screamed or something. Don't worry about it," Kimber said.

We made our way to the back door and found that, just

as we'd expected, it was locked. Scarlett May checked the windows as we made our way around the cabin. The front door was also locked, as well as the garage. But Scarlett May found a small window in the bathroom that had been left cracked open. She signaled us with a flicker of her flashlight.

Kimber and I boosted her up, and she crawled through the window. There was nothing graceful about it. She floundered, halfway in and halfway out. Kicking her legs, she landed on top of the toilet. The three of us froze, two on the outside, one on the inside. But nothing else sounded throughout the cabin. No voices. No alarms. And no lights.

I helped Kimber next. I lifted her light frame with ease, and she crawled through the tiny window without so much as a sound. I was next. But there was nobody to help me scale the wall. The window was just tall enough to where I couldn't pull myself up. I tried twice, my feet kicking against the wood shingles. I was determined to get in. Kimber and Scarlett May spat suggestions at me until somebody had the bright idea to open the front door.

I found myself lurking around the side of the cabin by my lonesome. And it was then that something rumbled in the bushes. I was several strides from safety when I saw the bush sway from side to side. I took off running, and a darkness lifted from the bush into the air. A cloud of my own personal fear came from the woodwork to greet me. As I lunged forward, the front door opened, and I tumbled inside just in time to escape my dreaded imagination.

My breaths came in short, shallow pants as the cabin door closed behind me. I didn't have long to catch my breath as the girls wandered throughout the cabin, arms linked and whispering. It smelled like the cuddy cabin of a small boat, or the abandoned grandparents' basement with periodic water leaks. It was dank and musty. Whatever it was, it didn't smell like a home two people were living in.

Their sofa was draped in a white sheet, and most of their furniture was clumped together in the middle of the room. A painting tarp crinkled beneath my shoes. I found it odd that the cabin was not freshly painted nor stained. It would have smelled better if it was. Boxes lined the kitchen counters with various appliances stuffed inside neatly. A bread machine. Wrapped coffee mugs. A blender.

"Do you see anything?" Kimber asked. The truth was, I saw nothing incriminating. This didn't look like the den of a wolf. This looked like the cabin of two people in the middle of a move, selling their vacation home for something more manageable in their later years. But I didn't want to admit it. Because admitting that there was nothing wrong with the Vandals meant there was everything wrong with me. And I didn't want to take that blame. Not today. Not ever.

Perhaps, I didn't know what I was looking for. Had I expected to find a pile of carcasses? Bunny rabbit tails, a bobcat's hide, putrid fish skins with flaking scales that glimmered like glitter across the cabin floor? Had I expected to find a warm spot in the living room where the wolf curled up to sleep? Had I thought the walls would be covered in claw marks and the cabin would reek of wet dog? No . . . I hadn't expected any of those things. But I simply hadn't expected this either. I didn't expect the Vandals to be *so* boring.

And then it hit me like a lightning bolt. This wasn't the den at all. "The garden!" I hissed.

"What?"

"That's where it all happens. Mrs. Vandal's pottery shed out back. It's got to be where all the evidence is."

Kimber shook her head slowly.

"Go outside? Are you stupid?" Scarlett May asked.

I thought for a moment—maybe I was. But I knew trekking out to the shed could clear my name. We would find the Baylor Butcher. The wolf. Whatever the threat was that still haunted me and my friends long after Big Jimmy had died. I was sure of it.

"Come on you guys. We've already come this far . . ."

"You mean across the lawn?" Scarlett May scoffed.

"No!" Kimber said in a voice that was anything but a whisper.

As if waking a giant, the floorboards creaked above our heads. The three of us froze, heads tilted toward the ceiling. My eyes followed along the ceiling as the steps crossed from one side of the cabin to the other. Scarlett May clicked her flashlight off, and we waited in the dark listening until the footsteps approached the staircase. Then all hell broke loose.

The three of us scampered like mice on a kitchen counter after the lights flickered on. No longer were we careful or quiet. We bolted for the back door, the three of us fighting over the doorknob. Yelling and pushing, we bolted outside, off the back deck, and into the grass. That's where we divided. Kimber and Scarlett May headed for the safety of our cabin. I was the only one who ran toward the potting shed.

"Wait!" I hissed. The whisper was lost in the heat of the moment. They didn't hear me, or maybe they didn't care. "Wait!" I yelled.

The girls stopped in the middle of the clearing as the floodlights illuminated them. Scarlett May waved me on and Kimber clung to her arm. "Come on Kinsley!"

My body locked up. I wanted to join them. I wanted to run far away from here. I wanted to run straight out of Baylor. But I was frozen. Frozen in fear. Frozen in time. I just stood there unable to move. The girls fled the scene as the Vandals' porch light came on and a figure peered out the window. The girls ran full speed back to safety as I dropped to my stomach and lay in the shadows.

I watched as Emma's figure appeared on the back patio underneath the porch light. She waved the girls forward then peered out into the blackness, looking for me. My heart pounded, and I felt like I was sinking into the wet grass. The Vandals' patio door swung open, and I sucked in a gasp of the chilly night air and a mission gone wrong.

With no thought at all, I army crawled to the potting shed. Once I hit the soil surrounding the shed, I popped to my feet and patted the door down in search of a way in. My hand wrapped around the cold metal handles, and I pulled the door open and shut myself inside. Once inside, I slowed my breathing and tried to think.

I tried to steady my trembling body, but I felt the unknown closing in on me. It was pitch black inside the shed, and Scarlett May had the only flashlight. I had no way of knowing if I'd found the wolf's den or not. Unlike the vast dark cove, this confined space was small and suffocating. I didn't know how long I would have to wait inside the shed, but I already itched to leave.

Slowly, I checked over my shoulder, but I couldn't see a single thing. I told myself there should be nothing there except rakes, shovels, potting soil, and seeds, but I didn't believe it. There *should* be shelves of tools, like bush-trimming clippers and rooting powders and plant growth nutrients. In a normal shed, there wouldn't be anything mysterious. Nothing paranormal. And definitely not malevolent. And under no circumstances would there ever be a large, hairy, grizzly wolf . . . standing behind me.

I scrunched my eyes shut and pressed the palms of my

hands against my sockets. But *should be* and *probably* were two very different things, and I knew that, with my luck, I'd just run straight into the wolf's mouth and asked him to swallow me whole.

Stop! Stop thinking of that . . .

I knew by now that I would conjure my fears if I fed my mind nothing but worry. But wasn't that what I was doing now? Wasn't that why my heart was racing? Wasn't it why the potting shed felt like it was closing in on me? Because the fear was growing? It was changing and morphing to life before me?

I felt it come together, pull itself from thin air behind my back. The tiny hairs on my neck prickled. My pupils dilated and my hearing piqued. Had I ever really been in control? Or was this all happening *to* me? Was I the victim? Because I certainly wasn't the hero. I felt like a victim now, in the dank, dark shed that felt more like a coffin with every passing minute. I was going to die in here. *Die again.*

Footsteps slinked through the wet grass, the sound growing further away. I tried to push it all out of my mind and stay focused on the facts. Listen to the footfalls. Mr. Vandal had chased the girls away. He was probably at my cabin now, pounding on the back door. The girls were probably hiding behind the pool table or upstairs in the master bedroom. It was the perfect time to escape. If there was evidence in the shed, I couldn't see it anyway. I took a deep breath and gripped the handle. I turned the lever just as I heard a twig snap outside the door.

I stilled, pushing my ear to the door. It was quiet. Too quiet. The door ripped open. I screamed. I pulled the door shut as I jumped backward. Once a coffin closing in on me, the shed was now my sanctuary.

I gripped the doorknob with two hands leveraging my weight to keep the door shut. My body jerked violently back and forth as the thing shook the door on its hinges. I held on for dear life. It took everything I had, and more.

As quickly as it started, it stopped. Everything stilled in the dark. But my dread only grew. I remained rigid, holding the door shut with all my might. I counted the seconds—the calm before the storm.

One. My breaths were quick and shallow.

Two. My joints were locked, my body braced.

Three. "Kinsley?" A deep voice called from the other side of the door.

It wasn't the wolf. It was Mason. *Mason?* Slowly, I straightened. I kept my hands on the doorknob but loosened my grip. Blood rushed back into my fingers like tiny pins sticking me.

"Mason? Is that you?" I asked.

"Yeah. It's me."

My shoulders dropped, and my body slackened. He was here to rescue me.

"Open the door!" he said eagerly.

I began to do as he said, but then I questioned—was he *too* eager?

Why would Mason come to save me, and not Noah?

"Why?" I said, wincing as it left my mouth.

"Why do you think? Don't you want to get out of there? Or are you going to hide in the neighbor's shed all night?"

I didn't answer.

"Come on, hurry up. He's almost back," Mason said.

My heart walloped in my chest. I knew Mr. Vandal would be back soon. A matter of seconds was all I had to escape unseen. But there was something holding me back.

How much did I really trust Mason?

Could he be the wolf?

He was the one who had told Walker I was taken. He was the one who had spread the lies and sent him home. He was the one who had threatened my relationship. I felt the weight of my scowl before I even realized I was upset. I wasn't suspicious of Mason; I was downright angry.

I'd done nothing to Mason. Why would he treat me that way? Is this how he repaid me for inviting him to my cabin for the summer? By eating my light bulbs? By getting in the way of Walker and me? He wasn't just a wolf in sheep's clothing; he was an *asshole!*

"No!" I yelled.

"Seriously, Kins? Come on!"

"No! I'm not opening the door. I'll stay here all night if I must!"

The doorknob jiggled lightly, and I tightened my grip. And then the storm hit.

A snarl ripped through the night, and the commotion rattled the shed. The whole door shook with such force it could topple the entire shack over. *I was right.* Mason *was* the wolf! And that made me his prey.

The door was pulled halfway open and then slammed shut, forcing in a brief gust of cool air. I threw my weight backward and felt a sticky web kiss my cheek. I yelped and flinched, letting my guard down for a split second.

Screams echoed in the distance. Three girls. I couldn't make out what they were saying, but I knew that Emma, Scarlett May, and Kimber were watching the whole thing from next door.

The wolf grumbled ferociously. Its snarls cascaded down from ten feet, maybe more. The slick drool gurgled in its growl. I could hear something rip, the tare of something salacious. I imagined Mason breaking out of his skin and growing to twice his height, into a beast this world had never known.

Eight tiny legs tiptoed down my neck and across my clavicle, forcing me to let go of the handle and flail about.

I screamed, scraping at my neck and clawing at my hair. My body danced beyond my control. The door sprang open when I let go, and I toppled out of the shed, rolling on the ground like I was on fire. Wet smudged across my chest and balled under my hand. The miniature threat gave way to the enormous one standing in front of me.

A large, grotesque wolf stood on its hind legs. Upright, like a human. The edge of its fur was lit by the moonlight and glinted a silvery white. Its eyes glowed fluorescent yellow flanked by fire orange. And its drool shimmered like a prism of promised pain.

It took a large breath, expanding its beastly chest and growing impossibly taller. I scooted back on my butt. My hands dug into the soil beneath me as I tried to push away. I gained inches, nothing more.

I scampered backward whimpering until I ran into something. A body. Still warm, but eerily still. And wet.

The girls continued to scream in the background as I pried my eyes away from the wolf to the warm body. I expected to see Mr. Vandal beside me, but it was Mason. *Mason!*

My heart stopped. He wasn't the wolf—he was a victim.

I coughed as my heart kicked back to life. The wolf pounced down upon me—its paws on either side of my shoulders—and it let out a growl so deafening that my ears rang and my blood turned to ice.

Its jaws seemed to unhinge, and its mouth gaped wide open. It could easily fit my entire head inside of its mouth. I winced from its hot breath, like I'd stuck my face inside an oven. I closed my eyes and tensed for my last moments. I'd died once or twice before; I thought I could do it again.

In that moment, when the sharp teeth grazed my chin, all I could think about was how wrong I'd been about Mason. That maybe he'd be alive if I'd trusted him more. And that guilt was the last thing I would ever know . . .

The wolf's jaws snapped shut, engulfing me in the pits of guilt. I startled. My eyes flew open to a calm, starry night. Crisp, cold air rest upon my cheeks and swirled in my lungs. A shooting star blazed across the sky and covered me in shame.

In that moment, I realized one thing. I'd rather die of fear than guilt. Because if the guilt didn't kill you—the regret would eat you alive.

The wolf was gone now, but the threat was far from over. I was shoulder to shoulder with Mason, and only one of us was breathing.

CHAPTER 9

As I lay next to Mason under the dazzling starlit sky, I didn't think of Mr. Vandal or the repercussions of our break-in. I didn't think much at all. I'd just been swallowed whole by the tallest, meanest wolf I'd ever seen, and all that was left was the intrusive self-doubt. I should have believed in Mason. I should have opened the door. I should have escaped when I had the chance. But instead, I ran right into this mess. It was a habit of mine. *So predictably me.*

One by one, my friends were being picked off. They were disappearing. They were turning into crows, sinking to the bottom of the lake, and being mauled by ten-foot-tall wolves. And, somehow, *I* was supposed to have the power to combat it. *I* was supposed to control the Baylor phenomenon and turn it into something pleasurable. *I* was single-handedly supposed to turn this world upside down.

If that seemed like an impossible feat, it's because it was. I wasn't as optimistic as Walker was. And I was pretty sure that I'd burn the forest down if *I* was left in charge. It was a frightening thought.

I wasn't the right fit for the job. But what if I didn't have to be? What if I gave that title to someone else? Walker would be excellent. But he was dead, of course, and I was pretty sure a living mind was a prerequisite.

Emma would be perfect. She'd be the main character in whatever book she wanted. But, unquestionably, she'd turn everybody in this town into oil slicked cover models. Shirts would be a thing of the past. I could live with that. It'd be far better than whatever I'd done here tonight.

The warmth from Mason's body was fading fast. Several footsteps swished through the wet grass and whispers floated in the air. They were coming for me. And I was ashamed of what they'd find when they did.

Gunner got to Mason first. He sniffed all around. His tail tucked between his legs. "It's okay, boy." *It wasn't okay.*

"Is that?"

"Is he?"

Kimber whimpered, stifling a cry in the palm of her hand. I lay helpless right where the wolf had left me. I couldn't cry for Mason. I'd gone numb. Something Kimber could never do.

Scarlett May picked up Mason's arms. She threw all

her weight backward, and he moved a mere inch. "Are you just going to stargaze? Or are you going to help me?"

"What are you doing?" Emma asked.

Scarlett May said nothing, but her cold stare and clenched jaw said enough. The worry trickled back in, and I became very aware that Mr. Vandal was somewhere in the clearing, and we had to get this body out of his yard before bad things got worse.

I took one of Mason's wrists and Scarlett May took the other. Gunner wagged his tail as if things had just become exciting. We started to drag Mason, but in opposite directions.

"Where are you going?" I hissed. Mason's arms were spread wide.

"We can't go that way! The floodlights will turn on!" Scarlett May said.

"We can't just drag him a mile out of our way. We *have to* go this way. The cabin is right there. If we all help, we can have him across this lawn in a couple of minutes," I said.

Gunner barked.

"Shhhh!"

"No!"

Gunner sat, cocking his head to the side.

"But what about Mr. Vandal?" Emma asked.

"What about him?"

"He was banging on all the doors; he's probably still

over there. We can't come back like this," Emma said, waving her hand at Mason.

"What else are we going to do? We have to act now." The seconds were ticking by at an alarming rate. We didn't have time to fight about it.

"Kimber, Emma, grab his ankles. Let's just get him across the clearing to the cabin. We can fight about what to do later," Scarlett May said.

They did as they were told, and we were moving Mason a little quicker than before, though his butt still grazed the grass, slowing us down. The four of us wobbled back and forth for what seemed like an eternity until the floodlights kicked on and revealed Mr. Vandal standing before us. That's when the slow crawl of time stopped altogether.

"What the hell have you girls been doing? Did you break into my home?" Mr. Vandal demanded answers.

His balled fists were clenched by his sides. Half his scowl was lit from motion-sensor light. The other half was hidden in the shadows, like Mason's body behind us. We bumped up next to each other, the four of us forming a wall in an attempt to hide the truth.

"Mr. Vandal, I am . . . I am so sorry about earlier," I stuttered, my eyes shifting, looking for lies to pluck from thin air. We'd broken into the man's home. There was no real excuse to give.

"You're sorry?" he yelled, with his hands in the air. "Do you have any idea what time it is?"

"We're sorry. We thought maybe . . . that maybe something was wrong. Like the house was abandoned, or you guys were out on vacation . . ."

"And what if we were? You have no right to break into my home! Did you steal something? Were you stealing from us?" Mr. Vandal's swarthy face grew closer with each accusation. But the girls and I couldn't take a single step backward. Our heels were already pressed against Mason's body.

"What's going on over there?" Noah yelled across the yard. All of us looked to find the guys standing half-asleep on the back patio of the cabin. All the yelling and pounding on the doors must have woken them. It was over now. We were caught. How could I explain this to any of them? Their best friend had been killed by a creature that didn't exist.

I felt the hollowness in my chest. Mr. Vandal yelled some more, but I could no longer hear the words coming out of his mouth. The idea of Kai, Noah, and Asher trying to get a better look at us and seeing the situation for what it was . . . was terrifying. The more they looked, the more they'd see, and it was an awful sight. One I couldn't shield them from but wished I could.

I tuned back in to hear Mr. Vandal threatening to call the cops. He stared at the four of us with a threatening glare. There was nothing we could say, so we just stood there silently eyeing one another. When he made his first move back toward his cabin, we flinched. He froze once more and glared at us one last time. Scarlett May tried to cover the corner of our man-made wall as he walked away. Fortunately, Mason was well hidden in the shadows, and out of sight. We didn't move an inch until Mr. Vandal's back door slammed shut, and then we each took a breath of relief.

Gunner whimpered, not understanding the rules of the game we were playing.

"Seriously, what the hell you guys?" Asher grumbled throwing his hands in the air and making a big show of his frustration. Noah shook his head and went back inside. Kai followed.

"Wait, we need you," Kimber said. Asher was the only one to hear her. He paused with his hand on the open door and then came back to the edge of the porch, lifting to his toes and craning his neck. He couldn't see what we were hiding, but he would soon find out. He jogged down the stairs, made his way across the clearing, and joined us in the bright floodlights.

"It's okay, guys. He can help us," Kimber's voice trembled.

I sighed heavily in anticipation of Asher's devastation. I glanced back at Mason, but he wasn't there. I squinted, searching the damp grass around us. *Impossible . . .*

"What's going on you guys?" Asher asked. Kimber immediately wailed and ran into his arms.

I looked all around us, but I could only see as far as the floodlights' illumination. Beyond that was a mystery of darkness.

Had Mason gotten better? Had he crawled off on his own?

Asher pushed Kimber aside and came at us. We parted, unable to speak. It was show and tell, only there was nothing left to show.

The girls gasped upon seeing the bare grass, and Asher grew frustrated.

"What?" he demanded.

"Where is he?" Emma asked me.

"You guys? Seriously, this isn't funny," Scarlett May said. But none of us were laughing.

I was chewing a hole in my cheek the size of a green pea. We scattered in the yard searching near and far. Gunner pranced about looking for a ball. None of us wanted to explain to Asher what had happened.

"Can we go home?" Kimber whimpered, pulling on Asher's arm.

We followed behind them in the wake of her tears. They reminded me of flower petals dropped down the aisle of a chapel. Our footsteps passed over the salty tears and blood-stained grass. It certainly wasn't the happiest night of our lives, but it was one we'd never forget. Or at least I wouldn't forget it, the others might.

When we were under the bright lights of the kitchen, Kimber really let loose. Asher wrapped his brawny arms around her tiny waist, and she snuffed her nose into his neck. I stood awkwardly staring at them as Kimber seemed to sink into herself. And I knew she was simply too weak to endure this kind of torture. Maybe she could draw strength from Asher. She would have to if she wanted to survive.

"Mason is gone, you guys. *Gone,* gone," Scarlett May said.

"What are you even talking about? What happened out there?" Asher asked, pulling Kimber off his neck. She quivered by his side, rubbing her arms.

"We broke into the neighbors'—"

"You what!" Asher's voice deepened.

"They have been doing all sorts of weird stuff. This entire summer, they've been gardening at midnight. Dragging bags back and forth through their garden. They've been watching us through the windows at night," Scarlett May said, pointing toward their cabin.

"So what?" he replied.

"We thought maybe there was a threat. You guys said it looked like nobody was living there. But clearly, they are. We wanted to see for ourselves," I said.

"Are you guys stupid?" he asked.

"I am sick of waiting around for something bad to happen!" I said, my tone sharp as a knife.

"So, you went to go find it? Is that what you're telling me?" Asher scoffed. He was right. We'd done a stupid thing tonight, and worse yet, I'd been the one to convince the girls to do it with me. I wasn't a leader and never should be.

"At least we're trying," Emma said, her eyes trained on the floor.

"Trying? You didn't even make it over there! You left us high and dry!" Kimber said, wiping her nose on the back of her hand.

"Okay, stop! Everybody stop! Just tell me what happened." Asher held his hand in the middle of the group like a traffic cop. Nobody spoke. We just looked at one another, not wanting to say it out loud. The things we'd seen. The things we'd endured. The things we'd let happen.

"You're up, Kinsley," he said, waiting. Everyone looked at me.

I took a deep breath and searched the floor for words. My voice was meek as I tried to recap all I'd done, and all I hadn't.

"We broke in—" Emma sucked in a sharp breath.

"All of us except Emma." I corrected.

"We'd looked around the cabin for only a few minutes when we heard something and ran outside. I ran into the shed where Mason found me. He wanted to help me, but I wouldn't open the door."

"Why?" he asked.

"Because. I don't know. I was scared . . . I didn't trust him." The truth was a tiny whisper from my lips. I didn't want to give it any more merit than that.

"A wolf attacked him," I said.

"A wolf?" Asher frowned.

"It's true! We saw it!" Scarlett May said.

My back straightened with surprise. They'd seen it? For the first time, my friends had seen the monster. It wasn't all in my head. That thing was really out there, lurking in the woods.

"It looked like a werewolf!" Kimber added, her hand pressed against her temple as if the very memory was making her suffer all over again.

"Well, technically, if it were a werewolf, it would have to transition in and out of being human, and we have no evidence of that," Emma said.

Scarlett May shot her an exasperated look. "The beast was on two legs! And it was gigantic!"

"Okay, okay. Everybody settle down. Kinsley, what happened next?" Asher asked.

"What's going on?" Kai asked, rubbing his eyes as he walked into the kitchen wearing only his boxers.

Nobody wanted to say it. Everyone's eyes turned away, pushing the responsibility off to someone else.

"The girls broke into the neighbors' cabin, and

supposedly got Mason killed. Yet there is absolutely no evidence—"

"We didn't do it! We didn't kill him! The wolf did it—" I slapped my hand down on the kitchen counter, and it sent a zing of pain through each finger. Everybody stopped to look at me. I couldn't think with my heart pounding so wildly in my chest.

"I didn't mean *you* killed him," Asher said, just as Noah walked in. *Great. Now everybody's here.*

"I didn't open the door. I should have, but I didn't trust him. He lied to Walker. He spread rumors that Noah and I were together, and we're not! We're not!" My voice cracked into something inaudible as the tears flowed down my cheeks.

For a moment, I felt everyone's gaze leave me for Noah, but it didn't last long. There was something in the way they were all staring that felt like I was being interrogated in front of a jury. Only I knew how guilty I really was, and they were just on the cusp of realizing it.

Emma wrapped her arms around me and patted my shoulder. Everybody else mumbled in the background. Accusations. Assumptions. But mostly questions. What happened to Mason? Where was he now? What did we do?

The guilt boiled up inside. At first it was a simmer, like a stew on the stove being prepared for dinner. The questions filled the open space around me. Their voices became louder and louder until I couldn't take one more second.

"Stop it!" I yelled.

They continued despite my plea.

"A wolf?"

"What kind of wolf?"

"Is he out there now? Does he have Mason?"

"Stop it! Stop it, stop it, stop it!" I couldn't believe the shrill voice was my own. I was screaming. My fists were balled tightly next to my temples, and my eyes squeezed shut. The stew was a rolling boil, the pot forgotten, and dinner ruined.

The lights flickered and clapped overhead. The light bulbs exploded, and glass rained down on us in the now dark kitchen. I covered my head with my hands.

In the blackness, everyone's breath became audible. My stomach churned as the shock settled. *I did that.* I was capable of terrible things. Somewhere, hidden deep within me, were pockets of darkness, places I'd yet to see or know.

I closed my eyes and clenched my jaw. I drowned out the whispers that something was wrong with me and the sounds of broken glass under moving feet. I hadn't wanted this to happen. I wanted us to be a team. I wanted us to work together. To be there for one another. I wanted this to feel like a family away from home. I wanted Walker.

"Hello?" Walker's voice penetrated my thoughts.

I opened my eyes to see the lights back on and

everyone looking around the room in awe. Walker was in the doorway, just as confused as the rest of them.

There was no glass shattered on the kitchen counters, no glass shards on the floor beneath my shoes. I squinted up at the bright light to see everything was perfectly intact, as if the explosion had never happened.

I did that, too.

I'd broken the lights, but more importantly, I'd put them back together. But before I let my mind run away with possibilities, I saw I hadn't changed everything. The scowls remained on the faces of my friends. The one thing I couldn't do was change the minds and hearts of everyone around me. And they were more suspicious now than ever before.

CHAPTER 10

My hands trembled and my fingers jammed in the wrong holes on the dial of the old rotary phone. I choked back tears as I frantically tried to call my gran. This needed to stop. It needed to stop *now*. I was *done* with it. I was done with feeling out of control. I was hurting the people I loved most, and if there was a power deep inside me, now was the time it needed to come out. My gran was the only one who could help me. I knew she had the answers. A simple call was all it would take—if I could ever get this old telephone to work.

"Wilde?" Walker asked softly as he pushed the bedroom door open.

My chin wobbled as I messed with the phone. Was it six nine? Or nine six?

"Wilde, what are you doing?" he asked.

I sniffled, shoving my fat fingers into the tiny holes and

trying desperately to circle the dial around the face of the phone. Each number took an eternity to wind back, and I kept forgetting Gran's phone number and how far into the sequence I had dialed. I slammed the receiver down not once, but twice, and then I closed my eyes tightly, letting the tears fall to my lap. I didn't want Walker to see me break down, but more importantly, I didn't want him to see the guilt I harbored for what I'd done to Mason. He crossed the room and sat next to me with his hand on my back, soothing me with slow, methodical strokes. I fought the urge to break down completely. I opened my eyes to face him and bare my heartache. I felt so small for all that I was. In the face of great expectations, I was falling short.

"What is it?" Walker asked.

I took a deep breath and glared at him through burning eyes. "I can't do this."

My eyes flickered to the phone and picked up the receiver again. Walker stopped me with his hand on mine. Slowly, we put the receiver down. I didn't have it in me to fight for a phone call I knew I wouldn't go through. She probably wouldn't have answered anyway. Walker held my hand until I gave him my full attention.

"You can't do what?" he asked calmly.

"Everything. Anything. All of it," I stared him dead in the eyes. If eyes were the windows to the soul, I was exposing just how weak I really was. And I hated to face my vulnerability.

I was afraid I was going to let all my friends die, right here in Baylor. I was afraid they were going to get picked off, one by one. Not only would I be unable to help them, but I'd be the one who set them up. The one who served them a cold plate of my poisonous mind. I didn't have the power Walker saw in me, and I never would. I was scared he would figure out that he was wasting his time with me. I was sure of these fears and so much more.

I didn't tell him I was afraid he would never love me, or that I was afraid he was using me to help him find Layla. The entire world was crashing down on my shoulders, and I wasn't strong enough to keep standing.

"We can do this, Wilde. I can help you." He rubbed his thumb methodically across my knuckles.

I shook my head, protesting.

"I need to talk to my gran."

"Here. What's her number?" Walker picked up the phone to dial for me. I rattled off her number effortlessly. It seemed so easy when he did it. He handed me the receiver, and I waited miserably through the never-ending rings.

"Try again," I said, when she didn't answer.

I waited as the phone rang, the tone growing louder, mocking me and my failure.

"Try it again," I said.

With each ring, I felt more and more alone. I was lost between the realms of the dead and living, and I wasn't sure I'd ever find my way. My answers were on the other end of this old Victorian phone—if she'd only pick up.

She didn't.

"Try it again!" I snapped. My hands shook when he took the receiver from me, and I wanted to pry it out of his hands and hold it to my chest. Why wouldn't she answer my call? Why wasn't she there when I needed her? Didn't she know she was being summoned? Was she gone forever? What if I never got to speak to her again?

Walker pulled me into a tight embrace. It was the straw that broke the camel's back. "I need to talk to her . . . I need to . . ."

"Shhh." He ran his hands up the nape of my neck and scratched the back of my head, tangling my hair into a mess.

"I know you think you need your gran to get you out of this mess. But I'm here. I might be all you have, but I promise you, it's enough. I can help . . . you just have to let me."

"Did you hear what I did to Mason?" I asked. He'd probably leave me when he heard, just like my gran had. If he knew what a monster I was, he wouldn't want to help me. And I didn't deserve it anyway. "Did you hear that I locked him out of the shed and let a wolf attack him?"

Walker's head tilted to the side as he looked at me empathetically. "Kinsley, you didn't *do* anything. You didn't do it," he repeated firmly, with his hands pressed against my cheeks as he held my head to stare into my eyes. "*You* didn't do it," he said again. Clear as day.

"It was gigantic. It ripped him apart, and I did nothing to help him . . ."

"Shhh."

I quivered, opening and closing my mouth like a fish out of water.

"Shhh."

I let him hold me for a long while as my emotions ran the gamut. We didn't speak for some time. I let the silence wash over me until every single emotion battling inside me solidified into one sole winner: defeat.

"Look, if you want to turn this thing around, you have to start slow. You're going to have to work at it. There's no other way around it," he said.

"I'm going to," I promised. "I'll work all night if I have to." If there was a way to right my wrongs, I'd do it.

Walker smirked. "It's going to take longer than that. You'll have to be patient."

"Well, I'm free now. Should we get started? I'm not going to sleep tonight anyway. I have nothing but suspicious friends downstairs—and not that many of them left. For all I know, they could barge through that door at any moment brandishing sage and pitchforks. If they don't go hunting for a wolf tonight, they're likely going to come for me. I saw the way they were looking at me . . . like I did it. Like I was doing it on purpose. But I'm not. I swear." I begged him to believe me.

"I know you're not."

"I have to harness this power. It must be now." I was determined to strong-arm the magic. Walker smiled from one side of his mouth, and a dimple appeared. He was somewhere between pitying me and being sincere. But I didn't care. I needed this. I needed to show my friends that I could turn it around. Otherwise, each one of them would fear me until the day they died.

Walker looked around the room and stepped away, snatching something from the dresser. He sat on the floor and placed a small peach-scented candle in front of him. He took a lighter from his pocket and lit it. Eagerly, I took a seat across from him on the carpet.

"To control this power, you need to harness your focus. There is a small stream of smoke rising from this flame. I want you to bend it."

It seemed kind of boring. I'd rather work on changing its color or scent. And to be honest, it took me longer than I'd like to be able to find the stream of smoke in the first place. But there it was, a small shadow that rose from the white-tipped flame. It was small and steady, so it should be easily pliable. *This was a joke.*

I took my time staring at the smoke without results. And then I imagined that I had cupped it with my hand. Immediately, the smoke flickered.

"Hey, I think it's working," Walker said eagerly.

I frowned. It wasn't quite what I was imagining. I tried again. The flame flickered slightly to the side. The scent of peaches danced in the space between us, reminding me that this should be fun.

"Good job, keep going," he whispered, careful not to distract me.

But the only thing distracting was how pathetic this was. It was only smoke; it should be easy.

I could extinguish the flame with my breath if I wanted to. I tried again. This time, I imagined my hand was made of steel, and I was forcing the smoke to contour to the curves of my palm. But clearly, by the lack of transformation, strong-arming this manifestation wasn't the way to succeed. I sighed and peeked up at Walker. He hadn't lost a single ounce of patience. His eyes beamed with excitement. He looked as if he could do this *all* night long. He believed in me, far more than I ever had.

I tried again. I imagined a pencil in my hand, and the flame was my drawing. I pictured drawing it in a different angle and smudging the smoke off to the side with my thumb. If anything, I was getting worse at this. Nothing happened at all.

"I just don't understand. I've done more than bend smoke before. Why can't I do this?" I leaned back on my hands.

"It's complicated. You must be in the right mindset.

You've got to believe in yourself. If you can't do that, then nothing will ever change. You've got to find that something inside of you that won't take no for an answer. You've got to change your entire identity if you want to believe in yourself. Are you the kind of person who can bend smoke? Or not?"

That was the problem. I'd never believed in myself. From the day I began school, I learned I couldn't keep up with the masses. There was something fundamentally wrong with me. The funny part was, in the eye of that disappointment, I never totally gave up. I kept trucking along, meeting failure at every step. It was the only path I'd ever known. Regardless of whether I believed I could do it or not, I knew I would never give up.

I tried to think about that feeling now. What was it that had made the magic work before? How had I stopped time to enjoy a moment I never wanted to forget? Slowly, I looked up from the candle to marvel at Walker. His encouragement was palpable. His patience was everlasting. *It was him.* It was the way he made me feel. It was the way he made me feel . . . about myself.

I'd told him many terrible things about myself. I'd told him I'd killed a man. He'd said it wasn't my fault. I'd told him I was a monster. He'd said I had to believe in myself. Walker had always made me feel like I was more worthy than I gave myself credit for. He was my biggest fan. And I wanted to live up to the image he had of me.

The girl he thought I was. I wanted to be better. I could identify with that, right? I could be all powerful? Magical?

I turned to the candle again, imagining the smoke sprawling off to the side. I squinted my eyes, focusing all my energy toward the tiny flame. And when the stream of smoke didn't so much as flicker, I blew it out, just like I had the candles on my eighteenth birthday cake.

The room went dark. I could hear Walker's lips part in a smile.

My cheeks warmed with embarrassment. I couldn't do it. It was such a stupid small thing, and I couldn't do it. If I failed at the start, the lowest point of entry, then where could I go from here? Flying was clearly far too advanced, but so was smoke bending. I didn't understand myself, and I never would. My mind was a labyrinth of locked boxes.

"What?" Walker chuckled.

I rubbed my eyes, and a small smile formed.

"What was that?" He laughed openly.

"What? I couldn't do it." I said, thankful the room was dark, and he couldn't see my face very well.

"Oh, but you did! You certainly found a way." He said laughing even harder now.

That I had. I'd found a way. He always saw the good in me. I wasn't dumb in his eyes. I wasn't powerless. I was the girl who found a way.

His laughter was like music to my ears, and I wished I

could see his dimples, because I knew they would be glorious. A treat sweeter than any summer peach.

The room illuminated in a soft orange glow. *There they are.* Those dimples, his smile. It warmed my heart, and I got lost in his presence.

His laughter dwindled, and his dazzling smile faded. His eyes dropped to the floor between us, and I grew alarmed.

"Did you do that?" he asked looking at the candle.

"Do what—"

The candle was lit. I froze. When did that happen? More importantly, *how* had it happened?

"Wow . . ."

"You didn't bend the smoke; you lit the flame. You're amazing!" Walker bounded to his feet, arms spread wide. I leapt up and hugged him, drawing in his coastal scent, and filling my lungs with pride.

I didn't know how I'd done it, but that correlated with all the times before. I never knew how. It sort of just happened all on its own. When my mind turned off and my heart swelled . . . that's when the magic happened.

I began to pull away so that I could tell Walker what I had just realized when his arms tightened around me. I froze momentarily and then sank back into his hold. He didn't want to let go. He wanted to hold on to me a little while longer. Did he have feelings for me? It felt less of a celebratory hug and more like the hug you'd give somebody that you missed. Like he was soaking up all of me. Like he'd missed me, even though I'd been right here all along.

I laid my head down on his chest, and he rested his chin on top of my head. His hands slowly rubbed the middle of my back, diving a little deeper with each stroke. *What was happening?*

My heart beat against him. The low thuds were audible, and I knew he could hear it hammering between us. Hell, he could probably feel it. But it wasn't just my heart; it was his too. Whatever I was feeling, I wasn't alone. I dared to raise my head, afraid to snap us out of whatever this was, but longing for a kiss. Slowly, I lifted my eyes, trailing up his neck to his stubbled chin and resting my gaze on the bow of his lips. I swallowed the lump in my throat and then took the leap, looking deep into his golden eyes.

His gaze was intense. Like he was at war with himself. I swore he was trying to tell me something, but what? Did he want to kiss me?

He winced as if he was in physical pain and then pulled away abruptly. Just as quickly as it came, the moment was gone. He ran his hands through his hair, turning away from me. Had I done something wrong?

"Is everything okay?" I asked softly. I slid my hands into my back pockets and gnawed on my lip.

"Yeah. Yeah. No, it's great. We're getting somewhere. Pretty soon . . . we'll be able to find Layla again." My stomach sank with the sound of her name on his lips. The room turned icy and hollow. It was stupid for me to think there was room in his heart for anything other than her.

"That's right. I'm sure we'll find her soon." I did what I could to reassure him and not look like a fool.

I thought back to the last time I'd seen her. She hadn't even been interested in Walker. I didn't know what was worse, knowing that he didn't want me, or knowing that he'd chosen her. All I wanted was for him to be happy. And sure, in a perfect world, I'd get what I wanted too. *But why her?*

"So, what do you think is going to happen when you find her?" I pried.

"Well, shit . . . . I guess I'll apologize," he said, like it had knocked the breath out of him.

"For what!?" I snapped. Didn't he know he'd done nothing wrong? That it was an *accident?*

"If it hadn't been for me, she would have lived a long, full life. She's out there, lost and probably scared, because of what I did. It doesn't matter if it was an accident, it was my fault. I did it. I stole her life." His voice sank into a pit so deep I wasn't sure he could crawl out. Maybe he never had.

I didn't like the way this sounded. Somehow, it felt personal. "Wait a minute, if you think you killed her . . . Then you think I killed Mason." I cocked my head to one side.

Walker spun around in shock. "Whoa. No, no, no. I didn't say that . . ."

"Yes, you did. That's exactly what you're saying. Oh my god, you think I killed them? All of them? Trinity? Big Jimmy? Lainey? Ethan and Mason? Oh my god . . ." I pressed my fingers to my temples as I took it all in. He thought I was a mass murderer. Was I?

"No!" he snapped.

"You've just been pretending that you think I'm amazing so that I don't lose my magic. You've been trying to keep me on track so I would find Layla for you!" I took a step back.

The flame flickered madly, and Walker held his hands out in front of him. "Wilde . . . That's not what I said, and that's certainly not what I think. Don't put words into my mouth."

"It was an accident. They all were," I said.

"I know . . ."

"Are you using me?" My heart stilled in anticipation of his answer. I didn't know what I would do if the answer was yes. I certainly hadn't been prepared to ask.

"Wilde, listen to me . . ." he began, as several other candles in the bedroom lit, casting dancing shadows on the walls surrounding us. "While it's true I'm trying to keep you on track, and that I'm trying to teach you to find yourself and your power, it's for you. I care about you. I . . . I *love* you, Wilde!"

The flames froze, and the shadows fixed in place.

"You're the only family I've got left. You're my only friend here. And it just so happens, you're the only hope I have to find Layla."

My heart thumped with disappointment. The flames grew tall, thrashing frantically about. Of course, he didn't love me romantically. But was I so wrong to latch onto those three little words?

"Do you think I killed those people? Do you think I'm capable of bad things?" I asked.

"I think we're all capable of making mistakes. Grave mistakes that have outcomes far beyond any premeditated measures. I know what happened was an accident. It's just hard for me to admit that to myself." Walker shook his head and swiped a finger at the corner of his eye. He wasn't using me. He was just a guy riddled with guilt, in the same way that I'd been. We really were two of a kind, and I couldn't believe I'd thought otherwise.

"You can't call it an accident when I did it then take the blame when you do it. Either we're *both* killers, or we're *both* total screw-ups. You choose," I said.

Walker closed the distance between us and wrapped his arms around me. We'd been doing a lot of touching tonight, but I wasn't complaining. Maybe it was the new normal? This one was different yet again. It wasn't passionate like the last one, and it wasn't celebratory like the first. This hug was . . . *brotherly*. It was the kind of hug you give to somebody that you both love and love to hate. It was firm and a little aggressive.

"Come here, you screw-up," he said. I laughed and slapped his back with my own frustration.

"I love you too, *buddy*," I said with a laugh. Walker flinched. It was barely noticeable, but it was there. That jab stung. He didn't want me to love him like a buddy any more than I wanted the same from him. And I couldn't help but wonder, what would our relationship be like if Layla ceased to exist?

"You think you can turn down your flames of rage now?" Walker joked as he eyed the candles. The room shook with the furious silhouettes of my heightened emotions. The light of a half-dozen candles burning like tiny torches.

"Oh my god! That's what I wanted to tell you. I think I figured it out. The magic isn't made from thought. The magic is made from feeling."

"What does that mean?"

"Well, all this time I've been trying to make things happen by imagining them, but it always seemed like it was when I stopped trying that the magic happened. I realized it was a feeling—an emotion—that turned the magic on."

"Do you think you can control your feelings?"

"I don't know?"

"Try it! You have about one, two, six candles lit in this room. Try to blow them out."

I considered the half dozen candles spread throughout the master bedroom. Walker placed a finger over my lips. "No cheating," he said.

I smirked and closed my eyes. It was hard to think of anything other than his skin upon my lips. I promised myself I could relive all the moments another time—if I got this right.

This time I didn't think about the candles at all. I knew I wanted to blow them out; I didn't have to imagine it. Instead, I chose to feel the subtle warmth leach from the room, envision the dim glow fade to black behind my eyelids as the flames extinguished, and feel the pride swell in my lungs like fresh air. And just like magic, the room went dark with victory.

The next morning, I woke to a low hum outside my window. I thought little of it as I got ready to meet Walker. But just as I was about to leave the bedroom, the buzzing noise nagged at me. What was it? It was too quiet for a lawnmower, too constant for a plane. I crossed the room and slid the window open, sticking my head outside to look around. The hum turned to a buzz, and I noticed tons of tiny dots flying frantically about. Several of them took notice of me and swarmed, trying to scare me off.

I pulled back, slamming the window shut and windmilling my arms through the air. There was a massive beehive tucked into the eaves of the cabin just outside my window. And now there were several bees inside, buzzing around me as I darted in wild bursts around the bedroom. I swatted and twirled, but it only made them angrier. I let out a yelp and ran into the hallway, slamming the door shut behind me. I came face to face with Emma.

"What's all that about?" she asked, eyeing me suspiciously.

"So many bees. There are *so* many bees outside my window right now," I said breathlessly. I thought I felt something on the back of my arm, and I swiped at it violently and craned my head to see if it was a bee.

"Really? Oh my god," Emma said, flinching from my wild theatrics. She'd tied her hair back in a ponytail. Her black leggings and hot pink sports bra under a loose muscle tank told me she was on her way out. Her sneakers were caked with dried mud from all the hiking she'd gotten in while being in Baylor.

"Are you taking Gunner out?" I asked.

"Yeah, do you want to come?"

"I would love to, but I have plans to meet Walker this morning. We're starting my training. There's a theory I want to test today, and I'm hoping for a breakthrough." I rolled my eyes, knowing my breakthrough wasn't coming anytime soon.

"Oh yeah?" she joked, as we walked downstairs. Kai and Asher were in the middle of an intense video game in the living room. Kai was still half tucked in his sleeping bag, like a butterfly only half emerged, stopping his metamorphosis to play Night of Emerald's Kingdom.

The coffee pot was only halfway filled, and Emma

didn't bother waiting for it to finish before she got on with her hike. Gunner did pirouettes out the back door as I waved goodbye to them. I wished I could get that excited about exercise. But right now, caffeine was the only thing I was enthusiastic about.

"Oh! You can't do that!" Asher yelled, and a sleeping Noah stirred.

"Shut up, dude. You can't wake up the entire house just because you're losing," Kai said.

I curled up on the sofa and watched the guys battle it out in the Castle of Greenland. I knew the game all too well. My little brother used to make me play with him. I used to pretend it was such a bother, but I secretly enjoyed it. But the one who'd liked the video games the most was Mason. It seemed odd that he wasn't sprawled out on the sofa, controller in hand.

The cabin seemed a little quieter in his absence. Smaller, in a sense. The guys were so captivated by their game. Had they forgotten what had happened to Mason? And why wasn't anybody blaming me? Surely, with my breaking all the lights in the cabin last night, somebody would have recognized me as a monster. I wanted to ask why they weren't sad, but I knew I'd be getting myself into trouble if I did. Forgetting about Mason was better for everybody. And honestly, I was jealous. I wished I could unpack the guilt and grief, the worry and shame, and spend my day in the Castle of Greenland. I supposed I would have to mourn alone. That's how it always felt, anyway.

The coffee maker beeped, and I leapt from the sofa. "Coffee?" I asked. I poured four mugs—two of them to go. As the coffee swirled at the top of the mug, I had a bad feeling about Asher. I mixed in creamer and sugar while I contemplated saying anything. I didn't want to give any credence to the thought, as that's when the bad things would happen. I handed the guys their coffee and said, "Hey, be really careful today. There's a beehive outside," as if it were nothing.

"Wait, what?" Asher asked. I rolled my eyes. It wasn't nothing when he was deathly allergic. I knew that. He knew that.

"There is a huge beehive in the eaves of the cabin. Right outside. We need to call a fumigator or something."

"Shit," Asher said, raking a hand through his hair.

"Looks like you're staying inside today," Kai laughed.

"I'll call somebody. I just don't know who takes care of these kinds of things. But I'll figure it out," I said, taking the to-go coffees and backing out the patio door.

"Be careful!" Kai yelled.

"Dude, shut up!" Noah grumbled from within his sleeping bag. The door slammed shut and I flinched, hearing the muffled groaning inside. I turned away and ducked my head while I hurried off the patio. The coffee spilled down my knuckles as I reached the lawn.

It was going to be a warm day. There wasn't a cloud in the sky, and the waters were calm. I sat on the end of the dock, sipping my coffee and searching my phone for bee removal in the Baylor Lake area. There were a few chat threads, but nothing official to be found in the small town. What did these people do when a swarm of bees moved in? I scrolled, searching for answers, and ended up calling the only option I found. Bobby Keller, a retired fumigator who still did side jobs for neighbors. I shrugged; it would have to do. I couldn't have hundreds of bees swarming the cabin, especially when Asher was allergic—and I had a propensity to make bad things happen.

I scheduled Bobby for that evening.

When I heard the gentle lapping of lake water against a canoe, I knew that Walker was paddling into the cove. I could only make out a baseball cap and an amber-colored T-shirt, but I felt his smile.

That guy right there, he loves me.

Maybe like a sister, but still. I'd been holding onto the thought that maybe he'd been lying to himself. I bit my lip in anticipation and watched him slowly glide toward the dock. Today was going to be a good day.

"Are you ready for this?" I asked, clapping my hands together.

"Am *I* ready? Are *you* ready?" he smirked.

"What have we got planned today, boss?" I was eager to test my theory.

"I don't know, how do explosions sound?" He took the coffee from my hand and helped me into the canoe.

"Explosions?" Now that was exciting. Way better than the elementary task of smoke-bending.

"Have you ever gone trapshooting?" he asked, pushing away from the dock.

"No, what's that?"

"It's when a machine throws clay pigeons and you try to shoot them while they're in the air."

"Oh, no. I've never shot a gun before." I searched the canoe for a shotgun.

"Who needs a gun when you have magic?" he said, a twinkle in his eye.

What? Was I the smoking gun? Did he expect me to shatter a clay pigeon with my mind? And then I remembered, that's exactly what I'd done to the light bulbs in the cabin last night. I shrugged, unsure of myself. "I guess we could try it." I eyed a small fishing boat near shore.

It took twice as long to get to our destination as I had expected. Maybe it was the performance anxiety, or maybe it was because I had drunk a large coffee on the way over, but either way, I had to pee. *Bad.* When the canoe bumped against the shore, I leapt out and ran into the forest to find a spot completely hidden from Walker.

I sighed in relief, zipped my shorts, and peered around. I'd been so focused on hiding from Walker, I hadn't realized what a great job I'd done. I must have gone farther than I thought, because I couldn't even tell which direction the lake was. The forest was dense with trees and seemed to go on forever. I listened for the water and the distant sound of motors on the lake, but all I heard were the bird songs emanating from the treetops.

"Walker!?" I yelled. My voice echoed in a way it shouldn't. Like my call had bounced off an invisible bubble and ricocheted back to me. Tiny goosebumps prickled my arms. Something was off.

Was I in the void? I spun around, trying to read between the lines. What was I not seeing here? What was right in front of my face?

I heard her before I saw her. A giggle that sounded pure as the songbirds and as joyous as a child playing in sprinkler water on a hot summer day. But Layla's echo was cut short. The sound was not traveling the distance as it should. Whatever was happening, we were trapped in it together.

It wasn't until I saw the red cloak from the corner of my eye that I realized she *wanted* it to be like this. She took pleasure in it. She wasn't trapped like I was; she reveled in the twisted shapes of the Baylor phenomenon.

Layla darted behind trees and dropped behind large rocks. She hid behind things that were a quarter of her size, and yet, no red peeked out for me to see. She slipped behind a sapling no wider than my wrist and disappeared completely. I sucked in a sharp breath. It was impossibly frustrating and magnificent all at the same time. What *was* she? And why wasn't Walker like that? Maybe he didn't want to spook me like she did.

"You're really good at hide and seek. You must have been playing for a long time," I said, stepping cautiously through the forest.

Layla giggled behind me, and just as I spun around, the red fabric passed in front of my eyes with lightning speed.

I groaned deep in my throat, feeling trapped and disadvantaged. I followed her deeper into the forest, not because I wanted to, but because I *had* to. She'd been so elusive that I couldn't ignore her, even if I tried.

But with every flash of red, and every turn, I might as well have been walking in circles. There was no way of telling which way I had come or how to get back. And there was no way I'd ever win this game if she was the one I was playing against.

I became more and more tense with every sighting of the red cloak. When she stilled long enough to deliver a genuine, mischievous smile, her eyes pierced mine, grabbing hold and refusing to let go.

Her long hair danced behind her as if she were floating in water. She was like a majestic animal, beautiful, but dangerous. We both stood still, sizing each other up. My heart hammered in my chest. She was a good several strides away, but I knew that even if I caught her, I'd be unable to hold her for long.

What did she want? Why did she provoke me like this?

"I don't want to play anymore, Layla," I said through gritted teeth. "I'm done!" I turned away, severing the intense eye contact, and stomped off. I became hyperaware that I'd just turned my back on her, and I feared what she might do to me because of it.

I wasn't sure where I was headed, but I knew it was away from her. Until, of course, it wasn't.

She materialized in front of me, blocking the path. I startled but tried not to show it. I put my hands on my hips, more frustrated than intrigued for the first time. I hated what she did to me. The way I felt around her. I didn't need her like I used to. I didn't want to find my way out of this mess. If anything, I was looking for a way to secure a life here amidst the weirdness. And I had a special day planned with *her* boyfriend that I didn't want to miss. My decision was made; I wanted to stay in Baylor. And she could go away now.

Layla's stare was playful at first, but quickly turned menacing, as if she'd read my thoughts. Her pupils dilated, darkening her eyes to coal. She pulled the *Waking Dreams* book out of her cloak, and I instinctively lunged for it.

But Layla wasn't an apparition of my mind like most of them. She was a true ghost, and my hands swiped right through her. She threw her head back and laughed, loud and boisterous. I hoped Walker wouldn't hear. This was the only time I wished he wouldn't come save me.

"That's mine!" I snarled.

She tilted her head to the side, and her lips curled upward.

All my gran wanted from me was to find this girl. And now that I had, I couldn't help but wonder *why?* I was expecting a wise old mage. One who knew the secrets of the world and would bestow a single answer to the one burning question inside my heart. But what I got instead was a twisted joker, a funhouse of disappearing acts, and more questions than I knew what to do with.

Did I have the wrong girl?

Gran said she needed my help. But this girl didn't need help, and if she did, she certainly didn't want it from *me*. She loathed me. She was like the Cheshire Cat, and I was her mouse. Little more than entertainment to bat around in the afterlife.

A branch snapped, stealing my attention. Walker sspun around on a ridge, far in the distance. He was looking for me. I saw him cup his hands to the corners of his mouth and call out. I couldn't hear a single word.

"What have you done!?" I demanded, taking another swipe at the book. We squared off. She held the book out of reach, and I was ready to pounce on it.

This time, Layla didn't look as amused. I could tell that she didn't like Walker here. It was her intention to bait me, and *only* me. Walker's eyes scanned right past where Layla and I stood without ever stopping. Couldn't he see us?

"Walker!" I yelled, stepping out and waving my hands overhead. He ran both his hands through his hair and then called out in silence once again.

"Walker . . ." I whispered. A loneliness coiled in the pit of my stomach, and for some reason, it made me miss home.

He wandered aimlessly, weaving in and out of the trees and yelling my name silently. He came so close I could reach out and touch him, but I didn't dare. The way his frightened eyes passed right through me sent a never-ending chill down my spine. Was this what it was like to be a ghost? I hated it. I hated everything about it.

Baylor had become my dreams, and my nightmares . . . and everything in between. But if there was a chance that I'd live here like Layla, unseen and unloved, this truly would be hell. I winced at the very thought. The *torture* she must bear . . .

My eyes watered as I pulled my gaze from Walker back to Layla. She looked just as frightened as he was. I no longer saw the twisted dark joker, but a lonesome girl who had lost her way. *No, no, no.* I couldn't feel bad for her. She was the enemy.

My heart sank even deeper as Walker passed by me, searching for something right in front of him. I lifted my hand, ever so slightly, and felt the wake of cold air pass by.

Sure, being unseen hurt, but it was downright agonizing to think of Walker losing both Layla and me.

If he had to roam Baylor for another twenty years looking for me, my heart would crack in half. I'd go absolutely crazy. I'd be just like Layla—playing adult hide-and-seek with the only person who wanted to find her.

Had she been right in front of Walker this entire time? Unseen? That would drive anybody mad.

It was so sad to think he'd been tortured with the guilt of the accident for all this time when she was right here with him. Layla had probably tried to get messages through but couldn't.

I now knew why Layla needed my help.

My chest squeezed, causing me to bring a hand to my heart. Walker spun around, eyes wide and mouth agape. Something had happened in his world that hadn't happened in the bubble with Layla. He frantically ran back the way he had come, leaving Layla and me alone.

I whipped my head around to see that Layla had vanished. In her wake were a dozen pages from the book fluttering to the ground. I lunged for them, falling to my knees and grabbing them, pulling them close.

Walker was out of sight, and Layla was gone. It was just me and the pages. I flipped them over, looking for titles, but they were all bodies of text. Tiny print from top to bottom. An anxiousness passed through me. How was I supposed to read all these pages and get back to Walker in time?

And then something changed. The print was getting lighter. I frantically looked through all the pages, and they too were changing. The words were fading, the ink leaching from the pages. I started scanning as fast as I could before there was nothing left for me to consume. But they were just words. Random words. And I wasn't fast enough to read them. All faded but a single line.

You don't belong here.

I sat back on my heels. The phrase stung the back of my throat. I knew she thought I didn't belong here, but that wasn't the complete story. I looked back, afraid that Walker would find me, and I would have to explain that his beloved had been sending me letters. Little notes telling me to leave him behind, the same way that she had. Were there more girls like me? Had Walker met other girls in this realm who Layla had scared away?

Fearing Walker's family curse—that love would never find him—I dug a hole in the dry soil. Staring at the page with a single line left, full of insult and judgment, I ripped it into tiny pieces, letting them fall into the hole. Layla didn't know me. She had no right to tell me where I belonged or who I belonged with. I pushed the dirt on top of the ripped pages and covered the evidence from Layla's visit.

I walked back in the direction I had last seen Walker

heading, wiping the dirt from my hands onto my shorts. It wasn't long before I found the clearing and our canoe.

"Kinsley! Are you all right?" Walker came running up to me.

I should have felt relieved that he could see me and I could hear him, but all I really felt was sadness for both Walker and Layla. Coming so close and failing to unite all these years. Tortured side by side and not even knowing it. At least *he* hadn't. She, on the other hand, she knew it, and that had been enough to make her crazy. I rubbed at the ache in my chest. Layla wasn't the threat I'd always imagined her to be. She was the girl who needed my help.

"What happened?" Walker asked, flipping my hand over and examining the dirt underneath my fingernails.

I pulled my hand back. "Sorry. I just hid behind a tree and kind of stumbled down a slope. I'm okay." I said hiding my hands in my back pockets.

"God, I've been looking everywhere for you. Didn't you hear me?" he asked.

"No." It wasn't a lie. But it wasn't the complete truth either. It was better he didn't know. It would only hurt him more. At least, that's what I told myself.

"Didn't you hear the explosion?" Walker scratched at his head, confused.

"Explosion?" I suddenly noticed the pieces of clay pigeons scattered around the canoe. "No. What happened?"

"I don't know. I was out there looking for you, and I heard an explosion. They all spontaneously burst. Now I have nothing for you to practice on." I thought back to when Walker had looked surprised and taken off running. The box of clay discs had burst, but why? How?

"Is something wrong with your chest?" he asked, eyeing me.

"Oh, it's nothing." I dropped my dirty hand. But the truth was, there was an ache in my chest. Call it guilt, call it sorrow, but I'd had it when the explosion happened. Maybe I had already completed today's mission, and I didn't even know it. I picked up a tiny piece of clay that fit in the palm of my hand and flipped it over. "We could still use these, right?"

Walker shrugged, taking the piece from my hand. He looked at it for a moment and then chucked it as hard as he could out over the water. Without hesitation, I let the excitement spark something inside of me, and the piece of clay shattered over the water.

"Whoa, did you see that!" he exclaimed.

Somehow, his excitement was contagious. I stifled a giggle behind my hand as Walker picked up another piece. Before I could let the fear of disappointment if I failed enter my mind, Walker had thrown the piece of clay and it was breaking into dozens of pieces.

With each piece we broke together, the ache in my chest became lighter. But I knew it would never fully fade.

There would always be a doubt that refused to disappear as the single passage had. And the worry that I wasn't where I belonged would fester until it became infected. But for right now, while Walker had a huge smile on his face and I was getting the hang of this thing we called magic, I would let that piece of me rest.

CHAPTER 12

Walker and I cleared the shore of broken clay pigeons that had been created in the explosion. I'd shattered every single one. Even the sneaky one he threw while trying to tickle me. I hadn't missed a beat. And with every little win, my confidence grew stronger. That seemed to be the key to it all. Locking in on a feeling and working it like a muscle. Once I trusted that I could break the next piece of clay, the explosions were bigger and louder, like thunder cracking overhead.

I got so good that, about halfway through, one clay chip exploded after it had barely left Walker's hand, and I had to pull back a bit. I learned to wait for the piece to be far away from Walker's hand, and at the highest point above the water, before shattering it into thousands of pieces. I couldn't have our fun end short with a burned hand.

Though, knowing Walker, it probably wouldn't have affected him anyway.

It was the most successful day I'd had yet. I'd learned not only how to work the magic, but I'd also learned how to hold back, even if it was just for a few seconds. I had tapped into the spot inside me that made everything possible. It was the trickiest spot of all—my confidence— but at least I knew it was there, fickle as it may be. I didn't want to leave when we ran out of clay pigeons, but I had to get back before the fumigator came.

The ride back was quick and left me longing for more time with Walker. I hardly thought about the eerie sighting of Layla in the forest; I wanted to forget about it all together. Feeling sorry for her would not help me win her boyfriend. And I couldn't possibly survive being torn in another direction.

When we paddled into the cove and found Noah and Kai running around the clearing like little boys playing tag, I knew our magical day was over. There was always tomorrow, I supposed. And as long as I played my cards right, my tomorrows would be endless. We would build a life here, so full of magic that *nobody* would want to leave. And nobody would have to.

"What are they doing?" Walker asked, stifling a laugh. I frowned as I watched Kai take his shirt off and swing it around his head. Gunner ran around barking at all the commotion. Were they drunk? What on earth was happening? I started to laugh, but the feeling faded fast.

"Oh my god, oh my god! It's the bees!" All I could see from the water were the two guys. Asher was nowhere to be found, and I prayed he was safe inside. I watched Noah pick up a rock and chuck it into the eaves near my window. "No! Don't do that!" I yelled, standing and making the canoe rock. Walker grabbed the sides and held on tight.

As soon as we could tie up, I hopped out onto the dock, but the boys had disappeared into the cabin. "Sometimes I think they left their brains back in Clover," I said with a sigh.

"Now the bees are going to be angry when you walk up the hill. How are you going to get into the cabin without getting stung?" Walker asked. It was a fair question; one I didn't have an answer to.

"You mean I can't just explode my way out of this?" I asked.

"Please don't," he said, laughing. I smiled, taking in his dimples.

"I had a lot of fun today," I said.

"I did too."

"What are we going to work on tomorrow?" I asked, lingering on the dock as Walker remained in the canoe. He was heading back home, and I wanted him to stay.

"Well, now that you're a professional—"

"Hey, I wouldn't go *that* far." I could feel the heat creeping into my cheeks.

"Seriously, you did really well today. I'm proud of you."

"Thank you," I said, softly enough to be a whisper. I wrapped a lock of hair around my finger and let his words soak in so deep, I'd never forget them.

"I'll come up with a plan tonight, but I think it's fair to say we get to move on to something more advanced tomorrow. You've earned it." He winked.

I smiled, but the hoots and hollers coming from the cabin interrupted the moment. The back door slammed shut. Kai and Noah came outside looking oddly thicker than before. "What are they doing now?" I mumbled under my breath. Gunner was chasing them, barking with excitement. We had to be careful, otherwise the neighbors would call Animal Control again. I swiped my brow and gritted my teeth.

Emma stormed outside, shielding her head with her hand as she ran down to the dock. "Kinsley, you have to make them stop. They're trying to knock the beehive down to get the honey! They're wearing like five pairs of pants just so they don't get stung!"

"They don't need to do that; I've got it covered. There's a fumigator coming this evening," I said, looking at my watch.

"What! You can't do that!" She marched down the dock waving her hands in the air.

"Why not?"

"Because that's inhumane!"

"But it's Bobby Keller, and the neighbors love him . . ." I said, reciting one review. Now that she was right in front of me, I could see her eyes were narrowed and her cheeks flushed.

"But what about Lainey?"

I felt a tinge of pain in my chest and sucked in a breath, looking back at Walker. "What about Lainey?"

"Lainey loved all things nature. How do you think she would've felt if she knew you hired a fumigator to *kill* the bees?"

"But Bobby—"

"*Bobby . . . Freaking . . . Keller . . .* How do you think she would feel?" she repeated.

I sighed. She was right. Lainey would've hated this idea. With her love for flowers, I could only imagine how crazy she was about the bees. I thought back to the time she'd rescued a bee from our swimming pool.

"Okay," I said with a shrug.

"Okay?" she asked.

"Okay. I'm canceling the fumigator." I pulled out my phone and sent him a text.

"What are we going to do about these fools?" Emma asked, still fired up. That was a whole other problem.

I looked back to Walker for answers, but he shrugged. "Don't look at me." He held his hands up. He reached over and released the rope from the dock, and I knew he was leaving me to deal with this disaster alone.

Just then, Kai yelped, and his gleeful dance turned into one of panic. One cry became two, as he ran around hysterically, waving his arms all about like a sky-dancer at a used car lot.

Noah was quick on his heels as they chased each other onto the lawn. "This is like watching a train crash in slow motion," Walker said.

Emma shot me a look, and my blood ran cold. We'd never told the guys about our incident on the train, and the complete scene unwillingly played through my head despite my best efforts to stop it.

"Can't you do something?" Emma asked. But this didn't feel like shooting clay pigeons over the lake for fun. This felt like they were depending on me to save them, and there were a million ways it could go wrong.

"What do you expect *me* to do?" I asked.

"Yeah, Wilde, can you make the bees stop like you did with the fireworks?" Walker asked. This wasn't like the times before; it was intense. So much pressure came down on me that I nearly seized up. Instead, I forced myself not to think about it at all. Because if I'd learned one thing, it was that my thinking got me in trouble.

I acted quick like I had earlier when Walker was

tickling me, and things were fun and flirty. I threw my hand out like a gun and pretended I was shooting the clay pigeons, just like before. Only this time, it wasn't a clay pigeon that exploded; it was the beehive. Pieces of the hive blew apart and thousands upon thousands of angry bees flew out.

A dark swarm gathered in the air as I took off running straight for Noah and Kai. Walker was quick on my heels, but Emma plunged into the lake. The buzzing of forty thousand bees vibrated in my very skull. The sound alone should have sent me running.

"Run! Run!" I screamed. I didn't know much about bees, but I knew they wouldn't chase you for very long. Less than a mile, my dad would say, and they'd be back with their swarm. "Run!"

Kai took off running straight into the forest. The dark cloud split in two, and half followed Kai into the woods. Gunner ran after him, barking hoarsely.

Noah fell to the ground and started rolling like he was on fire. I flung my hands wildly as I entered the killer swarm. I dropped to my knees by his side and tried to shield him, but it was too late. The bees were so tiny and fast. There was nothing I could do. He kicked and flailed as I tried to calm him.

The fear inside me rose, reminding me of when the lights had shattered in the cabin. The feeling grew as hundreds of bees pelted Noah. I didn't know if the bees *couldn't* sting me, or if I was so numb with adrenaline that I couldn't feel it, but there was no pain on my part. I sat by Noah's side unable to do anything to protect him.

"Kinsley, do something!" Walker yelled. I looked back, afraid to take my eyes off Noah. Walker was barely visible as the swarm dove straight through him. He was untouchable. Invincible. "Kinsley! Do. Something!" Walker's voice rang through my ears louder than the drone of the bees.

I don't know what to do!

I scrunched my eyes shut, the bees crawling over my face, and found a feeling. Not the feeling that I wasn't good enough, or that I might be a disappointment, but a feeling of protection. I tried to zero in on it, but the bees entangled in my hair kept me from concentrating. I tried to stay still. I tried to focus.

"Kinsley!" Walker yelled.

"I'm trying! I'm trying!"

Noah's writhing slowed beneath my hands. Tears streamed down my cheeks as he grew tired. He stilled, and I feared his time was over. "I'm trying . . ." I cried.

Nobody here could help me. And no matter how much Walker had tried to teach me, *I* was the only one holding my power back. I was holding them *all* back.

Everything grew louder. I heard Emma's screams from the lake, and I noticed banging on the windows for the first time. The drone of the bees waned, the crawling on my skin lessened, and the vibrating in my hair stilled. Everything calmed down. Except Walker. His voice was something I was tuned into, and I could hear him now.

"You're doing it! You're doing it!" he yelled. I used it like fuel to grow the magic.

Moments later, I dared to open my eyes, just as the last bee crawled across my lips and fluttered away. The large swarm lifted into the sky and left just as quickly as it had come. I looked down at Noah in utter shock. His arm was draped over his face, shielding him as best as he could. His lips were twice their normal size. Walker got behind his head and cradled it in his hands. Carefully, I lifted Noah's arm.

"Noah?" My voice strained.

Noah's face was red and swollen. His eyes were glued shut, but he was still breathing. A shallow breath, but there was hope. "What do we do?" I asked Walker. I heard Emma come up behind me, dripping. She was sopping wet with lake water. "What do we do?" I looked to her, pleading. But nobody had an answer.

"What do we do?" I whispered to myself. But even I didn't know. The back door slammed as Kimber barreled down the steps. I watched her fierce stride cross the yard. She dropped to her knees and stabbed Noah in the thigh with an EpiPen.

"Wow!" Walker gasped.

"Where'd you get that?" Emma asked.

"I picked it up today because I used Asher's other one. Thank god he stayed inside the cabin all day!" She pointed to the master bedroom, where Asher was watching from the window. His hand was pressed against the windowpane as he watched his best friend lying unconscious on the lawn. I couldn't be more relieved that he was okay. He never would have made it if he had been out here. I wasn't sure Noah would, and he wasn't allergic to anything.

"Thank you. Oh my god, thank you." I prayed that the medicine would work on him and that it wasn't too late.

"Yeah."

"We should do another. Is that the only one you have?" I asked.

"Yes, it's all that was prescribed. It *should* help. Where's Kai?" Kimber asked, worried.

We looked toward the wall of trees. Kai was a powerful athlete, and I was certain he could run until he was no longer being chased by death. "He'll be back. I know it," I said.

"Let's get him inside," Walker said, lifting Noah's shoulders.

We positioned ourselves to help move Noah when we heard a pounding on the window. All of us paused to look up. Asher cupped his hand over his neck as his face grew ashen. He stiffened as we all watched helplessly from the ground.

"What is he trying to—"

"The bees!" I jumped to my feet. Kimber popped up next to me.

"But he's inside. He's safe!"

"No!" I said running to the cabin. "There were several in my room this morning!"

"What are you talking about?" Kimber yelled frantically as we reached the deck and passed through the kitchen.

"This morning. A few bees had gotten inside, and I ran out of my bedroom. They were locked in all day." I gripped the banister and lunged up the stairs.

"But I used the last EpiPen!"

We pushed through the bedroom door just as Asher fell backward. There was a loud thud when he hit the floor, followed by Kimber's cry. My stomach sank. How could I be that stupid? How could I have forgotten there were bees inside the cabin too?

"Do something, Kinsley! Do something!" Kimber demanded.

I ran my hands through my hair and paced the length of the room. What could I do? I could barely get the bees to leave us alone; there was no way I could siphon the poison. The EpiPen was gone, and there was nothing left to help Asher . . . but me. It was too much. And I was drained from fighting off the swarm.

Asher began convulsing, and Kimber pounded on his

chest, tears running down her cheeks. "You can't leave me here! You can't!"

I crumbled under the pressure and ran out of the bedroom, shutting the door behind me. I pressed my back against the wall and cradled my head in my hands.

"This isn't real. This isn't real. This isn't real."

"No! No! No! Asher, no!" Kimber sobbed. I knew he was gone by the tone of her voice. I felt sick enough to vomit.

What was this world? What had I created here? And why? I grabbed at my stomach, clenching my T-shirt in my fists as I broke out into a cold sweat.

The door swung open and banged against the wall. Kimber stormed out. "What are you doing?" I asked, pushing off the wall and following her.

I expected her to be weaker than this. Smaller. So small that she would disappear in the wake of Asher's passing. But she was a lot stronger than she looked. She strode downstairs, her feet stomping with every step.

"Kimber what are you doing?" I asked again, trying to grab for her hand, but she yanked it away. I jogged to keep up with her stride as we went out the back door to where Noah lay.

"Is he okay?" Emma asked about Asher.

"I think he . . . I don't think he made it."

"This is bullshit!" Kimber said in a tone much deeper than I had known to be her own.

She strode right up to Noah lying on the ground. His skin was pale and, surprisingly, he didn't look any better. In fact, he looked . . . *Had he died too?*

His skin was purple and blue—bruised from the stings. His lips were large and his eyes swollen shut. I looked toward Walker, and my heart stuck in my throat. I knew Noah hadn't survived when Walker gave a small shake of his head. I cupped my mouth in shock. Then my knees hit the ground.

I'd grown up with Noah. I knew his mother like a relative. We weren't just friends; we were so much more than that. I'd thought about him all the time. This summer was supposed to be about us. I had wished for his kiss . . .

"I'm not staying here for one more second without Asher!" Kimber announced. Her tone was sharp as knives and her face determined.

Everybody froze, watching and waiting. If there was anybody who could find their way out of this realm, it would be that of a person with a broken heart. For they would forge a path where there was none before, just to find their other half.

CHAPTER 13

I'm *not* staying here without him," Kimber said maniacally. She turned in front of Noah's body so that they were heels to heels and lifted her arms out from her sides.

I couldn't pry my eyes off her. My focus narrowed and my mouth fell open. *What was she doing?*

Kimber closed her eyes and tipped back onto her heels. Only she never quite stopped herself. With arms spread wide, she did a trust fall back on top of Noah's lifeless body.

Nobody was there to catch her. Nobody alive anyhow.

"Wait!" I yelled, reaching my hand out.

As Kimber landed, she appeared to sink through Noah, hitting the ground with a muffled thump. At that exact moment . . . Noah sat up, gasping for air.

He grabbed his chest and patted his legs—which were

oddly both hers and his at the same time. He shuddered and scrambled to his feet, sidestepping away from Kimber's body, which now lay motionless in his place.

Her skin bubbled and bruised with the wounds of a thousand bee stings. Her lips swelled, and the color of her skin darkened to a swarthy mix of purple and blue.

Noah ran his hands through his hair and patted his face, chest, and thighs, checking that his body was in fact his own.

My eyes bulged. I couldn't believe what I was seeing. *A life for a life.*

"How did she—" spilled from my lips.

Kimber had given Noah his life back. I hadn't even known that was possible. My question echoed on the lips around me as everyone muttered the same thing: *how did she do that?*

Even Walker was taken aback, as he now cradled Kimber's head and shoulders, instead of Noah's.

"Is she . . . ?" Emma asked. My eyes flickered, meeting everybody else's disbelieving gaze. Nobody could believe what had just happened, and Noah looked like he was going to be sick.

"I don't know. I think . . . I think she sacrificed herself," I said, my eyes meeting Noah's for the first time.

"She can't do that. Oh god, she can't do that." Noah grabbed his stomach and staggered forward. He made it to some nearby bushes and dry heaved over weak knees.

"But she did," I said, my eyes meeting Walker's. His eyes were a burning blaze of amber gold, and his eyebrow dripped with fresh blood.

Kimber didn't give her life so that Noah could live instead of her. She'd given her life so that she could be with Asher—wherever that may be. Regardless of why she'd done it, Noah was alive. And I knew, by Walker's fresh wound, that if he had known this was possible, he would have sacrificed himself for Layla.

He would've taken her place in a heartbeat. He would have lived his life in the shadows, and he would have done it happily, knowing that she was alive and well. If Layla could feel the sun on her face and her heart beat in her chest, it would have been enough for him. I could see the wheels turning in his pained eyes, and I knew he was wondering the same thing I was: was it too late now?

I looked over as I heard Gunner's bark from the woods. Kai came running through the dense forest and into the clearing. He was still thick with several layers of clothing and visibly exhausted. Seconds after breaking through the woods, a thick shadow ballooned out behind him.

There had been three casualties and one revival in the brief span since he had taken off, but I wasn't worried about that now. There were thousands of bees flying after Kai and Gunner, and they were headed straight for us. In the real world, they never would've followed him for that long. At least that's what my dad had always told me. But we weren't anywhere near the real world, and these weren't regular bees.

"Run! Everybody, get inside the house!" Walker yelled, as he lowered Kimber's head to the ground.

Emma took off running, and Noah staggered from the bushes up the stairs slower than I would have liked. But I was the slowest of all—I was frozen. All the power I had to blast the clay discs was not enough here. There was no amount of training that I could ever achieve to prepare for each unique situation that arose in Baylor. And yet, somehow, some way, Kimber had known. She'd known exactly how to get what she wanted, and she hadn't had to read a single book to get it.

Layla's words echoed in my mind: *You don't belong here.*

Walker grabbed my arm, snapping me from my trance and pulling me inside the cabin. Once inside, I collapsed like Noah had on the floor. Walker held the door open for Kai and Gunner as they barreled across the threshold, and he slammed the door shut behind them. An army of bees pelted into the door, sounding like hail in a torrential storm.

Kai fell forward onto the floor, barely able to hold himself up on hands and knees and panting in pure exhaustion. His face was red, and he had purple welts where the bees had stung him. There were two on his forehead, one on his cheek, and, as far as I could see, one on the nape of his neck. I peeled myself off the floor and placed my hand on his back. I could feel the sweat that had soaked through his many layers.

"He's overheating! Help me get him out of these clothes!" I said. Walker pulled at one of his many shirts. Noah—still layered himself—helped peel layers off Kai. I crawled to Kai's feet and unlaced his shoes. I'd heard once that heat escapes from the head and feet.

"Is he going to be okay?" Emma asked, cowering in the corner.

"Emma, help us out. Grab his pants," Walker ordered.

I yanked off Kai's other shoe, and Emma came to my side to help me peel off his sweatpants. There must've been five layers of pajamas and sweats over a pair of jeans. All damp. He needed water, and maybe a cool wet washcloth on the base of his neck.

We worked together to strip Kai down to a single layer. Kai wasn't saying anything at all, and his breathing had yet to calm down. The entire cabin buzzed with the army of bees outside, making it sound like we were inside the hive ourselves. They bashed themselves against the windows, making small knocking noises. My mind splintered thinking of all the ways they could get inside. I paused to look around the room on high alert, and a chill ran down my spine.

The knocking bounced from one window to the next as the swarm of bees tried desperately to get in. They moved around the cabin, and I watched the darkness leave the living room and eclipse the front entry windows. My mind raced. Something was there . . . something important that I couldn't quite remember. Every second mattered as I tried my best to pin down the thought pestering my brain. It hit me like a ton of bricks. The bathroom window near the front of the cabin. It was completely open, and there was no screen.

"The window!" I yelled, as I leapt over Kai. Running full speed through the kitchen, I grabbed the banister and swung around the stairs. It was a race against the bees, and as far as I could tell, I was coming in last.

I barged into the small bathroom. The bees had just found the opening. I froze for a second, and without thinking, I slammed the door shut—trapping myself inside.

I let out a yelp as the bees swarmed around me. I flung my hands around and spun in tiny circles. The bees surrounded me. I squinted to keep them out of my eyes and tried to shield my face. I wanted to run, but opening the door wasn't an option.

There was nothing I could do. Spinning in circles wasn't getting me anywhere, and I refused to unleash them onto my friends. I couldn't see. I couldn't run. I couldn't yell. They covered my face, looking for ways in. Yet, never once was I stung. Which only worried me more.

They wanted something else from me. It didn't matter what it was, because I wasn't giving up without a fight. I was done with this. I was so angry with myself for not being enough to fight this world. I was so, so angry. I opened my mouth to scream a deep guttural shriek, but the bees filled my mouth before I could make a sound.

Angst tightened in my chest as I held my breath—the scream trapped somewhere inside.

Wings thrashed against the roof of my mouth. I hunched over as they packed in tight, pressing alongside my cheeks and pushing against tongue. My mouth had become their hive, and I had become their creator. Were they searching for a new queen bee? I didn't have time to think about it. All I knew was I was in danger, and my power to explode things would not help me here.

Walker barged into the bathroom, and the second he did, the second I saw him, the bees vaporized into a fine black-and-yellow mist. I sucked in several shallow breaths.

The mist was oddly beautiful. It swirled, catching bits of light. The yellows turned golden, and the blacks were just a shadow. The vapor danced like a slow whirlwind as it lifted out the window. Walker and I watched in silence. The cabin was no longer buzzing, and the knocking on the windows had finally stopped.

"*You* did that. How did you do that?" I asked Walker, as I tried to catch my breath. I grabbed his shoulder for support, and he embraced me.

"I didn't do that. You did." He stabilized me as I leaned over the sink and spat several times. I wiped my mouth still feeling the tiny legs crawling across my lips, but there was nothing there. "Are you okay?" he asked.

My insides were shaking, and I was fighting back tears. I had become a human hive—I wasn't okay. None of it was okay. In that moment, there was a part of me that envied Kimber. I didn't know where she'd gone when she'd taken Noah's place, but it had to be better than this.

I wiped my lips with shaky hands, and Walker wrapped his arm around my waist, ushering me to join the others. But as soon as I stepped into the entryway, I heard them talking about the calendar. I stopped immediately. "I can't do this. Don't make me do this." It was too much.

"What's wrong?"

"They're talking about the calendar again. They know that I'm doing this to them. They're judging me for it. I'm a damn *monster*, and they know it," I hissed, tears stinging the back of my throat.

"Wilde, you're not a monster. Nobody is judging you . . . We're in this mess together." His arm tightened in a comforting hug.

"I am," I said. I was. All this time, I was. Every second of the day. I was my own worst enemy. And in some ways, my judgment of myself was worse than theirs. Simply because it was the loudest. A constant echo in my head.

"We're going to get through this. You did so amazing today with the clay pigeons. And you did it again with the bees. Under pressure, too." I could hear the hope in his voice.

"I exploded the hive and released thousands of angry killer bees upon my friends."

"You *stopped* the bees. That's what I saw. You made them disappear. You turned them to a fine mist. I know it's hard, but you're doing it. And with more practice, there won't be a limit for you. Don't give up now. We're so close . . ."

I took in a deep breath and nodded, even though I swore he was the one who had vaporized the bees. I stole one more moment of quiet before joining the others. A moment to stare into Walker's eyes just a little longer. My friends were still arguing over the numbers on the calendar, and it was time to face them. Those that were left.

"The bees are gone," Emma said with a nod of hope. I gave her a small smile.

"Yeah, I noticed that," I said, scratching the back of my head. I didn't know how it had happened, and I was uncomfortable taking the credit.

Kai was sitting up against the base of the couch taking small sips of water. His black hair was plastered to his forehead, and his skin was covered in a thin sheen of sweat. He looked ill—but he would survive. "How are you feeling?" I asked.

Kai tried to clear his throat but struggled to get any words out. He patted his chest a few times and winced.

"It's okay. Just rest," I said. Noah took off one of his many shirts and tossed it to the ground. It landed near my feet, and a weird feeling swirled in my belly. I was both happy he was alive and conflicted by the turmoil I'd felt when I'd thought he had passed. He still meant more to me than a friend. Part of me wanted to run straight into his arms and give him the biggest hug ever. But I knew my loyalty lay with Walker, which made it all feel so wrong. Either way, I was grateful for what Kimber had done.

"Hey, Kins, did you see the calendar?" Noah asked with a pained expression. He suffered no bee stings, causing me to think his pain was purely guilt. He was probably happy to be alive but feeling guilty that Kimber had sacrificed herself. He pulled his shirt off, revealing a thin white ribbed tank underneath. I caught my eyes skimming over his torso the way they used to when I'd liked him, and I frowned.

"How are you feeling, Noah?" I asked. I averted my eyes from both the calendar and his physique.

"I'm fine. I'm better than fine. I'm just hot. But did you see the calendar?" His denim-blue eyes bore into mine as he peeled off his tank. I felt my skin flush and immediately peeked at Walker. How uncomfortable would it be if they all died except the three of us? Leaving me with Walker and Noah to roam the realms of eternity together. I really had to find a way to keep everybody safe.

"I haven't," I said. Noah nodded his head toward the wall. The calendar had eight slashes through it. Only five were left unmarked. I looked around the room and counted on my fingers to be certain. There were more than five of us left.

"Where's Scarlett May?" I asked.

"I don't know. She's probably with Sampson," Noah said.

"There's thirteen days, and eight of them have been crossed off. But only seven of us are gone. Who is the eighth?" Noah asked, scowling at the calendar.

"I thought we went through this? It was that store clerk who went missing. Right?" Emma asked, looking to me for clarity.

"So, there are five of us left? Kinsley, Emma, Scarlett May, Kai, and me?" Noah pointed to each of us, his brows stitched. "Why isn't *he* on the list?" He stared at Walker enviously.

"How do you know I'm not?" Walker asked.

"I just don't understand how the store clerk is on there. Does that mean that it doesn't have to be us on that list? It could be anybody?" Emma asked.

I knew that was wrong. Something about it was very wrong. I had already crashed a plane with over a hundred people on it. They weren't on the list. So why was Big

Jimmy? And was I on the list? Or Walker? It was either both of us, or we were going to be separated, and I would not let that happen. I wouldn't leave Walker to this realm all alone. No, there was something off about this calendar, but I couldn't put my finger on it. I didn't want to tell anybody about the plane crash, but there was another accident that I could talk about. Make an example out of.

"Hey Emma, remember when we were on the train? What about all those people? Why aren't they on the calendar?" I asked. It was enough to shatter the whole theory. We were missing something here. But more importantly, maybe we weren't all doomed to be picked off, one by one.

"What train? What people?" Noah asked.

Emma's eyes searched the calendar. "You're right. If this isn't the calendar for how many people are going to die, then what's the calendar of?" she asked, a horrified look in her eyes. Somehow, that question seemed scarier than a calendar hit list. It was the unknown that we feared most of all.

"I'm not sure, but we need to find out," I said.

"What train? What people?" Noah repeated.

Emma told the story of our trip to the depths of the canyon, only to reappear here as if it had never happened. But it had. And my physiology could attest to that. My heart rate picked up speed. I couldn't bear to listen to it again. I left the kitchen and joined Kai on the floor. Walker came and sat by my side.

"I'm just so sick of it all. When is it going to click?" I asked.

"We're going to get it. This is a unique mess that we're in. It's twisted. If normal life was a linear line, this mess is a tangled knot. It's going to take time," Walker said, with all the patience in the world. I guess that's what happens when you have all of eternity.

"You've got that right," I said, slouching.

Kai made a sound in his throat, and I thought that he was trying to smile. Although his cheeks were so puffy, I couldn't be sure.

"We've got to stop thinking normally. This isn't a rational thought process here. There is no logic behind this mess. Or at least none that we can see. What we really need to do is start reading between the lines . . ." Walker shook his head, deep in thought. His dimples disappeared, and the sharp lines of his jaw popped.

Read between the lines? Why did that remind me of seeing Layla in the woods? Her notes telling me that I didn't belong. I already knew that my being here had caused this whole mess, but if I wanted to stop the chaos, maybe I needed somebody as crazy as her to help me figure it all out. Maybe that's why my gran had told me I needed to find her. She was like the Cheshire Cat; the loony one that actually isn't so crazy. She's a little different, but maybe that's because she sees what we don't. Maybe she's been trying to guide me all along. My throat ran dry at the thought of needing the one person I wanted most to stay away from. The one person who could take everything from me.

"We need a twisted mind," I said, thinking of Layla.

"Not a twisted mind, just a nonconforming one. We just need to look at the world a little differently than we're used to. Flip it on its side, or look at it upside down, or backward."

"You need one of those atypicals," Noah said from the kitchen.

"What's that?" I asked, taking in his bare chest and sorrow-filled eyes.

"Yeah. That's exactly what we need," Walker agreed. I whipped my head around. *Atypical?*

Emma joined us in the living room. She crawled onto the sofa and pulled a pillow onto her lap. "Well, Kinsley's dyslexic," she said.

"Hey! What does that have to do with anything?"

"Oh my god. You're right. Maybe that's why all of this is happening in the first place. You're atypical," Walker said, staring at me with wide golden eyes.

"What the hell, you guys? What does that even mean?" I already had one title. I didn't need two.

"It's just like being left-handed in a world full of rights.

You get the job done, but you come at it from a different angle. It's nothing bad, really," Noah said.

"Well, it's not nothing," Walker disagreed.

"What he means is that you have a distinct, creative pattern for processing information," Emma said. But what did that mean? I didn't want to be different.

"Um . . . If by creative you mean broken, then yeah, it's creative all right," I said. I couldn't process a three-letter word without switching the letters around like a magic trick; there was nothing creative about that, just sinister.

"No, seriously. I did a bunch of research on it the last time you wouldn't read one of the articles I showed you."

I frowned at Emma, like she had gone behind my back. She shrugged.

"Your dyslexia isn't *just* a learning disability. It's two-sided. It's a distinct pattern in the way your brain functions, so you learn and organize information differently than most people do."

I crossed my arms and rolled my eyes. I wasn't about to let somebody tell me I was gifted.

"Seriously! Dyslexic people are really advanced at three-dimensional spatial reasoning, and they can recognize complex and ever-shifting patterns." Emma made cubes out of her hands and rotated them.

I sighed, embarrassed by the entire conversation. If it was true, I would have figured this calendar out long ago.

"It's true, Wilde. That divergence might just be the ticket to unlocking your ability," Walker said.

Kai still wasn't talking, but he made it a point to look me in the eye and nod. Even Kai was jumping on this wagon?

"I don't know, you guys. It's been nothing but a hindrance for me. Maybe it is a special power for some, but it's only held me back. Sorry to disappoint." I grabbed Kai's water glass and headed to the kitchen to refill it.

"No, I think we might be onto something here. The stupid calendar makes little sense to any of us, but maybe you could figure it out. You know, because your brain is working off the beaten path and stuff," Noah said with a shrug. I scowled at him over my shoulder. Emma slapped his arm, and his eyes grew wide as he looked at her in confusion.

Good lord, was that how they thought of me?

We were interrupted by the sounds of boots stomping up the stairs on the back porch. "Oh shit, Scarlett May's home," Noah said.

The air in the cabin shifted as we waited for her to come inside. My stomach flipped in dread as the doorknob twisted. She came in like a breath of fresh air, but that all changed the moment she slid her sunglasses onto the top of her head.

"Um, hi guys?" she said, surveying the room.

She slid her phone into her back pocket and cautiously

walked into the kitchen. I tracked her eyes as they landed on the calendar, and I gnawed on my lip as she stared at each one of us, slowly counting down. When she took in the sight of Kai on the floor, she knew.

I came to her side and put my hand on her shoulder, but she shoved it off and stormed out of the room. Kimber had been one of her closest friends, and now she had nobody. It wasn't the kind of thing I wanted to connect with somebody over, but I understood how she felt. And it seemed like, for the first time, Scarlett May and I had something in common.

CHAPTER 14

Kai slumped over, his eyes shut, and his chest moving slowly. It could have been the stress from the chase, or the handful of antihistamines I had given him, but either way, he should sleep through the night. Hopefully, he'd feel better in the morning. What wouldn't heal come morning was Scarlett May. And I worried that she might try something like Kimber had.

Emma took a pillow from the sofa and placed it next to Kai. I helped her tip him over until his head rested gently on the pillow. His body was radiating heat. It must have been from the venom. Emma grabbed a throw blanket from the couch, and I shook my head. He'd been through enough; we didn't need to cook him too.

Once we got Kai situated, Emma left to get ready for bed and Noah turned on the TV, leaving Walker and me on our own. I didn't want him to leave, and by the way he was lingering, I could see that he didn't particularly want to go either. He clapped a fist into an open hand and nodded toward the back patio. I stole a glance at Noah as we slipped out into the night. I was on high alert for the bees. Not only the killer ones buzzing around, but the dead ones that lay on the floor, dusted the seats, and sprinkled the railings with their little bee bodies and their sharp stingers. In the glow of the porch light, I scoured every inch of that patio. There wasn't a single bee to be found, though the hive still lay cracked open on the ground. It looked petrified as if it had fallen months ago and dried out in the day's light.

"There are no bees," I said, still looking.

"No. I think you took care of that," Walker said with a chuckle.

"What do you mean?" I asked.

"Wilde, you turned them to smoke. You vaporized them into a fine mist. They disintegrated—all of them. You know, I don't think you realize how badass you are." He rubbed my tense shoulders.

Badass? That would be the very last way I would describe myself. "I'm not all that you think I am," I said, careful not to disrupt the massage with too much movement.

It didn't matter, his hands left my neck as he craned to get a better look at me. "Are we going to do this again? Are you serious?" He breathed a deep sigh and wiped his lips with his hand. "What's it going to take for you to realize just how special you are?"

A laugh escaped me. This was ridiculous. "You guys literally just told me that my biggest weakness in life was actually a superpower. Who's trying to pull the wool over whose eyes here? Me? Or you?" I asked, cocking my head to the side.

"Don't you realize? It's true. Whereas most people have a processing pattern that goes one way through the woods, yours takes another path and—"

"—Yeah, yeah, yeah. I heard you guys. But what you failed to mention is, it's the wrong way."

"It's not the wrong way! It might be . . . longer, sure."

I laughed and rolled my eyes. I didn't need him to sugarcoat this. I'd had plenty of years to get used to it. I knew what dyslexia was and what it wasn't.

"Listen to me. It may take you a little longer, but that's only for the reading and writing. You're missing the whole other half here. Your kind of processing allows you to see things that most people don't and never will. It's backward, it's upside down, and it's exactly what we need in a situation like this."

It never felt good to be called backward, no matter how much of a light was cast upon it.

"Like this?" I asked.

"We're fighting your subconscious demons, Wilde. Whether you like it or not, this is a world of your making.

If only you could realize that, while it is your weakness, it's also your strength, then we might have more dreams than nightmares. That's all I'm saying." Walker stared out at the full moon in a pensive gaze. I could tell he was getting tired of trying to convince me.

I looked at the moon too. We sat in silence for a little while, watching the night pass by. Noah's TV show flickered a neon blue that reflected on the cabin windows, and I let myself breathe deeply in the silence. I doubted I would get much sleep tonight, and I didn't want to be alone to try. But I didn't think Walker would spend the night if I asked. It might be crossing the line that he'd drawn for our friendship. So, this is what I had instead: moon gazing until our eyes burned and we parted ways. I'd go off to bed and stare at my ceiling while he did whatever he did at night. I just wanted him to stay. I wanted to stretch this part of the night out. If only till the sun came up and there were no more shadows to steal my mind away —telling me lies about my worth.

"I wish . . . I wish you believed in yourself how I did," Walker said, in a whisper. It floated like a failed spell that just wouldn't stick—in one ear, out the other.

"If my dyslexia were a strength of any kind, then I'd be powerful. I'd be this almighty witch who could freeze time. Just like this. Right now. I'd freeze it. I'd keep this moment in a bottle locked up tight, so I'd be able to have you by my side whenever I wanted. Whenever I needed. Then I wouldn't be left alone with my thoughts at night. It can be so haunting." I smiled shyly at him and then looked back to the low-hanging moon.

"The bees would never have snuck inside the cabin. They certainly wouldn't have crawled inside my mouth. They wouldn't have stung Asher. And if I was a witch, I wouldn't be afraid of Baylor Lake. I'd swim right down to the bottom, and I'd throw a party there with Lainey."

I dropped my head as the heartache gripped my chest. "I'd go back home and tell my mom and dad I was all right. I'd tell them not to worry about me, because I had something I was doing here on the other side. Something important that I couldn't walk away from. I would tell them I was with my gran."

Walker was silent, taking it all in, and it felt good to speak freely. No judgment.

I examined my fingers, picking at my nails. "You know, Walker, I know I can't go home right now, but if I could, I don't know that I would want to. If it was a chance I had, I'm not sure I'd take it. There's just so much here that I feel is within my grasp. And I don't think I could ever leave you. The thought of leaving you behind, leaving my gran behind . . . It makes me sick. Physically sick. I can't imagine my life without you." My eyes burned. I was afraid if I blinked, a tear might roll down my cheek.

Still, Walker said nothing. I could see from my peripheral vision he was still staring at the moon. It was a beautiful moon; a gigantic one. I could see the craters from here, and it almost looked like a face. Even so, I had expected a response of some type. He seemed to be deep in thought. His brows were knitted and his eyes glossy. The gash in his eyebrow glistened just a little, and I could tell that his wound was opening again from our conversation. I didn't want that. I didn't want to open his wounds. I'd done it again. I hurt the people I cared about most.

But when I looked more closely, Walker was eerily still, and I realized he hadn't even blinked, let alone responded. I flinched. "Walker?" I asked.

He said nothing. Did nothing.

I spun around to see the TV's glow hadn't flickered in some time. The cabin windows were lit by a constant blue haze. I turned back to Walker and reached my hand out, shaking his shoulder. He was still and stiff. Stiff, like he'd been turned to stone. I grabbed at his face to pull him close, but I couldn't get him to move.

"What the hell . . ." I whispered. Looking out at the night sky, not even the stars were twinkling. And that's when I realized what I'd said. That if I were a witch, I would freeze time.

If I were a witch . . . If my weakness was my strength . . . *Was my weakness my strength?*

Oh my god, my weakness *was* my strength! I'd been so conditioned to think I was broken because I couldn't perform like the other kids in school. But I had never been in a situation like this before. I was only eighteen. And this was no longer the classroom. I looked toward the woods and the world seemed so vast. Here, I could be my own wizard. I could control the dimensional space around me to my liking. Maybe I wasn't lost like I had always thought? Maybe I was simply on the scenic route.

I laughed out loud in embarrassment. It was absurd.

But was it? Could I really be in control of all this?

I scampered down the grassy knoll to the sandy shore, checking over my shoulder often to see Walker's silhouette. It surprised me how the lake ceased to lap against the sand. I kicked off my shoes and peeled off my socks. I touched a single toe to the water, and it was a hard, glass-like surface. I pushed my weight down on top of the frozen lake water, and it felt sturdy. I stole a glance back at Walker. He was like a statue leaning against the deck railing. I smiled before stepping out onto the water. It wasn't slippery like I'd imagined it would be, but chalky and dry. It was still cold, though, and incredibly strong. I eased into my first few steps and then took off.

I ran. My heart beat thunderously in my chest. The cool night air kissed my face as I ran on top of the lake. Time was frozen, and I had no fear of being chased by a predator of the night. For I had cast them all to stone in my spell and they lay motionless in the shadows. I was a free spirit. I must've run a half mile before I stopped to lie on my back. Breathless, I stared up at the frozen stars. And after a while, I found the tail end of a falling star. A constant shimmer of gold etched in the sky.

I made a wish. But not like the wish I'd made when I blew out my eighteenth birthday candles. No, this wish wasn't for a kiss from Noah. And I'd be lying if I said I hadn't considered wishing for a kiss from Walker. But if I'd learned one thing here in Baylor, it was that a wish was not to be wasted on a fleeting moment such as a kiss. Don't get me wrong, I wanted it. I dreamed of the day where my lips would touch Walker's. But it was far more important to me now that he find happiness. I took my time crafting the perfect wish. Because who knows, if I was a witch after all, it might come true. Maybe . . .

I wished that Walker's curse would be lifted and that he would find love to carry him through the rest of his life. *Afterlife?* Whatever path he was on, it made little sense for him to walk it alone. And if he truly believed that I wasn't the person for him, then I would help him and Layla reconnect. But, luckily for me, I *knew* I was the one. And I was pretty sure he did too.

I walked back to the cabin deep in thought, remembering the time that fireworks had glimmered around Walker and me like streamers in a magical lagoon. I guessed this time I just needed to be alone. Time to think. To explore. I promised myself I'd try this freezing spell again, but during the daylight, so I could explore further into the forest and deeper into the lake.

With each step, I watched my feet meet the hard, glass-like surface of the lake, and I wondered what it was like below. I thought of the red door glued to the bottom of the lake, and I felt a subtle pull drawing me downward. Like the door was made for me and only me. Like my hand turning the doorknob was its life purpose. Sure, I was curious, but I think more than anything I was afraid.

What was the door? My door. The question created a feeling in my belly that I didn't particularly like. I didn't let myself think about it any longer because, somewhere inside me, I think I knew the answer. And it scared the living hell out of me.

Living hell . . .

If I had to guess, this was the very definition: a place you lived in that was evil in nature. In the real world, there might not be wolves that stand on their hind legs or killer bees looking to inhabit your body. There might not be bodies in the lake that whisper secrets. But hell was hell, and I supposed it was different for everybody.

I wasn't sure what hell was like for adults . . . Taxes or something. I guessed I would never find out. I'd just go on living here, in my own personal hell, trying my damnedest to make it my heaven. And if what I had always considered to be my biggest weakness was indeed a strength, then that should be an easy feat. In no time, the nightmares would dissipate, and the accidents would wane.

I looked near and far, searching the trees in the

distance. The glow of the cabin was nothing but a small dot in front of me. But with my yearning to see Walker so far away, my sight strengthened. Magnified. Walker was leaning against the back railing deep in thought. I saw it before I could even think it. A simple feeling. A dyslexic thought . . .

If I could see clearly, then what if I didn't have to walk all the way to the cabin? What if I was already there?

Startled, as if I was teetering on the edge of a cliff, I windmilled my arms and slowly lifted my gaze from my bare feet to the stairs of the patio. Behind me, the lake was calm and placid. A smiled creeped up on me, and for the first time I started to believe. To believe that maybe I *was* the person for the job. Maybe I *did* have the power to unlock the Baylor phenomenon.

If I were a witch . . . Maybe I didn't have to be a witch at all? Witches were inherently evil, weren't they? That's what I'd always thought I was in Baylor: evil. That part of my soul was steeped in the black malignant water. Why else would everybody die on my watch? Go missing in the woods or sink to the bottom of the lake? Why would birds flock from the sky and steal my friends from below? Because I was bad. I was wrong. I was the dreamer.

But what if I could control it? Then I no longer had to be bad. And I could stop thinking of myself as an ugly girl, with a long, pointy, and crooked nose. Green-hued skin covered in warts the size of grapes. A girl with a cackle so unnerving it sent chills up your spine. I didn't have to be that girl at all.

Standing there with a goofy smile on my face and nobody to see it, I thought of all the mischievous, glorious things I could do right now at the whim of a thought. A feeling. I could spy on everybody. Even the neighbors. I could hunt for the ever-fleeting tower. I could get free ice cream from the store. I could go to the mall . . . *The mall?* How far was the mall? Could I leave Baylor? If time was frozen, and I could do anything, then could I leave Baylor? Could I go home? Could I check on my parents? My body?

I felt the sudden pull. The wanting. The ties I had to my family beckoning me to come back. I looked at my hands as the odd feeling crept through my body, and they began to disappear. I felt the sucking of my soul drawing me.

No, no, no! I didn't want this! I didn't want to leave. I'd only thought about it.

But just as I had crossed the lake with a simple thought, I was abruptly standing in the corner of the hospital room.

I sucked in a ragged breath as I surveyed the room, afraid. It was dim and quiet. The monitors beeped rhythmically. My mom slept against my bed. Her chair was pulled close and her head on the edge of my thin mattress. Her arms stretched over my legs.

My dad was there too. He was semiconscious, dozing

off in a chair in the corner. His head was slipping from his balled fist. He looked broken in a way I'd never seen before. Weaker by unseen measures.

And then there was me. A version of me; one I couldn't identify with any longer. There was so much pain in the room that I could hardly stand it. I didn't want to see it. I didn't want to smell the antiseptic. I didn't want to know anything about it. I just wanted to go back to the world where I was in love, where I was learning to conquer myself.

The now familiar feeling of transporting my soul into another realm began. It started with the sinking in my stomach and moved to a crawling under my skin. Then it felt like my insides were lifting away from my shell. Like I was no longer standing there with my body. I felt like there were two of me, and one was invisible, separating to a new and distant land.

As my soul left, the outer parts of me crumbled in its wake, unable to live without the support. My hands wavered like a mirage until they were no longer there, and neither was I.

My eyes pressed shut as I took in a deep breath. I breathed in the smell of pine trees from the forest and the wood from the deck. It was a breath of fresh air after the antiseptic smell of the hospital. I took comfort in Walker's faint cologne that reminded me of the beach, and I knew I was home.

I opened my eyes slowly to see the guy of my dreams still frozen in place, and I was home. The life I'd left at the hospital didn't seem like my life at all. If anything, it was more like a past life. One I had begun to separate myself from as I dove deep into this one.

As much as I was afraid here in Baylor, it really wasn't very different from my real life. My past life. I'd been afraid there too, just for different reasons. Like not being noticed or getting a poor grade. The stress of an exam or what college to go to. It was nothing like this, of course, but the stress felt all the same. I might as well have been chased by a phantom wolf.

At least here in Baylor, under Walker's wing, I was learning the skills to combat these inherently evil threats. I only wished I'd been able to get training like this in my real life. I wished I'd believed in myself when I was back in school. Maybe then I'd have realized that classwork wasn't a one size fits all, and I was smarter than they led me to believe. How would that have changed my struggles? My dreams? My ambitions? I guess I'd never know.

CHAPTER 15

I stood on the deck staring at Walker. For the first time, I could gaze as long as I wanted without being noticed. Without being shy and having to avert my eyes. Without the embarrassment creeping into my cheeks and turning them warm. I looked at his broad shoulders stretching beneath his flannel. I took in his trim waist and strong stance. I walked around him, admiring his jawline, but when I came to his side, it wasn't how beautiful he was that stopped me in my tracks. It was the sadness that emanated from his eyes.

The tense way he balled one fist and hid it within the palm of his resting hand. It was the ache that poured from him, even though he was frozen, encapsulated in time. It was all the things I hadn't seen when I was so worried about what would come out of my mouth. I'd been so worried about how I came across to him, and the stress I carried, that I hadn't taken the time to notice how heartbroken he was.

I wanted to put my hand on his back and rub away all the stress. My hand lingered in the air, inches from his shoulder, and then dropped. I slipped it into my back pocket and leaned against the railing next to him. My eyes fell to my feet. If I stayed here in Baylor, would I be enough for him? Or would he always be looking for Layla? Would she always haunt us? There was a part of me that wanted to help Layla too, now that I knew her struggles. I couldn't help but wonder where my place was in this Baylor web. Where did I fit in? *How* did I fit in?

I sighed heavily and pushed off the railing. Inside the cabin, I found Noah fast asleep in front of the TV. I didn't linger long before heading upstairs. It was Scarlett May who I needed to check on. She'd been so hurt over Kimber leaving that I was afraid she might do something just like Kimber had. And if anybody was strong enough to do it, it would be her. I climbed the stairs, still in awe of how strong-willed Kimber had been. It made me wonder if I had imagined her all wrong. Maybe she wasn't the girl I'd always thought she was. And I wished she was here now for me to take a second look. A deeper look. One that I could only get by freezing time.

I grasped the bathroom doorknob with a light touch and turned it slowly. The door was unlocked, so I pushed it open just enough to peek my head inside. Nobody was in

there. It only left one more spot for Scarlett May to hide—
Kimber's room. I found her there on the floor, hunched
against the wall. She cradled Kimber's jacket in her arms.
Her chin was wrinkled, her face pink. A tear was glued to
her cheek, frozen mid fall.

It was a private moment of grief. One that I had
walked in on, unbeknownst to her. I took a single step
backward with the notion that I should leave. Give her the
privacy she deserved. But something stopped me from
leaving. She needed me. I crossed the room in a few long
strides and enveloped her in a hug.

It was difficult hugging her stiff body. But I let myself
mold into her hard crevices and sharp edges. I hugged her
tight, as if she were awake, so she'd know she wasn't alone.

"I'm sorry . . ." I whispered. I pressed the back of my
head against the wall, both of us mourning, but for
different reasons. Sure, I was gonna miss Kimber and
Asher. The loss of Lainey still weighed heavily on my
heart. But most of all, I was mourning the person I used to
be. The girl that I had always known no longer existed.
And in her place was somebody I had yet to know. Trust.
Love. I didn't know who I was in this dimension, and that
scared me most of all. I could be magical and powerful. I
could be in love and happy. Or I could be dangerous and
misunderstood.

I patted Scarlett May's knee and went to check on
Emma. It was no surprise that she was sitting at her

computer. Dressed in flannel pajamas, she hunched over the desk, a pen tucked between her fingers. Her cheek rest in the palm of her hand as she read an article, probably something about the inner workings of the dyslexic mind. I chewed my lip thinking the only thing worse than the pressure to succeed and the fear of failure was knowing you didn't try at all.

I stormed out of the room, across the hall, and into the master bedroom. I paced the length of the bedroom trying to think of ways to test the theory. Had being atypical always been a power? My eyes landed on the open window and then flickered to a framed picture of my brother when he was still in diapers. I didn't *want* to break it, and that wasn't the plan, but I had to test the theory, and it was the quickest way. I threw the framed memory hastily out the window, squeezing the windowsill as I leaned out into the open air to watch it fall.

When it stopped right before shattering against the patio, a wide smile crept across my face. I turned around and ran down the stairs, through the kitchen, and out the back door. Walker was still hunched over the railing, but this time, the picture was there too. It was suspended in air a mere inch above the patio. I marveled at it, touching the corner softly and watching it spin as if held by an invisible string. I chuckled and looked toward Walker, but my smile faded when I realized he hadn't seen it. The wonder still clung to me, despite not being able to share the magical moment. I grabbed the picture and ran back upstairs to do it again.

This time, it was going to be something bigger. I scoured the room. A million thoughts flooded my head. I grabbed my feather pillow. Twirling it around in my hands, I mused over the possibilities. Suddenly, I ripped off the pillowcase, grabbed a pair of scissors, and mindlessly cut a large slash through the center of the pillow. I tried not to think too much. I wanted it to be a feeling. And right now, I was excited, and hopeful. Maybe even a little playful. I hurled it out the window, and the feathers plumed into the air and fluttered both inside and outside the bedroom. I leaned out the window, full of hope, and I smiled with anticipation for a show unlike any other.

The white feathers stilled and separated. A glow deep within the veins of the feathers spread out to the soft edges. Each one lit in the dark. Like a million tiny lanterns, the feathers gleamed a warm golden radiance, lighting up the night. Unlike the picture of my little brother, I didn't want the feathers back. I wanted to send them out into the world. I wanted to free them—unleash them to spread the magic.

Go. Go now. A light wind ruffled my hair as I leaned out the window. The feathers stirred.

I watched as hundreds of golden feathers invaded the sky and sailed off into distant lands. Why would I want to give this up? How could I to go back to a life where magic didn't exist? A place where I was a nobody? I watched the feathers until I could no longer see a single glowing ember, and I wondered where they would end up. Who would find them? And who needed them most?

When the night sky was rid of magic, I thought I'd better wake up the rest of the world. To be honest, I was missing Walker. The magic was glorious, but it would have been better if he'd been awake to see it. I made my way through the cabin and resumed my position. I leaned my forearms on the railing and relaxed by his side. I was home. This was my *home*. I belonged here.

I wasn't sure if it was the magic of Baylor or the fact that my greatest weakness was a strength in this realm. It could have been that my gran lived here, and I had family on this side. And it very well could have been that I was falling in love with Walker. But I felt like I was in my forever home. And the longer I stayed here, the more my other life felt like a distant memory.

When I was good and ready, I willed my life to resume. Walker's still figure lifted ever so slightly with his first breath taken in hours. And I felt warmth touch my heart and a smile lift the corners of my eyes. He was back.

Walker dropped his head and looked at me with sad eyes, continuing the conversation we had been having before my adventure. "If you just believed, I know you could do great things, Wilde. You are the only one standing in your way."

I finally understood. I did believe. He'd been right the whole time, and I just hadn't been able to see it. I chewed on my nail nervously, afraid of how our relationship would change if he learned what I was capable of. I decided not to say anything about the mischief I had gotten into while time stood still. At least for now. He gazed back out at the moon.

"I know. I know. I hear that all the time . . . I'm trying," I said. I wasn't completely ready to take on this world, but I *was* trying. Just because I now believed that I *could* hone my manifestations didn't mean that I had mastered the process.

"I know you're trying. We'll get there. We just need more practice." Walker squeezed my shoulder and then turned to go home. He never gave up on me. It only made me feel guilty for keeping the secret from him.

I saw the remains of my pillow by the stairs. Walker bent down and picked it up, examining it. I swiped it from his hands and hid it behind my back. Obviously, it was too late. His brows rose and his mouth opened like he wanted to say something, but ultimately, he didn't. An embarrassed smile crossed his face and he turned away. I could only imagine what he was thinking. My face heated with humiliation.

"You're up to something . . ." His voice rang like a melody—taunting me.

"No! I'm not." But he knew better.

I heard him chuckle as he disappeared into the darkness. I pulled the pillow remnant from behind my back and examined it. A lone feather escaped through the tear. The golden glow rose before me and trailed off after Walker, following him home like a lost puppy.

I went inside and climbed the stairs to Kimber and Asher's bedroom. I knocked softly on the door, knowing that Scarlett May wouldn't answer. I knew she was huddled against the wall crying, and I could imagine her fretting over pretending that she wasn't. I imagined her wiping her tears and trying to catch her breath. I gave her a moment, not that she needed it. I wasn't judging her. I understood what she was going through. More than I would've liked to.

I opened the door slowly and walked inside. She didn't raise her head to look at me. I closed the door behind me and sat on the floor, just like when she'd been frozen. But this time, I didn't give her a hug. I didn't think she would be open to it. Scarlett May liked to appear tough. And I didn't want to do anything to threaten that. Out of the corner of my eye, I saw her swipe a tear quickly, but I pretended not to notice.

"Kimber and Trinity were my best friends," Scarlett May said in a shaky voice.

"I know."

"And they are just . . . gone." She waved a hand through the air.

"I know."

"I don't get it," she said, looking at me for the first time. Her eyes were flanked red with pain.

I wanted to help her, but the truth was, I didn't know how. When my gran had died, I'd shoved the pain deep down inside. I'd forced my mind to think of something else. Anything else. I'd refused to acknowledge any of it. It had simply hurt too badly. And I hadn't known where to start. How do you process death? How does it make any sense, that somebody could be there one second and gone the next? Where did they go? And what did that mean for the rest of us?

I chewed on my lip as the uncomfortable thoughts swirled in my head. I only wanted to be there for Scarlett May. I didn't want to confront my own grief. And a small part of me wished I hadn't come into the room. I hadn't thought that she would actually talk to me. And now that she had, the tightness in my throat was almost too much to bear.

"I don't either," I said, my voice wavering as I tried to keep from crying.

My vision turned blurry with tears, and I did everything in my power to stop the feeling. Stop thinking. Stop the hurt. The truth was, the more I thought about it, the more questions arose. The more I started to look at life like a cruel game. One where players were plucked away at any given time. Regardless of whether they were playing by the rules or not. I wanted to scream.

"What do we do now?" Scarlett May's forehead was creased with worry and confusion.

The only thing I knew how to do was to ignore it. And I knew that wasn't what I wanted to pass on to her. It wasn't helping me in the long run. I wanted better for Scarlett May. And the only thing that I could think of was the small power I had inside me. The power to make things happen before our very eyes. It paled in comparison to what she actually needed, but it was all I had. It wasn't going to bring Kimber back. And it wasn't going to send Scarlett May home. But maybe, at the very least, it could be a distraction. A bridge to get from one impossible moment to a time where it was more bearable.

I grabbed Scarlett May's hand and squeezed. She glanced over at me and then startled when the room turned pitch black. I heard her gasp when the ceiling lit with a billion sparkling stars. Hues of orange lit the galaxy where the ceiling fan would have been. The Milky Way streamed in aqua across the back wall. And the temperature dropped to match the outside air. I heard Scarlett May sniffle. But the best part was that she squeezed my hand tighter. This meant something to her. And even though it didn't take the pain away, I knew that we were getting through it. Together.

Scarlett May and I lay down on the bedroom floor

head-to-head. We took turns pointing out shooting stars for hours. We talked very little about the pain that we were living through. Mostly, she spoke about Sampson. She told me how she had always liked him far too much to date him. Because, in her words, he wasn't the dating type. He was the marrying type. She told me how she kept him close because she was waiting for the time when she was ready to settle down. That's when she would make her move. And I learned I had pegged Scarlett May all wrong. It was turning out to be a bad habit of mine. And it was only when the world had stopped that I was able to see Walker's pain, Scarlett May's heart, and my strength. And I wished the world could stop a little more often, giving me a chance to see all that I hadn't before.

CHAPTER 16

Several days passed, and with them my confidence grew. An instant pot of coffee brewed, a slide of a hairbrush in the bathroom, and clean socks when I'd had none before. It was the simple things that I put my mind to—the things I didn't care if I failed at—that I practiced with. And I was getting good at it.

When Sampson showed up at our door with several of his friends, I was excited to try my new tricks in a crowd. With the passing hours, the cabin grew thick with partygoers. More than I would have expected for the middle of the week. But it was summer, and ambitions were low. There weren't many job opportunities in Baylor, and I figured most of these people were here for summer vacations like we were.

I was pretty sure that every college-aged kid in Baylor

had come to my cabin, apart from Walker. I figured I would glimpse his flannel through the crowd later in the night. But I still didn't want to tell him about the night a golden feather had followed him home. So, it was good that he wasn't here to witness what I had planned. The cabin was crawling with distraction, and it was the perfect place for me to train. If I could master the magic in this environment, I would be a full believer in the power of my twisted mind.

And if I couldn't, I suppose I'd be disappointed. But with that disappointment would come the security of keeping Walker by my side. The responsibility I'd carry to save all my friends would be next to none. How could I save everybody if I was powerless after all? Although failure seemed like a terrible thing, I wasn't convinced it was all bad. Nonetheless, I was going to put it to the test. And all these people were test subjects tonight.

I found Emma fighting for space on the couch. She squeezed in, barely getting the back half of her butt on the sofa. She tried to take a drink but nearly spilled it after being bumped by the rowdy group next to her.

"Some party, huh?" I asked, leaning up against the arm of the couch.

"Yeah, it's something all right. Who invited all these people anyway?" she asked with a scowl.

I looked out into the crowd and found Scarlett May playing pool with Sampson and Skid. I smiled, remembering her feelings for him. "I have an idea," I said, nodding toward Scarlett May.

"It's always her," Emma said, finally managing to take a sip of her drink.

A boundless energy grew within me. It was time to play. "What's wrong Emma? Is this party not entertaining enough?" I said with a mischievous wink.

Emma's eyes sparkled with curiosity as she waited to see what I was going to do. I quickly scoured the living room and picked the closest guy to us. It wasn't much of a manifestation. Just a quick little yank in my mind, and his pants dropped to his ankles. Instant reward.

I peeked at Emma, and her eyes bulged as she cupped her hand over her mouth to stifle her laughter. Red boxers with little yellow bananas were thrust into Emma's face as he bent over to pull up his pants. All the girls nearby laughed, causing a bit of a commotion. Quick were the phones that drew to take pictures. Emma threw herself backward on the sofa, laughing and spilling her drink onto her chest.

I shouldn't have felt a surge of pride with my pantsing of an unsuspecting guest, but I did. And it was better than I'd imagined. It felt so good, I couldn't wait to do it again. I took Emma's cup from her as she stood and tried to swipe away an ice cube that had fallen down her shirt. I briefly wondered, if Walker were here, would he have known that *I* was behind the spontaneous pantsing episode?

"Cold. Cold. Cold," Emma said, pulling her bra away from her chest. The ice cube dropped to the floor and spun out. I couldn't help but laugh. Emma's shoulder slackened, and she looked at me helplessly. I grabbed her arm, beckoning her to follow me. As soon as we stepped away, a girl walking behind us slipped on the ice cube. I heard her scream just before she hit the floor with a thud. I flinched backward, tightening my grip on Emma as the girl startled me. A tall blonde girl knelt to help her up, and Emma looked at me with questioning eyes.

"Did you do that?" she asked.

"No," I said, though I was unsure. *Did I do that?* I didn't think so.

Emma aired out her shirt by pinching the fabric between her fingers and fanning it back and forth. I set my eyes on the pool table.

"So, it must be true then?" she prompted.

"What?" I asked, still staring at the green felt table.

"Your twisted little mind is actually a great power." Emma looked at me smugly.

"Well, I don't know about that . . ."

"Kins, you just dropped that guy's pants with the flicker of a thought," she deadpanned.

"Well!" I laughed, shrugging.

"Welllll?"

"I guess. Maybe. A little bit." I looked innocently at the ceiling. Emma squealed batting her hands on my shoulder.

"I knew it!" She hid her grin behind a balled fist. Even with the loud sounds of the party, I could still hear her excited whimper.

"Okay. But seriously, don't say anything." It was all so new that I didn't want it getting out.

"No, I wouldn't say anything." Emma stared at me, waiting.

"I'm just not ready to have everybody's eyes on me. All their expectations to send them home. It's too much, you know? I'm not ready."

I watched the dynamics at the pool table; Scarlett May looked upset. Angry even. I wasn't sure where Skid's girlfriend was, but there were two girls vying for his attention. One of them had a special interest in Sampson, too. I watched as she whispered something in her friend's ear and then made her way to him. Seductively, she trailed her finger down his cue stick. Scarlett May barked at him.

"Sampson! You're up!" she said, tongue-in-cheek.

He leaned over, positioning his cue stick. The girl stopped him, taking the cue stick from him.

"What's going on here?" I mumbled. Emma looked but was unamused. She didn't know how Scarlett May felt, so it didn't seem very significant to her. Still, it wasn't my place to say anything. Especially not after the night Scarlett May had spilled her secret to me under the make-believe starry night sky.

I had only turned to look at Emma for a split second,

but when my eyes returned to the pool table, Sampson had his arms around the girl, and he was attempting to teach her how to play. He drew the cue stick back and forth between the girl's knuckles, and I couldn't bear to look at Scarlett May.

"Who else should you pants?" Emma asked, trying to get my attention by patting me on the shoulder. I shook her hand off.

I didn't know how to remedy this. All I really wanted was for the girl to go away so that Scarlett May could play pool with Sampson. And I doubted very much that pantsing him was going to achieve that. Pantsing *her* would be even worse.

They drew the stick back one last time and drove it into the ball. To my surprise, the ball shot back and forth like a ping-pong ball. It hit the side wall and flew off the table, heading directly for Scarlett May's stomach. I gasped as she absorbed the blow to her gut. She wrapped her hands around her waist and dropped to her knees, breathless. Sampson rushed to her side.

"Oh no!" Emma said.

The flirty girl ran her hands through her hair, shrugging, as her friend laughed out loud. The two of them scampered off with Skid.

"Oh my God. That looked like it hurt," Emma said. She started for them, looking to help, but I caught her wrist as she passed by.

"I think Sampson has this," I said, watching him on his knees next to her. Emma looked at me and then back at Scarlett May huddled on the ground. She nodded, not thinking much of it, but I saw how he rubbed her back.

I was a little leery of getting involved when Scarlett May got hurt. And even though I'd achieved my primary goal of uniting her with Sampson, I hadn't intended to cause her any harm. It was a setback in my mind. Maybe I didn't possess the control that I thought I had. And just maybe I was playing with fire.

"Hey, Kins, you know what would be really cool? If you pantsed another guy." Emma said, scanning the crowd for another victim. I briefly joined her and then scrunched my eyes shut. *No.* Pointing this magic at somebody was like playing Russian roulette. You never knew if there was a bullet in the chamber.

"Yeah, until something bad happens," I said.

"Like what? You accidentally pull down his boxers too?" Emma giggled. Her amusement faded as an attractive guy walked by. Her eyebrows rose as she looked over his arms in a muscle tee. She gestured toward the guy. "Oh, come on! Just one more!" she whined.

It didn't take much for me to cave. After all, I didn't like ending on a grim note. You always hear you should quit while you're ahead, but how many times does it take to get ahead? How many times should you risk the failure?

"One more. Then were done," I said in my most serious tone.

Emma smiled and pointed to the guy with the shoulders. "That one!" she said.

"That cute boy? The one with the perfect smile and muscles sculpted from god?" I asked.

Emma nodded. Her eyes fixed on her target.

I licked my lips, getting ready. But Emma didn't really want me to pants the guy. She didn't want to embarrass him. She was attracted to him. She just didn't know it yet.

"Okay. Get ready. Here we go . . ." Like clockwork, the apple of her eye turned to face her. Emma's eyes darted to the floor, and then she spun to hide her red face in my shoulder, but I was already gone. I smiled, watching from a few people away as the guy strode right toward her. Emma spun in circles looking for me, and I hid behind a mountain of a man.

A group of guys made their way out of the living room, pushing me backward into the hall. By the time the sixth or seventh guy squeezed by, I made my way back inside to find Emma deep in conversation. I smiled, standing alone in the hallway, watching. Emma wasn't naturally comfortable with the opposite sex. She was a little clunky and a lot nervous, but right now she was killing it. And I wasn't going to interrupt her.

I was looking over the crowd for somebody to talk with when I noticed the garage door open and close out of the corner of my eye. I knew if any of these partygoers found the golf cart, there would be hell to pay. It wasn't going to happen on my watch.

I hurried down the hall, ready to do whatever it took to keep the golf cart parked but stopped five feet shy of the door. Something registered in my mind; a flash of red. I looked over my shoulder, shocked to see a red door in the middle of the hallway. I was pretty sure that on the other side of that wall was the office. And I knew, beyond a shadow of a doubt, that door was for my eyes only. Slowly, I turned. I approached the door, touching the doorknob. Its gold hardware matched nothing in the cabin. And there was something in the way the metal was lukewarm that made me hesitate.

Was it a trap? It reminded me of the door I had seen at the bottom of Baylor Lake, and it beckoned me to enter just the same. If I had felt any control over my power tonight, it was gone now. I was helpless when it came to the door. My curiosity was like the pull of a six-horse carriage—powerful and very much unstoppable. I never even looked back.

I opened the door and was immediately sucked in with a gravitational pull. My feet slid over the floor as if it was ice. The door slammed shut behind me. I spun to open it, but it had vanished. My heart pounded, and I immediately felt hot. I was now trapped within the walls of the cabin, and nobody knew it but me.

"Help! Let me out!" I yelled. The lights flickered and buzzed in the overhead two-by-fours. The sounds from the party faded on the other side of the wall into a muffled, distant murmur.

"Hello?" I called out, meekly. There was nothing but exposed beams and the backside of the drywall. I patted the wall in the dim flickering light, looking for a way out.

The door had vanished as quickly as it had appeared, and there was no way out. A short hallway led to something bigger, brighter. I had no choice but to walk it alone. I stretched my eyes as far as they could go. Where was the light coming from? What would I find when I rounded the corner? I could only hope my gran was there, waiting.

I took one step, and then another, leaning into my footsteps cautiously. As I walked down the narrow hall, unfamiliar voices arose.

These were not the voices of college-aged kids partying at a lakeside cabin for the summer. These were the voices of professionals. They belonged to another time, another place. Anywhere but here.

"Dan isn't going to make it here if he keeps running his mouth like that," a man's voice said, calm and collected.

"I'm so sick of these arrogant residents coming in here thinking they're god's gift. Every single one of them," a woman replied quietly.

"It gets worse every year. Maybe it's my age—"

"No. It really does get worse. This year is especially bad," she agreed, her voice a monotone, like the conversation was overly mundane.

I took another step. I didn't know who Dan was, but by the sound of it, I didn't want to. It seemed that my head ached more the closer I stepped toward the light. But by the time I rounded the corner and saw the doctors, it was my knees that threatened me the most. Quaking and weak, I almost collapsed.

Several doctors crowded around an operating table. Machines glowed, bags of blood and fluids hung on metal poles, and a continuous beeping chimed sharply. I sucked in a breath, but the air seemed so thin. There was so many of them, and only one of me. It reminded me of the night that Levi had been swept up in a tornado of crows, and I found myself at the foot of a hospital bed. *My* hospital bed.

Was that me? Was this happening in real life? Now?

The doctors talked like they were having coffee or lunch with a colleague, but the truth was, they were working on somebody's head. *In* somebody's head. My stomach turned sour when I saw the male doctor lift a portion of skull from the patient. He placed it on a metal tray draped in a blue napkin.

As if connected to the skull myself, my head screamed with pain. I reached up into my hair, grabbing my head, whimpering. I was only semi-aware that my head felt whole, and I continued to search for a missing piece—the cause of my pain.

It was one of the quiet men who noticed me first. As if he could hear my pain. He lifted his head and stared at me.

"Hello?" My voice cracked wearily through the pain.

He stared cautiously, unblinking. Sitting in a chair by the patient's head, he appeared to have little to do.

My face winced as the sharp pain grew unbearable. With nowhere else to go, I took a step toward him, looking for help. I was desperate and on the verge of passing out.

His eyes rounded and his face paled. He was the only one present who could see me. "Oww!" I groaned. My voice like that of a frightened little girl. A little girl calling out into the night when she was afraid a monster might reply but prayed it would be her mother instead.

The pain stabbed, and I sucked in a seething breath through my teeth.

"Patient is starting to wake. Pushing anesthesia," the man said, taking his eyes off me and focusing on his equipment.

But as soon as he said it, everybody in the room stopped. They all turned to look directly at me with wide eyes. My mouth dropped open as I stared back, just as surprised as they were. What was this place? Where was I?

I felt incredibly exposed, like I was being seen for the very first time, and I wasn't ready. The monitor's beeping slowed as the wooziness took over. The pain in my head subsided, and the bright lights dimmed. When the worst was over, the doctors went back to work, and I went back to being invisible. Invisible to all but the man in the chair, who watched me carefully.

Released from their snare, I turned and ran down the hall, away from the pain and exposure. The red door appeared between the exposed beams, summoning me. The golden handle called my name.

I barged through the door and shoved my way through the crowd, grabbing Emma by the shoulders and pulling her away from her beautiful stranger.

"Emma!"

"What! What is it?" she asked in annoyance. Her eyes flickered back to the brawny muscle tee as I pulled her away. "Kinsley, what?"

I dragged her all the way upstairs. Away from the crowd and into the bedroom. When I flipped on the lights, a couple lay tangled in each other on my bed. They made a show of protesting.

"Get out!" I yelled.

The couple scampered off the bed and out of the bedroom, mumbling choice words beneath their breath.

"What is going on?" Emma's voice rose as she demanded answers. The room was still, and the music was muffled through the walls.

"I went back!" I said, breathless.

CHAPTER 17

I ran my hands through my hair, pacing the length of the small bedroom. Emma stood still, trying to grasp it all.

"I went back. I saw it all as it was happening."

"You went back where? You saw what?" she asked.

"I went back to the hospital. They were performing surgery . . . Oh god . . . Was that me? Was that my head?" I patted my hair where the pain had pierced through.

Emma frantically examined my head. "What are you talking about? There's nothing here!" There was no dried blood, and most importantly, no missing skull. I turned around slowly as she sat on the foot of the bed, patiently waiting.

"Tell me what happened," she said softly.

"They pulled out this piece of bone and put it on a tray. They were talking like it was nothing. Like it was nothing to remove somebody's skull. Like they did it every day." I grabbed my stomach, afraid I was going to be sick, but the nausea passed by.

"Whose they?" Emma asked.

I pulled the computer chair out from the desk and wheeled it over to the edge of the bed. "The doctors. Me. My *other* me. The one that's real, back home. I saw them. For a moment, I was there. It was like I was spying on them." I sat in the chair and looked Emma in the eyes.

"How did you do that?"

"That's the thing. I didn't. It was like it summoned me. This door showed up out of nowhere and when I opened it, it pulled me through and then vanished, trapping me inside the walls." Oh god, I sounded like a lunatic.

"The walls?" Emma tried to keep up, but I could tell I wasn't making much sense.

"Yeah. The hallway downstairs by the garage. A mysterious red door appeared."

"The tapes! We have to watch the surveillance!" Emma said, popping to her feet and rushing to the computer. Relief washed over me when I realized she was on my side and not silently judging me like I did myself. It was nice to have a friend to count on.

"At first, they didn't see me, but then they all looked at me …" I was lost in the memory, my unfocused eyes staring at the corner of the room where the carpet met the baseboards.

Emma typed away on the computer.

"You said by the garage door? I wonder if the kitchen surveillance would have captured it." Emma was quickly sifting through video.

"The worst part was the way they looked at me. Like they were disgusted. Like there was something wrong with me. Like I shouldn't be there," I said in a whisper. But if I wasn't supposed to be there, then where the hell did I belong? Did they even want me back? Or had I been banished to the realm of dreams and nightmares, the realm of Baylor Lake—my phantom reality.

"Here! I found it!" Emma said, pointing to a tiny figure on the video feed. She zoomed in. The video showed me standing by a bare wall in the hallway. There was no red door.

"No. That can't be it. Rewind it. Start from the beginning when I came into the shot."

"That is the beginning," Emma said, scowling.

"Just do it!" I snapped. I wasn't crazy. I knew what I'd seen.

Emma rewound the video. I watched myself in reverse. There were only a few steps taken backward before I was out of the shot. She hit play, and I walked into the hallway and stopped. I froze, bawling my fists at my sides. I appeared to be in some sort of trance. I glanced at Emma nervously as I struggled to make sense of it. It wasn't her mind lost in translation. It wasn't her up on that screen proving that she was crazy.

The video showed me turning around and placing my hand against the wall, like I was trying to listen in on a conversation happening in the other room. I stayed there like that for long enough to feel the shame and embarrassment spread across my skin in waves of heat.

"That's not what happened! It's a lie!"

Emma gazed at the screen, her brows knitting together as she looked for clues.

"It's not real! There was a door, I went through it," I said, on the verge of hysterics. My voice didn't sound like my own as it was much higher than normal. Quicker, too.

Emma held her finger up, motioning for me to wait. Something seemed to snap inside me on the video, and I appeared to wake from my trance. I spun around and took off running through the crowd. That's probably when I'd gone looking for Emma.

Emma hit pause and turned to me with an open mouth, but she couldn't seem to find the words to say.

"I swear, Emma, it didn't happen like that."

"It's okay." Emma nodded. She didn't believe me, but she loved me all the same. She accepted me, even through my psychotic flaws. But I didn't.

"They looked at me! They looked at me like I wasn't supposed to be there!" I said fanning my face. It was so hot. My throat tightened, and my eyes watered. Where did all the time go? I had been trapped inside the walls for ten to fifteen minutes, but the video showed no more than sixty seconds pass before I fled in search of Emma.

A guy and a girl barged in, laughing. "Get out!" Emma and I yelled in unison.

I took a deep breath and sank to the floor, dropping my head to my bent knees.

"Hey. It's okay. Remember, if that video feed wasn't real—"

"It was real."

"*If* it wasn't real, then who's to say any of it is? Who's to say *this* is real right now?" she asked.

I looked up at Emma as she tried to give me her best *it's okay* speech, and I pinched her before she had a chance to finish. Just like a viper, I struck without warning.

"Ouch!" She rubbed her arm. If she hadn't thought I was nuts before, she did now. Her scowl said it all, and her mouth hung open in shock.

I rolled my eyes.

"Point taken. You didn't have to pinch me." She slumped on the floor next to me.

"I don't know where I belong anymore, Emma."

"I think we need to get you home," she said.

"I don't think they want me there. You should have seen how they looked at me." A tear dribbled down my cheek as I thought of how unwelcome my presence had been in the operating room. I didn't want to go back anyway, but regardless of choice, it still hurt to know I didn't belong. And I didn't want that choice made by anyone but me. Was it too much to ask to be the only one in control of my fate?

"Of course they want you. Your mom wants you there. Your dad does. Even your brother. Don't think for one second that you've been banished to Baylor because they looked at you weird."

"But I have been banished here, haven't I?"

"I think you're just here to heal. And when you get your strength back, you're going to set us free, and we're all going home. That's what I believe."

"And if I can't?" It was a tall order. What if I couldn't save everybody? What if I couldn't save Emma?

"I can't let myself think about that. You know, I'm trying to be strong here, but I really, really want to go home. You can't lose hope, Kinsley, because if you do, we all will. And I don't want to see Baylor with lost hope. It's already haunting enough."

I felt the weight of responsibility crash down on me. I needed to thrive, because there was no other way out for them. When the time came, I could send them home, and then I would stay here with Walker.

"Too haunted for *you*?" I asked, trying to lighten the mood.

"You know, it's one thing to read it, and it's an entirely different thing to live it. I can't close the book on this. I can't turn out the lights and go to sleep knowing that tomorrow will be a sunny day and breakfast will be waiting for me downstairs on the kitchen table come morning. I don't even know if there will be a morning here. I don't know if we will survive the night."

"I'm so sorry, Emma. I'm so sorry I'm putting you through this." What kind of friend was I?

Emma rested her head on my shoulder, and I heard her stifle a sniffle. The girl was homesick, and I knew the feeling.

"Can you just make it better? If only for tonight?" she asked. I sighed, knowing that it would only be a bandage. That I would be fixing the symptom and not the cause. That the fear would still be there tomorrow . . . *if she were to wake.*

"I think I can." It was one small thing I could do for her now.

I closed my eyes, and I imagined Emma curled up on her window seat with her favorite book in her bedroom at home. There was a candle lit on her nightstand, and her cat curled up by her side. It was her happy place, and right now, it was her safe haven. She didn't have that here, but she needed it.

"Ceecee," Emma exclaimed.

I opened my eyes to see that we were no longer in the guest bedroom of the cabin, but in Emma's bedroom sitting on the floor. Her cat, Ceecee, purred rhythmically. Emma scratched behind her ears and under her chin. Emma's eyes lit with wonder, and she stood up, spreading her arms wide. "It's been so long!" she exclaimed.

"Is it how you remembered?" I asked, paging through the book on the window seat.

"It's exactly how I remember it. How did you do it?"

"Don't worry about that. Just enjoy it." I made my way to her door.

"Hey Kins . . ." I had almost made it out of her room, escaping the question that I knew would come next. "Can I stay?" Emma's eyes were pleading when I glanced over my shoulder. I wanted so badly to tell her yes, that she was home now, and the nightmare was over. The truth was, I couldn't lie.

"Only for tonight," I sighed.

I watched a flicker of sadness cross Emma's face as I turned to leave. As soon as I closed the door to her bedroom, I was in the hallway of the cabin. I'd given her a dream to live in, but it was only temporary. The dream would turn back into a nightmare soon enough. There was only so much I could do, and I rode that guilt like a wave across the hall to my bedroom.

I vaguely remember a wandering girl stumbling through the hall looking for an extra bathroom. I pointed her in the right direction as I crossed into the master bedroom. A faint smell of raspberry and vodka wafted behind the girl. I locked the door behind me. If Emma could escape for a single night, could I escape too?

I dressed for bed and turned out the lights. I closed my eyes and thought about what I really wanted. If it was just for one night, which dream could I live in? I wanted to go home just like Emma had. I was homesick too. I wanted to see my mom, but there was a part of me that was afraid of knowing it was fake. Worrying that her love was disingenuous. A figment of my imagination. I presumed that would hurt more than not seeing her at all. For that reason, I chose to stick with my bedroom. I could pretend I was home for one night, just like Emma, and we could commiserate together come morning when we woke in the cabin.

I opened my eyes, and I was in my bedroom, just the way I'd left it. My bed was unmade, and my graduation gown hung from my windowsill. I smiled and touched the fabric of the navy-blue robe. My shoes were on the floor, still toe to heel, as if I had just stepped out of them yesterday. Several clean outfits lay scattered on the floor outside my closet.

It triggered a memory of me getting dressed on the night of my birthday. I was going to celebrate, and I remembered I was running late to pick up Lainey. My eyes drifted over my desk where my journals had been bookmarked. My backpack sat in my computer chair. It was just the way I remembered it, and it almost made me feel like I was home. It didn't take away the nagging homesick feeling completely, and I knew that had something to do with my family not being here. But even though the familiarity of my belongings eased the pain in my heart, in no way had it healed it.

Now that I was here, I felt the emptiness that lived inside me. It was never my home that made my heart full, but the people that lived within it. I paged through my journal, opening to the bookmarked entry. I read a passage full of my hope to steal the heart of Noah Hampton. I blushed thinking of the time when that was my biggest dream. I'd had big plans the night of my birthday, and I had hoped that he would kiss me. I had been so naïve. It seemed like years ago, but I had no way of telling just how long it had really been. I sighed, feeling almost lonelier here at home than I ever had in Baylor. Which was saying a lot, because nobody understood me there. Nobody but Walker.

I turned back to my bed and my heart seized. Walker St. James lay on my unmade bed. His fingers interlaced behind his head and his ankles crossed lazily over one another. He smiled a wicked smile, and his dimples burrowed into his cheeks. I swallowed the lump in my throat as my mind raced in a hundred different directions at once. How long had he been here? Had I summoned him? Was he real? I had so many questions, but the one overpowering thought was how he could single-handedly close the gap in my heart. My world wasn't complete if he wasn't in it, and that scared me more than the devil of Baylor himself.

"Walker," I said breathlessly.

"Wilde," he replied.

"What are you doing here?" I took in how glorious he looked sprawled across my bed. And I was suddenly utterly horrified at my dirty bedroom. I stepped on a pair of shorts on the floor and kicked them underneath the bed, thankful that they slid across the hardwood floor effortlessly.

"What are you talking about? You wanted me here. Right? Isn't that how this all works?" he asked. Did he know I was just thinking about him? Did he know how I felt right now? I was uncomfortably exposed.

"No! And yes. I mean . . . maybe?" My voice hitched as I dropped to the floor, crawling on hands and knees after the laundry strewn everywhere. I slid half of it underneath my bed, and after popping to my feet, I kicked the rest of it into my closet and shut the door with a huff. My eyes widened as Walker left my bed for my desk and picked up my journal.

"No!" I lunged for him, but he was much taller than me, and he held the journal high over my head.

I jumped like a child, trying to swipe it from his grasp. His proximity made my cheeks flush, and I took a step back. He already knew I wanted him here, and now here we stood, alone in my bedroom.

He held the journal in which I had described my feelings for Noah in depth high above his frame. If this wasn't vulnerability, I didn't know what was. I felt exposed, like I was naked in front of him. I was afraid of how he would respond, and if getting a deeper glimpse of who I was would change his mind about me. Sometimes, being naked could be a funny thing—sometimes it was anything but a joke. I didn't know how Walker really felt toward me, and that scared me to the very core. I knew he cared, but I was pretty sure I was the only one with romantic feelings.

"What? I can't read it?" he asked. I couldn't tell if he was being sarcastic or not.

"Are you *insane?*" I didn't like how frantic I had become. Walker saw it too. The only difference between him and me, was that he liked it.

"Maybe?" he said seductively, with one brow arched. My heart hammered in my chest.

I stood staring at him like he was a feral beast until he slowly lowered the journal. As soon as it was in reach, I snatched it protectively. Walker held his hands up and backed away slowly. I shoved the journal inside a desk drawer and slammed it shut, barricading it with my body. He'd have to go through me if he wanted it now.

Walker let his hands fall and turned his attention to a

painting hanging on my wall. I had painted it when I was eleven years old.

"No!" I stopped him again.

Walker laughed and held his hands up again. I stood between him and the painting, a small space for my exploding heart. I felt like the fireworks from the Fourth of July were bursting in my chest. I was nervous, excited, and petrified all at once. I couldn't tell if it was beautiful or horrific. I couldn't tell if having Walker in my home made me complete, or completely insane.

Walker smiled down at me as if feeling for himself what I had felt all along, and he backed up slowly, giving me space to breathe. He was amused, and I was about to have a breakdown. He turned around, spotting the collage of photos behind my nightstand.

A small whimper escaped my throat as I buried my head in my hands. *Please make it stop.*

"Is this you?" he asked, pointing to a photo of Lainey and me in sixth grade.

"Yep," I said, shoving my hands in my back pockets and chewing nervously on my lip. There was a photo of Noah and me when we were younger pinned right next to it. I hoped he hadn't seen that one, or at least didn't recognize him.

"So, this is your room?" he asked, turning around and taking it all in. I cringed seeing the strap of a pink bra underneath his shoe. I really should have kept my room clean like my mom always told me.

"This is my room," I squeaked out.

"I like it." I sucked in a breath, not realizing I'd been holding my breath until now. Why did this make me so nervous? Walker was my friend. We hung out almost every day in Baylor. But there was something about having him in my bedroom that made it all so real. Like he'd come to visit me in my realm and was really seeing me for the first time.

"So, Wilde, why did you bring me here?" he asked, the same smug look on his face as when he'd held my journal.

CHAPTER 18

My bedroom was dim. I almost never turned the lights on. The summer before I'd started high school, my mom had gotten me a light shaped like a giant branch that sprawled across my wall, and with each stem, there were dozens of twinkling lights intertwined in the twigs. If I was home, it was plugged in. It may be a little childish now, but I'd always adored the soft glow of light scattered throughout the corner of my room. It was on now, and it only made Walker's chiseled jaw more alluring . . . and more out of place.

Why had I brought him here? I guess because I couldn't live without him, or I didn't know how to anymore. He was still a ghost, and I was still a dreamer, regardless of which realm we drifted through. But if that wasn't hard enough to wrap my mind around, the truth was, this wasn't my bedroom at all. This wasn't my reality, but a phantom of one I used to know.

I couldn't walk out that door and converse with my mom and dad. My brother wouldn't barge in at any moment trying to find my candy stash. And if I walked out that door, I wouldn't see the spindled stair rail of my house or the family photos my mom made us take every year at Christmas. I'd see wandering strangers looking for a private bathroom in the cabin at Baylor Lake. If I jumped out my window, I'd land on the grassy knoll of Rock Creek Cove. It would probably be the party trick of the night, and I would be thrust up on the shoulders of two or three muscular guys and paraded around like I was a demigod. Maybe that wasn't a half-bad idea . . .

But the part that *was* real was the connection I had to Walker. My feelings for him, regardless of backdrop, were unmatchable. I'd never felt this way about anybody before. My feelings for Noah stemmed from attraction, friendship, and maybe even the need to fit in. Noah had always been so comfortable in his own skin and so popular that I felt like maybe, if he liked me back, I would finally have a chance to relax and be accepted. I wouldn't have to try so hard to fit in.

But all of that was different with Walker. Walker never tried to fit in. He couldn't. He wasn't even alive. Actually, he stuck out like a sore thumb, and he owned every bit of it. I think it was one of the things I'd fallen in love with first.

High school is hard. It has its own little ecosystem. It's delicate, and difficult to find your place. But from the moment you graduate, that little world opens up— growing on a scale that is impossible to imagine at the time. The ecosystem you live in becomes the one you create. But I was neither in high school nor out in the real world. I was somewhere else entirely. I had my own realm laid out in front of me with infinite possibilities to create . . . *and destroy*. If I'd thought the real world was a big place, it paled in comparison to the silo of my imagination.

Living in a realm where anything is possible, and the path you choose could go on indefinitely, is a scary thing. Worse when you must do it alone. I didn't just want somebody like Noah, where I could fit in by his side. I needed somebody like Walker, who knew himself and was confident enough to allow me to find myself. I didn't have to change for Walker; I only had to grow into my potential . . . I had to find *myself*. And he would be there to walk the winding paths with me while I grew.

"Wilde?" Walker asked, head cocked to the side with a patient gaze.

"Huh?"

"Why did you bring me here?"

"Oh." My throat ran dry as my eyes scanned the bedroom I'd grown up in. "I wanted you to see this," I said simply.

"Really?" He laughed, running his hand over the stubble on his cheek.

I raised my eyebrows and nodded. Was it so hard to believe?

"Then why won't you let me see any of it?" he asked.

"You mean my journal? You can't read that."

Walker turned back to the collage of photos and my heart thumped in my chest. He un-pinned a picture of Noah and me at one of our mothers' get-togethers. We were wearing aprons and serving hors d'oeuvres; we couldn't have been older than eight.

"No, no, no," I said, plucking the photo from his hand.

He didn't say I told you so, but he might as well have by the way he was looking at me. I plopped down on my bed with a heavy sigh.

"Look, I just wanted to try it. I wanted to try to see my old bedroom. I thought it might ease some of the homesick feeling I get in my chest. And once it worked, I didn't really want to be alone. I didn't want to see my parents, because I thought it would be heartbreaking to know that it was only my imagination."

"Did it work?"

"Well, you're here, aren't you?"

Walker smiled and sat down next to me. "No, I meant, do you feel less homesick?"

"It didn't work as well as I thought it would. It's nice to

be here, and it's comforting in its own right. But there was something missing."

"The home part?"

I nodded, feeling the burn in the back of my throat. "I can look out my window and see the row of houses . . . But I know nobody is home. It's as if, everywhere I go, I'm alone. Isolated. The cabin is filled with my friends, yet I'm the only one dreaming." I threw myself back onto the bed and stared up at my ceiling. Walker lay down next to me on his side, his elbow propping him up.

"I'm glad you brought me here. I don't want you to feel alone. You know, Wilde, we might be in different spaces, but we're connected here. I think our souls found each other for a reason."

My stomach dipped. I loved the way he was looking down at me. "And why is that?" I prompted him.

"I haven't figured that out yet. But if we're talking about home, you're the closest thing that I have felt to home in a very long time. I can't thank you enough."

I wanted him to lean down and kiss me so badly. I pled through my eyes. We were soul mates. He'd just said it. Yet he still didn't want to kiss me. I saw the sadness that I had grown accustomed to pass through his eyes. It was the same sadness I had seen when I'd frozen time and he was gazing up at the luminous moon. He was a hurting soul, and he didn't need kisses. He needed a friend.

He fell back on the bed, and for a moment we both lay

on our backs staring at the ceiling through the dim light of my twinkling branch. But then Walker pushed his arm under my shoulders and pulled me to his chest. I looked up to see his glassy eyes before my head landed on his shoulder. I wasn't sure if he needed a hug or if he didn't want me to see him cry, but I wrapped my arm around his chest and melted into him. I wasn't the only one missing home.

I breathed in his beachy, coastal cologne and closed my eyes. It brought me back to the night we'd met. I was just a scared, drowned girl he'd plucked from the lake. I had sat in the canoe in my underwear, my hair dripping down my back and chest as I checked for claw marks on my thigh. But in the time it took to see the sky had illuminated with stars, I'd inhaled his smell, and his warm presence had me forever snared in his trap.

We drifted off, each drowning in our own despair, and clinging to one another like life rafts in a turbulent ocean. We held each other, trying to stave off the homesickness. Our heartache was a shared well of pain. We were two lost souls seeking refuge in each other, and I never wanted to let go again. I fought sleep, but it was inevitable. Walker's chin fell heavily on the top of my head as my mind quieted and we fell asleep.

In what seemed like no time, the combination of heat and light coming through the window lifted me from slumber. But it was the heavy arm around my waist and the heat against my back that fully awakened me. My eyes flung open as I stared out the window at the magnificent view of Baylor Lake. Just like a pumpkin carriage created for a magical night, my bedroom back home had disintegrated with the stroke of dawn. But it wasn't the pumpkin that had made the night magical. It was the prince. And my prince, Walker, was holding onto me tighter than ever. He'd never left, and he never let go.

His breath was hot against the nape of my neck. His hand rested at my navel, and his thumb was tucked into the waist of my jeans. My eyes widened, and I sucked in an alarmed breath, causing Walker to stir behind me. It was the last thing I wanted. I wished I could stay like this forever. I would have pretended to sleep for the rest of eternity if he'd keep holding me. But as my luck would have it, I ruined it the second I realized it was even happening. Walker stretched behind me, pushing into me as he did. His thumb caressed the skin just below my belly button as he slowly withdrew his hand from my waist.

I dared to be brave. I turned around to face him, but he was just getting up. He leaned over and kissed the top of my head, causing my stomach to churn with excitement. But then he did something unexpected. He ran his hand back and forth over my head, messing up my hair. He leapt out of bed, stretching once more and taking in the view from the window.

I lay in bed utterly confused. The kiss on the top of my

head was something lovers did. But the ruffling of my hair was something that big brothers did to their annoying siblings. It said a lot of things, but it didn't say I think I'm falling in love with you. Why did he have to be so confusing? It was almost if he was fighting a battle within himself, and I wished he would just surrender already.

The way he'd held me while we'd slept would say something different entirely. I wasn't sure if it was a reflection of his true feelings unmasked as he'd slept, or if he was simply dreaming of somebody else. Somebody I had been avoiding. Somebody who had his heart but didn't want it. Part of me felt like Walker had been lying to himself. That he'd loved me all along but just wouldn't let himself admit it. But there was an even bigger part of me, a part driven by fear, that wondered if Walker really did have the curse of broken love. That he would always love somebody who didn't love him back, and furthermore, would be incapable of reciprocating the true love that I gave him.

When I found myself checking my morning breath in a stealthily cupped palm of my hand, I assumed I had been complicating things far too much—the guy just didn't like *me*. I rubbed my eyes and ran my hands through my hair, fixing the mess my dreams had left me with.

"So, Wilde, when did you master teleportation?" Walker asked, turning from the window to look at me. His mussed hair and wrinkled shirt were a good look on him. I liked the way he looked right after waking up, and I knew my nights would never be the same if he weren't in them.

"I guess, last night?"

"Really?"

"Yeah," I said with a shrug. He wasn't buying it. He knew I was omitting the truth, but he wasn't sure why. He didn't know I was afraid he'd ask me to use my magic to find Layla, and that if I did, he might finally move on, and I would be left to this web of dreams all alone.

"Okay." He didn't argue. I wished he would have. I wished I could scream *you don't want me* at the top of my lungs and burst into tears. But he was more the type to watch and wait. I would go on allowing the guilt to cannibalize me as he quietly collected evidence of my dishonesty. It would come out eventually, we *both* knew it. I sat in awkward silence as he waited calmly for me to change my mind. But my lips were sealed.

"I think we need to up your training." I didn't enjoy lying to him, but I simply couldn't tell him the truth. There was too much on the line for me to lose. He was the one thing that kept me sane, and I surely couldn't live without him. Or perhaps I would go crazy like Layla had. And I had already been banished from my real life back home.

"What did you have in mind?" I wasn't sure there was much else he could teach me now that I'd unlocked what had been holding me back.

"It's a good question. I guess I need to evaluate you first."

I swallowed, trying to moisten my dry throat. If I wasn't willing to tell him, he was going to make me show him.

Walker disappeared downstairs to brew a pot of coffee, and I ran to the bathroom to brush my teeth. I splashed cold water on my face and slapped some pinkness into my cheeks. I ran back out and jumped into the bed, pretending I'd never left, and waited for his return.

Emma screamed a long, drawn-out cry across the hall. It ended in a muffled gurgle. I knew that cry. I knew she'd fallen asleep at home and rudely awakened here. I also knew that she was screaming into her pillow, because that's exactly what I had done the first month I'd been trapped in Baylor. I worried she would come in and curse my very existence, but she didn't.

By the time Walker came back with two steaming mugs of coffee, I had a plan. I was going to hold my magic back. Dampen the manifestations. I wasn't going to show him what I was truly capable of. That, I would explore my own. And he would be none the wiser.

He handed me a cup of coffee, and I thanked him, taking a sip before resting it in my lap. He sat opposite me on the bed. "I want you to go back," he said in a serious tone.

"Go back where?"

"If you are truly lucid dreaming, you should be able to travel wherever you want. I want you to go back to your home, your body, to the life you used to have before you came here, no matter how hard it is."

"What are you even talking about? Why would I do that?" I asked in a flustered tone.

"Why?"

"I mean, how? *How* do you expect me to just go back? And what would I even do there?" I asked.

"Take me with you. We can try to figure it out together. Maybe you could just lie down on top of your body and your soul would reconnect?"

It hurt knowing he was trying to send me home. And it only confirmed my biggest fear, that he could never love me back. If that was the case, maybe I shouldn't stay. My heart ached at the thought of leaving.

"But then, I would never see you again." I scoured his golden eyes for answers. Was that what he wanted?

"No, perhaps you wouldn't. But Wilde, this isn't where you belong." Walker's face contorted the same way it had when he'd told me I had died. I was beginning to know it as his uncomfortable truth face.

"Honestly, I don't think I belong there either."

"What? Why would you ever say that? Of course you belong there. That's your body, your family, your home." It made sense to Walker, and I could see why, but he hadn't seen the looks the doctors had given me in the operating room.

"Maybe . . ." I lied.

"Let's go back. Together. Just to look around."

I couldn't let him down, not without at least trying. I nodded and closed my eyes. Walker reached forward and took my open hand in his. He waited for the magic to pull us through a wormhole, sending us to my battered body in the hospital bed. But me, I let the minutes tick by as I enjoyed holding his hand instead. I didn't let myself think of the hospital or the home I'd left behind. I stayed fully immersed in that moment, concentrating all my focus on his skin touching mine.

After quite some time, he squeezed my hand. "It's okay. We can try again another time." He'd been so patient and so supportive that it only made me feel worse for deceiving him.

"Sorry . . ."

"Don't be sorry. It's not your fault. You're just not ready," he said. He was taking half the blame for my failure, but he'd done nothing wrong. An uneasy knot formed in my stomach, and I was hating myself more and more with every chance I had to tell him the truth but didn't.

"Well, let's get this straight. You can't fly."

I broke into laughter. "Nope."

"You can't make yourself teleport."

I shrugged apologetically.

"But you *can* shoot down a clay pigeon telepathically," he said with pride.

"And apparently, beehives too," I added.

Walker laughed. "Yep. You have a real machine gun on that hand of yours."

His laughter died down to a small upturn of his lips as he gazed into his mug. His voice softened. "But you can't find Layla. And you can't find your way back home."

It felt like a punch to the gut. I averted my eyes, also looking into my coffee mug. I *could* find Layla. She'd been coming up to me, and it was I who had been avoiding her. Of course, he didn't know that because I'd been lying about it.

I could find my way home, too, although it wasn't a place I liked to be. The hospital scared me, and the doctors intimidated me. The bloated and bloodied patient I saw was not a girl I knew, or wanted to. My mom's tears made me feel sick to my stomach, and the bright lights hurt my eyes. I felt incredibly exposed and more invisible than ever all at once.

I never wanted to go back again. In fact, I would gladly stay here with the werewolves and wormholes, the haunted waters and the nightmares. I would stay here chasing after Walker for eternity if he'd let me.

CHAPTER 19

Several days had passed and not much happened. One evening, when I was sitting on the back deck with Kai and Gunner, we'd spotted a glimpse of red between the trees. I played it off as nothing, but I knew it was Layla in her red cloak checking up on me. I'd told Kai I was tired and went to bed. I forced myself not to look out the window at night for fear she'd be watching. Like a rabid animal, she was gaining confidence and getting closer. It was inevitable that she would strike, and it was better to keep my distance for as long as I could.

I stayed up half the night tossing and turning. The curiosity pushing me to jump to my feet and open the window, searching for the girl in red, was almost unbearable. I had made up my mind to stay, and I didn't need her or the *Waking Dreams* book any longer. I was getting good in my abilities and growing confident in myself. I hid most of it from Walker by avoiding him. I knew I couldn't hide forever, and I would have to come out to him eventually, but I was waiting for the right time. The right place. A feeling of certainty. I was so afraid that he would send me home, tell me I couldn't stay, that I just avoided him.

There was one thing nagging in the back of my mind that had been there for a while now, that had contributed to my hesitation. The red door at the bottom of Baylor Lake. Somehow, I got it in my head that if I knew where the door led, or what its purpose was, then I could tell Walker everything. How else was I supposed to tell him that I had found my strength and still wanted to stay when there were so many questions left unanswered? It didn't seem very responsible of me. I wanted to be prepared in case I had to argue my reasoning with him. I couldn't fight for my right to stay if I couldn't answer any of the questions he might ask.

Of course, Walker wouldn't be asking about the door in particular—I'd never told him about it. That was a question I had pondered all on my own. It had been smoldering in the back of my mind since the day I'd found it, since the day it had beckoned me to open it, but the idea had grown into a raging fire of curiosity after I'd found a similar red door in my hallway. If the cabin could open a portal to an operating room, a realm where half of me lived, I had to imagine that the red door at the bottom of the lake was the exact same thing. A gateway between worlds.

Training with Walker was like baring my soul to him. I'd been avoiding it since the night he'd slept over. Call me superstitious, but I've been waiting for a sign. A moment in time where I knew I could tell him everything and he would not turn me away. Today was the day I was going to investigate the red door. Because the more answers I got on my own, the more confident I would be to tell him I belonged here—and believe it myself.

I laced my shoes for a hike and pulled my ponytail through the back of a baseball cap. I was slightly afraid I would never come back, so I lingered in the kitchen when I saw Emma. She was feeding Gunner scraps from breakfast.

"Good morning," I said.

"Hey. Going for a hike?" she asked, taking me in.

"Yeah. I should be back this afternoon. I'm heading out to the cliffs," I said, pointing, and then standing awkwardly. I wasn't ready to leave, even though the door had been calling. Emma turned around and shot me a weird look. I chewed on my lip, but my feet didn't move an inch.

"Uh, did you want company?"

"Oh no, you don't have to do that," I said, waving a hand. Emma nodded and went back to cleaning up her mess on the countertop.

I stood quietly at her back as the seconds ticked by.

"That's it. I'm coming." Emma slammed the oven mitt down. "Let me get my shoes."

I shrugged as she left the room. I couldn't argue with that. When she came back, she walked right past me, grabbing the leash on the way out to the back patio.

"Looks like you get to go, buddy," I said to Gunner. He wagged his tail and barreled out the door, running like he was slipping on ice. His legs went twice the speed that his body carried him, and he whacked the door frame on his way out. "Ouch!"

Emma wrapped the leash around the back of her neck and Gunner ran out before us.

"Did you have a fight with Walker or something? I haven't seen him around lately."

"No. Everything's going good," I said defensively. She knew I was covering something up.

"Did you have a fight with Noah then?" she prodded.

"No, why?"

"You're acting weird. Don't think I don't notice."

I frowned. Of course she'd noticed. I'd practically begged her to come without ever saying a word. She must have known there was a reason.

Gunner locked up on a bush, his front leg bent in a pointing position. He was frozen still, his tail unwavering as an arrow. Emma and I giggled, breaking the tension. We stopped to watch for a bit. He dropped his foot slowly and inched forward, ever so slyly. He was a predator hunting his prey. Eventually, his creep turned into a lurch as he ran into the bush and a covey of birds fluttered out.

We laughed, clapping, and cheering him on. "Good boy!"

"Do you think he senses that something is off here?" Emma asked.

I watched Gunner look into the sky at his missed prey. "I don't think so. I think he's more of a hunt, eat, sleep, and dig kind of guy," I said.

"Yeah, you're probably right. I found some more holes in the front yard the other day."

"I'll have to fill them this weekend."

We got to the part of the hike where we ascended a steep dirt path. Both of us were breathing hard, and Gunner was nowhere to be found. Emma didn't seem like her regular self. She hadn't been since I'd sent her home for a night. I should have gifted her a starry night sky like I had Scarlett May, because allowing her to go home without any of the things that made it real, like a family, was probably more torture than it was worth. It was a shell of the life she used to have, and I think it made her withdraw from this one even more.

I had to reengage her, but how? "Hey Emma, I have a secret . . ." I said, dangling it in front of her like a carrot before a mule.

Emma stopped dead in her tracks and turned around

to wait for me. There was nothing quite like the power of a secret.

"I figured out how to stop time." I wasn't sure how she would take it, but I hoped it would give her something to look forward to.

"You did? How? When?" She cocked her head to the side and tucked some loose strands of hair behind her ear. She seemed more perplexed than anything else.

"I guess I did it when time ceased to exist for you. Remember that time?" I said, laughing.

"Wait, are you serious? You can stop time?" Her eyes grew wide with excitement.

"Yeah. You want to see?"

"Yes, please!"

It happened quickly. More quickly than ever before. I didn't have to concentrate this time or work with my breathing. I just leaned into that feeling of wanting to please Emma. I wanted to make her happy and proud of me. Everything froze except us.

"No way!" Emma said, turning to look at her surroundings. The leaves on the trees no longer swayed. The blades of grass were crisp and unwavering. Gunner's tail peeked through a bush in the distance. And the air was stagnant upon our skin. Emma ran her hands through the air feeling the drag for the first time.

"It's weird how the air stops too. It kind of becomes heavy in a way," I said, playing with it between my fingers.

"It's so weird. The entire world is like this? Frozen? It's just you and me?"

"I guess?" I said, shrugging. I didn't really know.

"Wow . . ." Emma mumbled under her breath as she walked off to investigate.

I smiled watching her like a child on Christmas morning as she walked through the clearing, full of wonder. But then I caught sight of the cliff where Walker and I had jumped. Where I had seen the red door for the first time. I was so scared to meet my fate that I froze Emma too. She didn't need to see this, and I didn't want her to worry. I'd be back by the time she even turned around. As far as she had to know, this wasn't anything more than a hike where I'd told her one of my secrets.

I left her in the clearing and made my way to the edge of the bluff. As I peered down to the lake below, I realized that it too was frozen. I looked back at Emma, wondering if I had enough time to unfreeze, jump in, and then freeze again before she turned around. I needed time to stand still, but I also needed the lake to be placid. Otherwise, I'd never get in. Could I stop time *above* the lake, but continue it *below*?

It was getting too complicated, and I could sense myself making up excuses. I couldn't talk myself out of this, and that's exactly what I had begun to do. I had to believe that everything would work out just the way I wanted, the way I needed.

I jumped before I had time to talk myself out of it.

Even though time was standing still, free falling felt like a rush. The stagnant air didn't riffle through my hair the way it would have if it was free flowing; it wrapped around me, as if I were a knife slicing through warmed butter. I windmilled my arms and held my breath as I prayed that the glassy lake would break, and I would fall into the water. But it remained solid, and it was fast approaching, and I feared I would splatter like a bug on a windshield.

I closed my eyes inches before the sheet of water, and felt the slap of the lake as I broke through and plunged beneath the surface.

Success.

As soon as I felt the cold water on my face, I knew Emma would be looking for me and my cover would be blown. I needed to freeze time again before she turned around to see that I had vanished.

My arms and legs were suddenly pinned between the layers of rock-hard water, and I wasn't able to move an inch. I'd stopped time, and the lake had frozen with it.

Like being stuck in dried cement, I couldn't move so much as a fingertip. My hair stretched out in front of me, and a million tiny bubbles had frozen mid-burst. My eyes were the only thing that could move, but I couldn't see much through the effervescent stir of the water. My chest had no room to rise, there was no air for me to breathe, and I couldn't expand my lungs, anyway.

Fear snatched me much like the water had, and I knew I was in over my head. What if this was it? What if this was the rest of my life? I knew I hadn't died yet, and I knew I couldn't, just as long as my body was appropriately taken care of in the hospital. I wanted to take a breath because it was my instinct to do so, but I didn't need it to survive.

My mind screamed for Emma to notice me trapped here, but I had frozen her too. How could I be so mindless? I was the only one who even knew I needed help, and the only one with the power to fix it.

My heart hammered in my chest; it was just about the only thing that could move. I remained still as stone as the adrenaline coursed through my veins telling me to run, to fight, to do anything but freeze. I was utterly powerless against the full weight of the lake. And I was in no mindset to manifest. My emotions had to rise and fall before I'd have the clarity to help myself.

It felt like an eternity all on its own. I felt like a fossil etched in stone and buried for a lifetime. My fear ran so hot I swore the water was starting to melt around me. But after a long and dreadful stint of terror, I started to calm.

I moved my fingers at first, and then a slight bend of my knee. I arched my back, and the water became like sludge. I dropped further into the wet-cement-like water, still falling from my jump. When my mind fully cleared, I was able to release my spell and resume time.

My hair covered my face, then lifted for me to see the lake and the trail of bubbles above me. I knew Emma would be looking for me, but I couldn't think of that now. I had one mission for the day, and I wasn't going to turn back after the hell I'd gone through to get here.

I desperately wanted a breath of air, but I didn't want to risk never coming back down, so I dipped my head down to my toes and started swimming to the bottom of the lake.

I swam hard and fast. Everything inside me told me it was wrong to swim downward with no air, but about halfway down something took over. Something began to pull on me, and the weight of the water itself pushed me down quicker than I could've swum. I sank like a ton of bricks.

I searched through the water, looking for the door, but everything was too murky to see. It felt like I'd been under the water for a solid year, and still, there was no end in sight.

I startled when I saw a hand breaking through the poor visibility, and I realized I wasn't alone in the haunted lake. I paddled fiercely as somebody neared, swimming next to me. A wave of emotion washed over me as I saw Lainey's freckled face paddling by my side.

I couldn't tell if she was real or a memory. She simply swam alongside me during the long and brutal trek through the water, like a good friend would. And it was at that moment I knew I was on the right track. I knew this door was something more than a figment of my imagination, and I was right to explore it.

A golden glimmer pierced the dark water, and like a string anchored directly to the door, I descended right on top of it. The red door grew more vibrant with the closing distance, and the pull grew stronger.

There, at the bottom of the lake, was a single red door set into the sand. The hinges latched to a pile of rocks. My feet planted heavily on the bottom of the lake next to Lainey's. The familiarity drew me in, and without thinking, I reached out and grabbed the doorknob. Lainey encouraged me excitedly. I twisted the knob and pulled the door open just a crack before stopping myself.

What was I doing? I didn't want to open the door, I only wanted answers. What if the draw was so strong, there was no escaping it? A bright light shone through the crack, but there were no answers to be had. I couldn't tell what was beyond, other than light. Lainey grabbed a hold of my hand over the doorknob and pulled with all her force.

No!

The door swung open all too fast, and Lainey's eyes lit up like fireworks on the Fourth of July. I too was dazzled by what was inside.

Through the door, white, fluffy clouds drifted by, and

the sound of an airplane hummed somewhere in the distance. The water warmed around me from the sunny day. I sucked in a deep luxurious breath of the fresh air that flowed through the door.

Cautiously, I kneeled on my hands and knees and peered over the edge of the door frame. Lainey did the same next to me, and we marveled at the sky. It was definitely another world, another realm. Without a shadow of doubt, I knew it was the world I had grown up in. The world I now called "The Real One."

But as I sat back on my heels, I wasn't quite as sure it was the one I belonged to. There was something in Baylor that called to me, something other than Walker. I was getting to know myself here, better than I ever had at home. I was starting to believe in myself, and I wasn't ready to give that up. I felt the pull in both directions equally. My soul yearned for its body, but my heart refused to follow.

Lainey nodded encouragingly. Slowly, I shook my head to communicate that I wasn't ready. That I didn't think I ever would be. I watched as Lainey's face fell into deep disappointment and then verge on the edge of something else entirely.

I reached forward to close the door, and I felt Lainey's knobby hands on my back as she pushed me through.

I screamed, falling through the open door and into the thin air, grasping the edge for dear life. My body dangled above the clouds as my arms grappled in the sand and water. Lainey stood above me as I screamed and fought to get back. I tried to hitch a leg onto the doorjamb but failed miserably.

She bent down and grabbed my hand, but not to help. She lifted my fingers off the sandy floor and bent them backward until I lost my grip.

"No! Lainey! Help!" I screamed out, hanging on by a single outstretched hand.

The weight of my drenched clothes made my body feel even heavier, and my wet skin erupted in goosebumps. I was helpless, and so very foolish.

I looked down between my dangling feet as the clouds parted, and I could see the tiny neighborhoods below. Immediately, I knew I was over my hometown of Clover.

My gut wrenched, and the air became difficult to breathe. She was supposed to be my friend. She was supposed to support me. But this wasn't the Lainey I knew and loved; this was the ghost of her. The thing that had grabbed me in the lake before, trying to drown me.

It reached down lifting my pinky finger, and I screamed. "Stop it!!"

My voice rumbled like thunder, and all the fear and anger of betrayal flew out of me like a storm, knocking Lainey backward into the deep water. I slung my free arm into the lake and reached for a rock to grab hold of. I thrust one leg over the doorjamb and wedged it into the corner of the frame. I struggled, kicking buckets of sand through the open door, stopping briefly to watch it fall into the sky. I mustered all the effort I had left, heaved my body through the open door, and rolled onto my back at the bottom of the lake.

Holding my breath, I rolled onto my side, looking for Lainey. I saw her in the distance, swimming toward me like a shark in the deep sea; unnaturally fast and alarmingly compelled. I scurried to my feet and trudged through the thick water to the door. I lifted the door from the rocks. It was as heavy as an iron boulder, and pushing it through the water made it even more difficult.

Lainey was closing in on me, and it took everything I had to get the door up and over the midpoint. Once it stood upright, it was easier to close, as gravity helped pull it shut. I pushed all my weight on top of the door and rode it to the ground as it fell.

Lainey was five feet from me as the door made its descent. And by the time it clicked shut, I could feel her hands upon my cheeks, reaching to ensnare. But instead of the hard nails and the deadly grasp that I had anticipated, her fingers turned to a whisper-light touch as she, and the door, faded into oblivion.

The door disintegrated into the sand. I whipped my head around and saw nothing but the strands of my dark hair floating around my face and tiny bubbles that escaped my nose pirouetting in the water.

There was no ghost of Lainey left, and there was no more portal to the life I'd once had. If I was unsure whether I belonged in this world, none of it mattered anymore, because my decision had been made for me in a heap of betrayal and rage.

I was here to stay . . .

CHAPTER 20

I broke through the surface of the lake, flailing my arms and gasping for air.

"Kinsley! Kinsley!" Emma screamed from the top of the bluff.

I hammered the water, fearful that Lainey's ghost would materialize once more beneath my feet.

"Kinsley are you okay?!" Emma yelled frantically.

"Yeah." But my small broken voice was much too quiet for her to hear. I tried to gather myself, brush the hair out of my face, and focus on her pacing back and forth at the top of the cliff. She was worried, and who knew how long I had been down there.

"I'm okay!" I yelled the best I could.

With all the strength I had left, I swam toward shore. Emma took off running, and it wasn't long before she and Gunner met me in the shallow water.

"Oh my god, Kinsley, you scared me! You were down there forever!" she said, tromping into the lake. Gunner barked excitedly and swam in circles, biting at the ripples in the water. Emma hugged me tight as I stood weakly in a foot of water.

"I'm sorry. I didn't mean to scare you. I tried not to, but it almost took my life." I sloshed my way to shore.

"What!?"

"I tried to freeze time so you wouldn't know how long I was gone and you wouldn't worry. But I froze the lake with me in it. It was like being stuck in cement."

Emma gasped.

"That wasn't even the worst part. The worst part was . . ." I pictured Lainey and how desperate she'd been to betray me. It wasn't how I wanted Emma to remember her, so I kept it to myself. "I think I died."

"I've heard that before. How many times do you think it's happened now? Two? Three?" Emma plopped down in the sand and unlaced her shoes.

"It's not something a person gets used to Emma," I snapped. I plopped down next to her, but I was too tired to take my socks and shoes off. I fell onto my back, closing my eyes to the sun and welcoming the warmth on my cheeks. "Not here . . . *there*. I think maybe my body died in the *real* world."

Emma looked me over and then poked my arm. "You don't seem any different?"

She couldn't possibly understand what I'd been through. "Okay. Promise not to say anything to anybody?" I asked rolling onto my side. The dry sand caked to my wet skin like a blanket of warmth.

"Yeah. Even Walker?" she asked.

"Especially Walker."

"Yeah, okay," Emma said, shielding her face from the sun with her hand.

"I think I found a way back home—"

"What! No way!" Emma's face lit up, and in that split second I realized I had made a devastating mistake by telling her. She would either want me to go through the door like Lainey had pushed me to do, or she would want to find it herself, and it no longer existed.

"No, it's not like that. I mean, it was. It was a portal of sorts, but it closed."

"Where is it? We can open it again." Emma stood, dusting the sand off her butt. She was ready to go home.

"No, it's not like that! You can't just open it," I argued.

"Noah is really strong, and Kai is super smart. We can do this as a team. We have to tell them! We have to go!" Gunner came tromping out of the water and shook off all the excess water, splattering us.

"The door isn't locked Emma. It's destroyed."

"We can put it back together!"

"It vanished. Disintegrated into nothing. It

disappeared, Emma. It is no longer at the bottom of the lake. It's gone."

"Well . . ." Emma began but couldn't finish. She placed her hands on her hips and bounced her foot up and down. She was trying not to cry, and I hated myself for not having the foresight to have seen this coming. I unlaced my shoes and peeled off my socks. I gathered them up in a heavy, sandy mess, and Emma and I started the long walk home—barefoot and drenched in defeat. She sniffled the entire way home as Gunner pranced happily before us, finding twigs to take as souvenirs.

I couldn't help but think that I had been the one to cause her so much pain. And maybe, if I had just dropped through the open door, I would have landed in my bed at home, recuperating from the accident. And then Emma would have gone home too. Maybe they all would have.

But what about Walker? He would stay here all by his lonesome. He'd wander around Baylor looking for Layla. And Layla would follow him around driving herself crazy because he couldn't see her. It was an impossible feat. On the one hand, I was torturing my friends, keeping them from their homes and their lives ahead. But on the other, I would be forcing Walker to be tortured with a life of solitude. He didn't deserve that. None of them did.

When we got back to the cabin, Emma gave me a half smile, dumped her shoes by the deck, and disappeared into the cabin. Gunner drank a gallon of water, and Kai made fun of me for going hiking and coming home in wet clothes.

"Kai, can I ask you a hypothetical question?" I tossed my shoes into a pile with Emma's. It wouldn't take long for them to dry in the summer heat.

"What's up? Did Emma push you into the lake or something?" he said, chuckling.

"Do you remember when you drove to the edge of the Baylor phenomenon?" I leaned against the patio railing next to him.

"Yeah. Did you find a new edge?" he asked, suddenly serious.

"Kind of. But it didn't send me back to the cabin. I think it was more like a portal. The gateway back home." I hated seeing the excitement light Kai's face. I was doing it again—giving false hope. "But it's gone now . . ."

"What happened, Kinsley?" He leaned in.

"There was a door. It was at the bottom of the lake—"

"How did you get there?" he asked, brows furrowed. Nothing got past Kai.

"I didn't really need to breathe. I guess I can hold my breath for quite some time here if I put my mind to it. But that's not the point."

"Right. Go on," he said eagerly.

"I opened the door, and on the other side was Clover. Well, I'm pretty sure it was Clover. I was high above the clouds, looking down on the neighborhood. Time seemed slower there, and the air was . . . different, familiar. I don't know how to explain it."

"No way . . ." His back stiffened, and I could tell he was ready to go on a hunt for the door, just like Emma had.

"But when I closed the door, it disappeared. It completely disintegrated into nothing."

"Maybe we can find it?" Kai asked hopefully.

I shook my head. "I think it's really gone."

Kai straightened, suddenly eager to end the conversation. He turned to head inside the cabin, and I realized I'd never asked my question.

"Hey, Kai?"

"Yeah?" He looked over his shoulder.

"If the gateway closed . . . hypothetically . . . does that mean there's no way back?" I was unable to say the word *died*.

"There's always a way back, Kinsley." He turned and headed inside, leaving me by myself.

I rested my forearms on the railing and gazed out at the lake. I wish I knew for certain. I had planned to stay here in Baylor either way, but if there truly was no way home, I think it would end the plague of uncertainty. I could tell Walker, and there would be no convincing me otherwise. It would be beyond my control. Noah, Kai, Emma, and Scarlett May could lay down roots here, and we could stop fighting. Maybe we could even have some fun. But I had to know. There was nothing worse than the uncertainty.

My clothes were nearly dry by the time I finally came up with a plan. I would need to find the hidden cemetery. When Trinity died, her headstone had appeared immediately. And I assumed it would be the same for me. I would have a headstone next to hers and Lainey's. The only problem was, I didn't want to go alone. The woods were a place of nightmares for me, and if I found my headstone, I didn't want to know what would happen when I felt my world closing in on me.

I couldn't bring Walker, not without telling him the truth first. Emma and Kai were freshly scarred, and I didn't want to put them through seeing headstones. What if they had headstones of their own? What I really needed was Scarlett May to come with me. She was strong, and I knew she could handle anything she saw in those woods.

By the time I had changed my clothes and started searching for Scarlett May, I couldn't find her anywhere. In fact, I couldn't find anybody. I was so desperate, I was willing to take Noah, but I couldn't find him either.

"Emma?" I yelled down the hall.

"Kai?" I called, jogging down the stairs.

"Gunner?" I peeked my head out the back door.

I paced the living room, wondering where they had gone in such a short time. "Noah?" I called, softer yet.

I would have taken him had he answered. I just didn't want to field questions about my feelings for him the entire time. Not that he would ask. I was sure he didn't even like me anymore. It had been weeks since we'd talked last. Still, I often felt his eyes on me. Especially when Walker was around. He didn't like him.

But he also didn't want to end up like Mason—missing after a wolf attack. A sickening feeling twisted my gut. Was that why Noah hadn't talked to me? Because he thought the incident with Mason was my fault? That I did it on purpose because I was angry they'd turned Walker away with a threat? Well, I guess I *was* still angry about that . . .

I was doing it again. I was stalling. Only this time, I didn't have Emma to fall back on. If I wanted to check out the graveyard, I was going to have to go alone. Asking Walker was not an option for me. Not now. I could do this. I could be brave and courageous. I could face the forest and its mysterious ways.

I scribbled down a message on a pad of paper. *On a walk.* And I left it on the kitchen counter where I thought it would be most visible. I caught a glimpse of Gunner's water bowl on the way out and wished I had him to come with me. But none of that mattered now. I was going to do this. I was going to see if I was dead or alive. If I had a chance of going home or if I was already there. I was going to march into those woods, and I was going to discover my fate. I just had to put one foot in front of the other.

As it turns out, fate is a hard thing to find. I must have walked for hours. Dusk had settled in, and my stomach growled from hunger. I'd stomped through so many rapunzel plants that my jeans had a hazy, light-purple dusting below the knee. I glanced up into the trees now and then to see the same crow watching me. It didn't matter how far I walked, it was always there, perched in a new tree high above me. It seemed a little wider than most crows and reminded me of the crow we'd seen flying overhead on our way to the library. It reminded me of Levi.

It was probably just my imagination. A way to protect myself from the evils that lurked deep within this forest. But I didn't care what it was, I only cared how it made me feel, and I no longer felt alone. I was still angry with Levi for how he had treated Emma, but I was more upset with myself. I'd caused the storm that night, and if it wasn't for me, Levi would still be here. And he deserved a chance to live. They all did. No one deserved my wrath.

The crow called out as it swooped down between the trees in my path. The bird was gigantic. Twice the size of any regular crow. It flew in front of me, so close that I could reach out and almost touch it. But it was faster than my walking gait, and I ended up jogging after it.

"Levi?" I called out. It was stupid. Of course, it wouldn't answer me. But could I at least get it to slow down?

"You're going too fast," I said, through burning lungs. I liked talking out loud. Like somehow I was less crazy because a bird might be listening, instead of nobody.

The bird took a sharp right, and I stopped briefly to analyze the change in path. But there wasn't much for me to figure out. The crow perched on a headstone. My fate had found me.

I walked slowly, catching my breath. My eyes flickered from the bird's black, beady eyes to the multitude of new headstones scattered throughout the trees. With every step I took, the temperature dropped, and I became more leery.

Another crow called out above us, and I saw a single black bird circling the cemetery. "Your friends are calling you," I said.

The bird didn't move. Its eyes were trained on me as I slowly dropped my gaze to the stone it was perched on. Its sharp claws dug into the stone. My heart sank when I read *Levi, taken unfaithfully.*

Oh no . . .

It was more than just a hunch now. I was convinced the crow was the embodiment of Levi. Why else had it taken me directly to his grave? I clenched my jaw, suddenly feeling awkward in front of the bird. Had it known what the headstone said?

"You shouldn't have hurt Emma like that. You messed up." I scowled at the bird, and it did nothing to show its remorse.

"You did this to yourself," I said, getting more upset with its silence than anything else.

I looked up at all the other headstones, crooked and

worn, and Levi turned to assess them with me. His claws made an unsettling scraping sound against the stone, and I cringed. I wanted to tell him to stop, but I seriously doubted he had the capacity to understand me.

The next stone I came to was blank. I was thankful for that. But I couldn't help wonder why it was here in the first place. Somebody or something had planted it here in anticipation, and that should have worried me. I think I was just so relieved that whoever it belonged to wasn't marked yet. So much so, that I didn't care about the expectation of another death on the horizon.

The next two stones I saw were for Kimber and Asher. It didn't seem like that long ago that the bees had invaded the cabin, but these headstones were decades upon decades old. Moss had grown up the sides, and the sun had stained patterns into the rock. *Asher was taken by weakness*, which wasn't his fault at all. He was genetically weaker than the rest of us when it came to the bee's venom. But what really surprised me was that Kimber's headstone said she was *taken a coward*. And Kimber had been anything but cowardly.

The way I saw it, Kimber was the bravest one yet. She was the only one who had known how to escape this place. And instinctively, she was the only one who had known how to bring Noah back. She'd sacrificed herself. She was courageous. I couldn't for the life of me understand why the legacy etched in her headstone would read that she was a coward. What was it that I hadn't seen before? I placed my hand on top of the headstone waiting for the answers to come, but they never did. When Levi flew to Kimber's marker, I scowled at the awful scraping noise and moved on to the next.

Ethan had a headstone now too, and apparently he was *taken by worry*. That I understood. I remembered how worried I had been on that walk. I remember looking for something to explain it all away. That unsettled feeling I had cinched my chest. When Ethan had jumped into the water, I had just assumed it was him. That he wasn't safe. That he wouldn't come back to the surface. And because I was worried—so dreadfully worried—he never had. My heart sat heavy in my chest, and there were so many things I wished I could take back. But I couldn't.

"I'm sorry, Ethan. You didn't deserve that," I said in a whisper.

I passed two more headstones with fresh clean slates. No lives claimed. Not yet. Levi flew overhead and perched on the next marker. Mason's marker. I rubbed my arms as the temperature continued to drop. New birds called above, and I could see that there were three or four of them now. Circling.

It didn't surprise me that *Mason was taken a liar*. He never should have told Walker that I belonged to Noah. It simply wasn't true, and he had no right to meddle in my affairs. But he wasn't just taken because he'd lied, he was taken because of my anger toward the lie. I shook my head, upset with the mass destruction I had caused.

"I'm sorry, Mason. I'm sorry," I said, patting the headstone. Suddenly, I was glad I'd come to the cemetery alone. This wasn't something I wanted my friends to see.

I looked into the distance to see another clean slate, and one with just the beginnings of a name. My stomach dropped, wondering if it was my name slowly being etched into the stone. I kneeled and examined the chiseled mark in the stone. One long line, the beginning of the name. The first of the letter was covered with a string of ivy. I reached out with a shaky hand and lifted the vine. My mouth ran dry as I lifted the strand of ivy, and a *K* was revealed.

I swiped my hands over the stone, desperately searching for more clues, lighter scrapes, anything that would tell me how I had died or why I was taken, but there was nothing left for me to see. Which could only mean one thing. It wasn't set in stone yet.

I sat back on my heels as Levi jumped to the ground next to me. *It wasn't set in stone.* Nothing was finalized. And if I wanted to go home, I would still have a body to return to. I hated the way relief washed over me. I hated it. It only confused me more. What did I want? What the *hell* did I want!?

Tears pricked the corners of my eyes as I realized that I would not get any answers today and the weight of the decision would come back to the cabin with me, resting heavily on my shoulders. The secrets I needed to keep from Walker were draining, and I was getting tired of keeping them. I was tired in general. I wanted it to be over, only I didn't know which life needed to end. I only knew that I couldn't keep living two lives at the same time. It wasn't fair to me, it wasn't fair to my family, and it was incredibly exhausting.

A name had clearly been started on this headstone, and if I had to guess, I'd say that the *K* was made when I'd shut the door in Lainey's face. When it disintegrated beneath me, and the gateway closed. But if that hadn't ended me right then and there, that could only mean one of two things.

Either there were more doors out there, more than one way to get back home, or I hadn't fully made up my mind up yet. I had thought I was stuck in Baylor, but the sense of relief that had washed over me when I saw the incomplete headstone had me second-guessing. I was torn. I needed to talk to my gran. She was the only one I trusted to have my best interests in mind while guiding me toward a decision.

The scraping grew louder, casting a shadow on my thoughts until it was all I could hear. I turned to yell at Levi, but he was perched quietly in the dirt. A dozen or more crows cawed above, creating the beginnings of a vortex. I had seen this before, and I didn't want to get caught in it. It was time to leave, but the scraping held me in place.

What was it? Where was it coming from? It was close, I knew that much. I got to my feet and dusted my hands on my jeans. The ivy twitched, drawing my attention back to the headstone. I reached out and gently lifted the vine one more time. The letter A was freshly carved into the stone, causing me to gasp and flinch backward.

I wrapped my hands around the ivy and tore it off the headstone. The grinding of the stone grew louder as Kai's name slowly etched its way into the rock.

"*No . . .*" I cried, wrapping my arms around myself.

Levi lifted into the air and joined the murder. I took off running.

CHAPTER 21

The crows circled above, calling out to one another and funneling in the sky, high above the cemetery. I ran through the rapunzel, weaving in and out of the pines as I tried not to look back. Whatever was happening in the sky was a bad omen, and I didn't want to stick around to find out what might happen on the ground.

It was dark enough that the colors had faded from the forest and the trees were just a blur of dark, muddy shadows. I couldn't tell if I was running deeper into the forest or if I was heading toward the cabin, but I knew the storm was brewing behind me in the graveyard, and I was doing everything I could to get far away. I was alone and afraid in the forest, and that was a terrible combination for me.

My lungs burned, but I refused to slow down. I was

going to run until I couldn't hear a single crow screeching in the distance. I hopped over fallen trees and small bushes. I checked behind me, my hair eclipsing my sight. But when I turned back around, I ran straight through a spider web. I opened my mouth to scream and flailed my hands about as the sticky string pulled across my lips and clung to my cheeks. I tried not to cry as I grasped the invisible threat, trying to free myself and run away at the same time. I felt the tears on my cheeks, anyway.

I swore to myself that I would never come into these woods again. Especially not alone. The forest had become the accumulation of my worry, and on the darkest of nights, my fear. It was no place for exploration, and I promised myself to stay far, far away. Some things were best left unknown. The etchings on the headstones were none of my business. There was probably nothing I could do to save Kai anyhow. He was probably already gone.

This couldn't have been my fault. I didn't even know where Kai was. Everybody had been gone when I'd left for the woods, and I certainly didn't have any ill will toward Kai. He was one of my favorite people. He was kind, intelligent, and he was a safe place for me in my rowdy group of friends. It *couldn't* have been my fault. Unless I had seen his name being etched into the stone for a reason. Maybe it wasn't over until the inscription was complete. Until the words *taken by* were followed by something obscure. Something speculative. A single word like kindness or courage. Could he be taken by kindness? I didn't doubt it.

My ankle rolled, and I lurched forward. My foot caught on a pile of rocks, and I tripped, driving my hands into the dirt. I let out a small grunt when I hit the ground. Sprawled in the dirt where no path had been, I listened for the birds. Their calls were growing louder and louder, drowning out the sound of my hammering heart.

I could see them in the distance. Small black dots against the darkening sky. Somehow, I was getting closer to them . . . or they were getting closer to me. I scrambled to my feet and took off in a hobble. I couldn't sustain a run any longer. My body was drained, and my mind was giving up. I couldn't run fast enough to save Kai. And if I could, I wouldn't even know where to look.

Running water babbled over rocks. A small stream appeared by my side, and I suddenly recognized where I was. The lake wasn't far, and down by the water was a small path that would eventually lead to the cabin. I picked up speed, being careful not to stumble again, and I ran alongside the stream. I gained distance on the crows, and the suffocating air began to lift as the dense trees opened to the clearing of the lake. I weaved through the last of the trees, relieved when my feet hit the sandy shore. I hunched over to catch my breath.

"Quick, get in!"

I barely had the energy to lift my eyes, but when I saw

my gran sitting in a canoe perched in the rocks, my back straightened with renewed hope. "Gran! Gran you're here!" I called out in a sob.

"Get in, child!" she said, holding her hand out for me to take. I mustered a fresh burst of energy and plunged into the water, soaking my shoes. I clambered into the canoe ungracefully and then lunged for my gran. I enveloped her in a tight hug, and I couldn't have been more thankful when she hugged me back. I didn't know what I would've done had she disintegrated or disappeared like times before. I needed her now, more than ever.

"Gran, I love you! I've missed you so much. You have no idea."

"Ohhh, I've got some idea. I love you too, dear. More than you'll ever know." Her voice was music to my ears.

Her eyes shifted from me to the sky, and it was then that I noticed the crows had grown louder again. They were catching up to us, but I didn't dare look back.

"It's time we get out of here," Gran said, taking the paddle. The canoe began to move swiftly through the water. Surprisingly, Gran was quite strong for her age. Strong like Walker. I wondered if strength prospered after death.

"I've been trying to get a hold of you. The phone didn't work, and you haven't been visiting. I was worried," I said, my grip tight on the sides of the canoe.

"I'm here now. It's difficult to reach you. Our planes

are more different than you can imagine." The canoe glided through the water faster than I thought possible.

"How? How are they different?" I asked hungrily. I wanted to ask everything in the world. I wanted *all* the information from her. I didn't know when I would see her next, or if I ever would again.

"Where I live, I can go anywhere and be everywhere, all at once. There are no rules or restrictions. But finding you has proven to be difficult. It must be the drugs. They keep your mind shut down and locked away. It's hard for me to break through. The dream state that you're in is like a prison. It's governed only by your emotions. Unfortunately, your fear seems to be the driving factor. It must be so scary for you." Gran tilted her head with empathy. "It's a dreary place, and I'm *so* sorry you must be here. But it shouldn't be much longer now."

A prison? Was Baylor my prison? If it was, then why was Walker here?

"What do you mean, it shouldn't be much longer?" I asked, suddenly worried my time was coming to an end.

"You'll wake soon. I promise it won't be much longer. You're healing quite nicely. There have been some . . . *hiccups* . . . along the way. It's been rough on your parents, your brother, and aunt. It's been rough on your grandpa. But when you wake up, everybody is going to be so happy. It won't be easy dear; I'm not saying that. But it will be better than this cold, dreary place." Her chin wrinkled and her brows creased with distaste. A visible shiver ran down her back, causing me to look away.

It wasn't *that* bad.

The guilt hit me like a tidal wave. I had no idea how to tell her that I planned to stay here forever. I was going to make a life for myself here. I didn't want to devastate her and my grandpa. I didn't want to hurt my family at all. But Baylor had become my home. Walker was my home. I couldn't leave him.

"But Gran, remember when you said *if* I come back." I chewed on my cheek nervously as I waited for her reply.

"Oh dear, you *will* make it. You were *always* going to survive this. I'm sorry if I made that unclear." Her forehead creased with pain.

"Then why did you say it? Was there ever a chance I wasn't going home?" I leaned in. The answers couldn't come fast enough.

"I said *if* because there was a small, very small, chance that you *theoretically* could *choose* to stay here. But that's not in the cards for you, dear," she said, searching my eyes.

"About that . . ." I hesitated. I was glad she'd brought it up, but I was still so scared to tell her how I felt.

"Oh dear, are you thinking about staying?" she asked. I thought I saw a flash of disgust pass through her green eyes.

"Gran . . . there's this guy." I said with tears in my eyes.

"I know. I know there is." She dropped the paddle to

the bottom of the canoe and held her arms out for a hug. I crossed to her and fell into her open arms. The canoe dipped but didn't slow. We propelled forward by an otherworldly force, as if Gran was still paddling.

"I can't tell you what to do, honey. You're going to have to make that decision on your own." She held me tight.

I cried on her shoulder. I cried for Walker, I cried for my family back home and all the pain I'd put them through, and I cried for my gran and how deeply I'd missed her. Nothing was ever going to be fair or easy. Whether I was living or not, I was imprisoned. I only wished the answers were clear, because it was the ambiguity that rattled my mind the most. I wished my path was laid out before me and I'd never come to a fork in the road. I feared I would choose wrong.

"I don't know what to do, Gran. *I love him.*" I looked deep into her eyes.

Her cataracts had cleared, revealing a brilliant emerald green with tiny glimmering flecks of gold. That was how I knew she was real. That this conversation I was having with my dead grandmother was real, and not one I had conjured from grief. I soaked it all up. I cherished every moment.

"I know you do. I can see that. Just like I know you love your family. But hearts are made to break, honey. And with each break they become stronger, and you love deeper.

Sometimes, if you love something, the best thing you can do is let it go."

The air left my lungs in a whoosh. *Let him go?*

"You need to take care of yourself, first and foremost. I wouldn't ask yourself who you love more, your family or a boy, I would ask yourself where you belong. Where do you belong, honey?"

My stomach churned. It was the question that haunted me most. I didn't know. "What if I belong in both places? . . . Or neither of them?" Was that possible?

Gran ran her gentle hands over mine. "You belong."

I closed my eyes, letting the two simple words wash over me. It hurt to hear them, and for the life of me, I couldn't understand why. If she was speaking the truth, then I had been lying to myself. Not just this whole summer, but my entire life.

"I want to stay . . ." I said in a whisper. "This world is different to me. I feel like I get to be somebody here that I never was back home."

Gran patted my hand, and I pulled away. She began to paddle again while she chose her next words carefully.

"There is no right or wrong here. But I will leave you with this: you will find your greatest happiness not from luck nor fate, but through hard work, grit, trials, and tribulations. Your fullest heart will come from breaking, time and time again, and loving despite the vulnerability."

I took a deep breath. Nobody wants to hear how hard it

will be. I had come so far here in Baylor, but she was talking like the journey had just begun, and it put the fear in me.

"When the time comes, go down the steepest, most treacherous path. Don't shy from the dark nights—lean into them. I know you will find your way. Whichever you choose, know you belong, wholeheartedly. I will be with you every step of the way, even if you can't see me." The canoe nudged the shore.

I arched my back, wondering where we had beached. I recognized the cove by the unique formation of boulders nearby. It was close to where I had dove early that morning.

"Don't leave, Gran. Stay," I pled. I wasn't ready to say goodbye.

"I'll be here," she said, smiling.

"Did you find him?!" Scarlett May's frantic voice traveled across the lake.

I looked from Gran to the lake, searching the open waters. Through the darkness I could see what I thought were two heads bobbing in the water. My heart sank. *Kai.*

"No!" Noah yelled.

I leapt off the canoe. My feet plunged into the water as I ran ashore. My instincts stopped me, held me still, as I remembered my gran sitting in the canoe. I was torn between helping Kai and knowing I may very well never see my gran again. I looked from her to my friends and back again. She encouraged me with a nod.

"Go . . ." she said, and then she was gone. Just like she'd never been. The canoe, everything had disappeared, and I was standing alone on the shore in the shadows.

"Kai?!" Noah screamed. The hoarseness of his voice told me they'd been searching for far too long.

I ran into the lake, dragging my legs through the resisting water until I was deep enough to dive in. I swam as hard and fast as I could, taking in my surroundings as I came up for air. Emma was on shore pacing back and forth, crying. Scarlett May and Noah were some distance apart, yelling to each other between diving for Kai.

"How long has he been missing?" I asked, breathlessly.

"He's gone! He's gone!" Scarlett May yelled, splashing around in hysterics.

"He's been under for ten, fifteen minutes now," Noah said.

It was bad news. I'd seen Kai's name etched into the gravestone, but I'd hoped it wasn't final yet. The inscription hadn't been complete when I took off, and a small part of me clung to the idea that maybe it never would be. That maybe Kai wouldn't be taken by the lake of dark secrets, and that he would come home with us tonight.

I gulped a giant breath and dove under the water. It was pitch black. Even if I could stay under all night searching, I couldn't see a damn thing. I swam straight down toward the bed of the lake, where the portal to my distant reality had once lived. Something brushed against my arm, and I startled, stalling momentarily before continuing. It happened several times on my way down, but I continued anyway. I couldn't be afraid of the dark any longer—I wouldn't be.

Lean into the darkness. . .

Suddenly, I feared the others would think that I'd drowned too, and it would send them searching deeper into the water. I worried that my prolonged absence would cause yet another death. I pushed it out of my mind, and I used the worry as fuel to swim deeper.

By the time I hit the bottom, it was obvious that I would never find Kai. I patted my hands against the soft, silty lake bottom, feeling around in the rocks and unseen plants. Something prickly, something muddy, something slimy. An open sandy floor, and gobs of seaweed. I couldn't see any of it, and feeling around in the dark brought on new challenges.

I was helpless under the weight of the lake. Hindered by the darkness. If Baylor was a phantom world where magic was real, then the forest was where the evil mist lived, and the lake was where the poisons drained and gathered.

I couldn't do it. I couldn't find Kai. There was something about being under the water that kept me from crying, and for that, I was thankful. I pushed off the bottom of the lake and started my ascent empty-handed. There were only three of them left. Only three. No matter how much training I received, I couldn't save them.

In the dead of the night, the four of us huddled on shore, shaking, soaking wet, and drenched with grief. Noah wrapped his arms around me and Emma, and I stroked Scarlett May's head on my lap. Now and then, a shiver would rack through one of us and extrapolate through the group as if it was contagious.

"We were trying to find the door . . ." I wasn't sure when Emma had said it, but her words played over and over in my head, haunting me for hours on end. The red door to Clover had claimed its first victim, sight unseen.

CHAPTER 22

It was early morning by the time we got back to the cabin. We were like a mob of zombies, cold and wet, beyond exhausted, and half asleep. We walked through the cabin door, and everybody scattered. Scarlett May had been sleeping in Kimber's room ever since she and Asher had left, and Emma was across the hall in her and Lainey's room. Noah took the couch, since it was now open. Every time somebody didn't come home, one of us got a better bed. Even though I was sure it didn't translate to a better night's sleep.

I lingered, watching Noah crawl into the sleeping bag and punch his pillow aggressively. It was almost like we didn't have tears left to cry. Like we had been through so much trauma in Baylor that it couldn't affect us any longer. Instead of breaking down, we hardened. We shut down, and we isolated ourselves. Maybe it was the path of least resistance. I felt the effects of it too.

When Trinity had died, I'd wanted to run far, far away. I'd felt a very deep sense of danger, and all I'd wanted to do was flee. But so many times later, all I wanted now was to crawl into bed. By the looks of it, everybody else felt the same way. We didn't love Kai any less; we just didn't have the strength to feel the pain, and we didn't have the energy to run. There was nowhere left for us to go.

I waited till Noah settled before turning out the lights. And with my hand on the light switch, my eyes wandered helplessly to the calendar on the wall. Out of thirteen days, there were only four left. I didn't know who the fourth was going to be. My jaw hardened when I remembered my gran saying I was always going to survive this. I was starting to gather that, when she said survival, it actually meant death in Baylor. The last thing I wanted was to be another X on that calendar.

She'd said I would be waking soon, and it was hard for me to comprehend what that meant for this realm. What would happen to Emma and Noah if I woke up? What would happen to Scarlett May and Sampson? Would they disappear? Would they die? Would they disintegrate like the door on the bottom of the lake? Or get swept up in some extravagant vortex like Levi? There was no way to know. I had to come up with a plan to set them free before anything else bad happened. I needed them to go home alive. I flipped the switch, and the lights went out. My feet were heavy on the stairs as I dragged myself to bed.

From the moment my head hit the pillow, I was asleep, and I didn't wake until late the next morning. But I remembered dreaming of a war.

There was a battlefield under ominous gray clouds filled with thunder and lightning. There were hundreds of doctors dressed in light blue scrubs holding their scalpels and syringes as weapons. Their first line of defense was . . . my family. My little brother and his buddies were covered in war paint, striped across their cheeks and the bridges of their noses. My parents, my aunt, and my grandpa stood front and center. Even in the distance, I could see the anger on their faces. They were ready to fight, and they would show no mercy.

On the opposing side, my side, stood Noah, Sampson, Scarlett May, Emma, Walker, Layla, and me. It was a far cry from the hundreds they had on their side. But we had heart, and I knew I had a secret weapon that would put their needles to shame. I could manifest anything I wanted, and I could end the battle with the drop of a hat, if that's what my heart really desired.

We were getting ready to fight. The seconds were ticking down when something terrible happened; Layla crossed over.

I wasn't entirely surprised; I knew she didn't want me in Baylor. I was falling for her soulmate after all. But when she joined the opposing side, Emma, Scarlett May, and Sampson did too. It broke my heart that Emma wouldn't stand behind me, but I understood why she wanted me to go home. Because she was stuck here until I did. They were only a quarter of the way across the clearing when Noah turned to me and shrugged. He didn't walk; he ran.

By that time, only Walker and I stood against what felt like the rest of the world. I remembered the worry I'd seen when I looked to him with questioning eyes. Whose side was he really on? Because it was now or never.

That's when I woke up. I never got to see what Walker chose, and I never got to see the war between my past life and my phantom reality. But I had to imagine it was a dirty fight.

I rolled over in bed and stared at the white wall, playing the dream over and over in my head. Any way I reworked it, the battle ended when Walker chose the other side. Because when he left, there was nothing left worth fighting for. I let the doctors uproot me from this realm and take me back to Clover.

Several days passed in a blur. Even though the sun and moon danced across the sky, time never really existed here. No parties raged at the house, no video games played on the TV, no cues hit winning balls into the pockets of the pool table. Walker's dimples never came, and my heart began to freeze over. I was so devastated by the idea of leaving that I pulled back from everything. It was clear my mood affected the others too. The once lively cabin was quiet and still.

The Baylor Balloon Festival was the following day. It was the day we were to capture Layla. I recalled the picture of her and Walker in a hot air balloon. She had been gorgeous and very much in love. They both were. We were supposed to go to the festival, find Layla, and then what? They would go off happily ever after, and I would have no choice but to return home? Suddenly, I wished it was Layla who had disappeared in the lake instead of Kai.

I'd been avoiding Walker because I knew he wanted to send me home too. I knew which side of the war he was on. And the rejection I'd feel from him would be far worse than anything I had experienced so far this summer. But something changed on the morning before the festival. The fight inside of me smoldered with the simple question —*what if?*

If my days were limited here, I wanted to spend them with the person I loved most. I was done hiding from all of it. I laced my shoes and grabbed Walker's flannel, tying it around my waist. I planned to take the golf cart straight to his cabin and demand answers. I was going to tell him that I wanted to stay. I was going to bare my soul to him, and if he didn't want me . . . I guess I wouldn't fight the war.

As soon as I made my decision to see Walker, I heard a commotion outside at the dock and peered out the window. Walker was tying up. I immediately took off running down the stairs. I hadn't realized how much I'd missed him until this very moment. I swung the door open and ran halfway down the grassy hill before calling out, "Walker!"

He threw the rope down and froze when he heard my voice. "Wilde?" His voice rang with something I'd never heard before. Anger?

He marched down the dock and I slowed, cautiously. "Where the hell have you been?" He waved his hands in the air.

"I've been here. What do you mean?" I flinched.

"I haven't been able to get over here. I haven't been able to get close to Rock Creek Cove at all!"

It could have been a week since I had seen him last. Maybe longer. I searched his eyes, trying to understand why he was so angry with me.

"You used to summon me. You used to want me with you so badly that I had no choice but to come. And now? Now I can't even get across the lake? It's like you put up an invisible shield. What the hell is going on Kinsley?" he asked, hands on his hips.

I hated when he used my first name.

"I . . . I . . . I didn't know it worked like that. I'm sorry." I had no idea that being afraid to see Walker would keep him from me.

"You didn't know it worked like that? Why don't you want me around? I thought we were *friends*.."

An ache settled in my chest.

"If we are *just friends*, then why are you so mad?" I took a step forward, the smoldering in my belly igniting to a small flame.

"Because we're a team. You don't shut out your team."

"But what does that even mean?" I asked, needing more.

Walker ran his hands through his hair and spun around. He dropped his hands to his hips as I stared at his rigid back. I wanted to reach out and touch him. I wanted to run my fingertips down his back and rest my forehead between his shoulders . . . I didn't dare. I waited patiently for him to turn around while the flame in my belly flickered with insecurity.

"It means, we do this together." Walker turned around, his face softer now. Saddened almost. "In a world of smoke and mirrors, you are the only thing that's real to me. Don't shut me out." Walker's eyes fixed on mine.

"I'm *not* shutting you out, I promise."

"But you're hiding stuff from me. There are things that you don't share with me. Why?" he asked, his face contorted in a mix of emotions that I couldn't read.

"I'm not hiding anything from you," I lied. So much for being brave.

The pain on Walker's face melted to disappointment. That look I knew. I didn't know which hurt worse. He reached behind him, pulling something from his back pocket. A glow radiated from his hand as he held the golden feather between us. My eyes flickered back and forth, from the feather to his face. And as my thoughts raced over the secrets I hid from Walker, his jaw hardened.

"You've been hiding *this* from me."

The fire in my belly snuffed immediately. I was marked a coward. I certainly couldn't tell him that I was going to spend the rest of my life with him now. "That's nothing." One more lie toppled out.

His eyebrows arched. "Nothing? You think I don't know what this is? This is a Wish of Warmth. The floating element, the warm golden glow."

Walker let go of the feather and it gently floated between us.

"This wish followed me home one night. When I took my clothes off, the feather slipped out from behind my jeans and hovered in the corner of my room. The damn thing has been following me ever since. I've only seen you once since that night. It was the time you summoned me to your childhood bedroom. And you were hiding stuff from me then, too." He reached out, his hands hovering over my shoulders, before he gave up, dropping them to his sides.

"I've done a lot of research on this wish. The Wish of Warmth. It's typically given as a parting gift. A wish for good fortune and happiness. Did you give it to me? Or does somebody else in Baylor possess the same power as you?"

I remembered sending the feathers out by the

hundreds. Those wishes were for anybody who needed them. I shouldn't have been surprised that Walker needed it. "I sent it with you," I admitted.

He snatched the feather and stepped closer to me. I could feel the intensity of his gaze and the heat of his breath on my face. "Is this, or is this not, a parting gift?" he asked sternly.

The proximity between us heated the nape of my neck, and I fought the urge to fan my face and step away. Was this the time to tell him? I didn't know. I was afraid. I dropped my gaze to the round marbled button of his flannel. "It's not a parting gift." I would stay forever . . . If he let me.

He took a deep breath. While he was relieved, I was bound by my lies tighter than ever. I was surprised by the bear hug he gave me. Startled with shock, and suffocated by his shoulder, I adjusted my head for air and then wrapped my arms around him. He held me like he was never going to let go. I held him like I was halfway gone.

"Just promise me one thing?" he asked.

I said nothing.

"Don't leave without saying goodbye first."

"Um, Walker?" I asked. *Now or never . . .*

Before I could get the words out, he continued, "We're still going to the Baylor Balloon Festival tomorrow, right? You'll let me come over?" I felt his chin rest on the top of my head, and a part of me melted into him.

"Yeah. Of course. We've got to catch Layla, right?" I pulled my armor back on, shielding my heart from the unknown. I knew it was what he needed to hear.

"Yeah." His tone was slightly higher than normal. Excitement to find her? Or was I reading too much into it? Was there something else he wasn't saying? I bit my tongue.

"We have less than twenty-four hours before the festival." Walker pulled away and checked his watch. "To be honest, I'm afraid to go home. I'm afraid you won't let me back over." He shot me a half-joking smile, but it didn't reach his eyes.

"Of course, I'll let you back. I just . . ."

"What is it?"

"I was afraid to see you, because I didn't want you to know about the magic."

Walker's brows rose, and he took a step back, forcing me to explain.

"Do you remember when you said this was a puzzle for somebody with a twisted mind?"

Walker nodded.

"Do you remember when Emma said that I was atypical, and that my mind worked in mysterious ways?"

Walker nodded again.

"I thought, if it was true, then the magic would come, and I could control it. The Baylor phenomenon would be what I made of it. And so it was. That very night, when we gazed at the full moon from the porch, I froze time. I walked across the lake. Not around it, but on top of it. I sent hundreds of Warm Wishes out into the world. I didn't know what I was doing, it was just a feeling of hope. The feathers traveled on their own, seeking a destination. And when you left that night, I was just as surprised as you were when one of them followed you home. I've been testing the atypical theory ever since, and most of the time it works."

"Why would you hide that from me? Isn't that what we were trying to achieve together through your training?" Walker shook his head, completely confused.

"Well, yeah, but what would happen if I didn't need training anymore?" I asked.

"What do you mean?"

"What would happen to us if you no longer needed to teach me?"

"I don't know. I guess I would come up with more difficult challenges for you. And at some point, I assume you would pretend that you still needed me as a teacher. And we would go on doing lessons that both of us secretly knew you didn't need. Maybe one day, *you* would teach *me*. And we would do that forever, because there's no way I'd be as quick of a learner as you—"

"You mean, you would still stick around if I mastered the magic?"

"Of course I would," he said, slightly offended.

I was too afraid to ask how this would change our hunt for Layla. I decided to quit while I was ahead. That would unfold tomorrow anyway.

"Come on. Did you think we would stop seeing each other or something?"

I shrugged.

"Don't do that. We're so much more than that. You mean the world to me. I'd never cast you away." He swiped his thumb across my cheek. "I mean, if you're here . . . I'm here, right?"

"Yeah, okay . . ."

When push comes to shove and we meet Layla face to face tomorrow night, I'd find out just how true that statement was.

"You said it only works *most* of the time. What about the other times? What happens then?"

"Oh, yeah. It seems that my fear blocks the magic. And when that fear comes, when it rises inside of me, there's nothing I can do. Kai—" His name stuck in my throat. It was too soon, too raw. "Kai drowned. And all the magic in the world couldn't bring him back."

"Kai?" Walker folded an arm around his waist and cupped his mouth.

"We can't even cry anymore. We're so numb to the pain . . . we can't even cry."

"I'm so sorry," he whispered.

"I have to send them home. I must get them out of here. I just don't know how," I said shaking my head.

"We're going to find a way."

"Will you help me?" I asked.

"Of course, I'll help. We can do this, especially now that you can freeze time. It can't be much more advanced than that. I keep checking on the *Waking Dreams* book, but it's never been returned to the library. I'll check again tomorrow. I know there is something in there that would help us figure this thing out."

I cringed thinking about the book but nodded regardless. I was hopeful we'd find a way, but something inside of me wondered at what cost? What sacrifices needed to be made to send the three of them home? The cabin door opened and closed with a slam, and it wasn't long before Gunner's wet nose pushed against my leg.

"Hey, we have a big day tomorrow. Let's take your mind off everything for a while. Do you want to take a break? I know of a great drive-in movie theater . . . We could take the golf cart?" Walker forced a smile as he absentmindedly petted Gunner.

"Actually, that sounds perfect." My heart pitter-pattered in my chest when I considered that maybe the movie was a date. But of course, it wasn't a date; it was only the two of us killing time before trying to find his ex-girlfriend. Twenty-four hours until I'd knew which side of the war he would fight on.

We parked the golf cart in the open field. About a half dozen vehicles were parked in a line, and several groups of moviegoers sat on blankets before them. The movie screen was gigantic, even from a distance. It didn't matter which movie played, only who you came with. And tonight, I'd come with the one person I wanted to spend my time with.

I grabbed the blanket from the back seat of the golf cart and left the keys in the ignition. Nobody came to the drive-in to steal. Especially not the people rocking the single cab truck with foggy windows. I smirked as I looked at the heated truck and then quickly averted my eyes. Walker and I found a spot halfway to the screen and placed our blanket in the dirt and sparse patches of grass among the others. Most of them looked to be on dates.

"Do you know what movie is playing tonight?" I asked, settling down on the blanket.

"*Between You and Me.*"

I forced a smile. *Between You and Me* wasn't just any movie. It was a popular movie about love and sacrifice. About a boy and his family who live in another world. He leaves everything behind to chase the girl of his dreams, even though she lives on a different planet. One day he realizes that being with that girl is costing him his life. He can't live outside of his world for any sustained time, and he has no other choice but to return home without her. He was willing to lay down everything he had, just to be with her. But in the end, he'd never really had a choice. He'd chosen to sacrifice, but fate chose otherwise.

I didn't want that to happen to me. I wanted to be the one in charge of my destiny. And I'd already chosen to sacrifice. The only thing that would send me packing would be Walker's rejection, and even then, it would be a tough choice.

"Have you seen this movie?" I asked.

"Yeah. It's a great one. Have you?"

"Yeah, but don't you think it's kind of sad?"

"Sad? Maybe. I kind of look at it as a journey, though. Samuel Chesson gets to experience another world, and he gets to fall in love, what could be better than that?" Walker settled on the blanket, perched on his elbows behind him. I leaned forward, grabbing my knees in a bear hug.

"Oh, I don't know, staying with the love of his life, and *not* having to leave her?" *Just a thought* . . .

Walker tilted his head, weighing the options. "When you're cursed in love, you take what you can get. The time he spent with her was way better than sitting in his world all alone," he said, staring at the blank screen.

It hurt thinking that Walker was so starved for affection that he would choose the broken heart over the lonely one. I was pretty sure that avoiding heartbreak was not only the safest bet, but the smartest one too. I would have done it, if I'd had a choice.

"So, you're saying you would rather fall in love and have your heart shatter a *million times over*, just for the experience?" I asked.

"I think so. Yeah. Isn't that what life is all about?"

"Heartbreak?" My voice squeaked.

"The ups and downs. The journey." Walker stole a glance in my direction then quickly looked away.

"Call me crazy, but my life's a little different. A little safer. My journey is all about avoiding land mines. I would like to be whole by the time it's complete." I rested my chin on my knees.

I wasn't really whole as it was. Half of my heart was in another realm; half was wrapped up in a ghost of a guy. I'd been in some sort of accident I couldn't even remember, and I'd fallen deeply for someone I could never keep.

"You can't go through life being so scared, Wilde. If

you're afraid a bomb is going to blow, then you stop seeing what's right in front of you." I thought I saw his pinky finger stretch toward me on the blanket.

"Is that how you felt with Layla?" I regretted the words the moment they slipped from my lips.

Walker's fingers withdrew as his hand clenched into a ball, and his face contorted.

"I mean, even though it hurt, you were thankful for the time you spent with her? Would you do it all over again?" I asked, reading him carefully.

"I . . . I *would* do it again." He reached up to touch his brow, and when he pulled his hand away, there was fresh blood on his fingertips.

"Oh!" I scrambled around the blanket looking for something to hand him to stop the bleeding.

"It's okay. I'm fine." He smeared the blood across his temple in an attempt to remove it, then rubbed his hands together.

I hated how the very mention of her name caused his wound to reopen. It wasn't something he would ever heal from; I knew that now. I had so many more questions to ask, but I didn't want to cause him more pain than I already had.

"You said that maybe I could teach you the magic one day. What would you do with it?" I asked, trying my hardest to take his mind off Layla.

It had the opposite effect. He took a moment to think about it, and then he dabbed at his brow again.

"Honestly? I would change the day it happened. I'd go back in time and stop the accident. I would do whatever it took to keep her safe."

I sighed heavily. I'd asked the wrong question again. "But what if it took not being with her anymore?"

"You mean like the movie?"

I looked up at the screen as it darkened. "Yeah, I guess."

"Absolutely. Whatever it took."

The movie screen flickered to life, and the sound was adjusted from too loud, to too quiet, to just right. Trailers for old movies I'd seen several times played in the background, and my mind wandered.

He certainly loved Layla, and I had to imagine she'd been a different person back when he knew her, because the Layla I knew was a little bit crazy. I lay back beside him as we watched the trailers in silence. I pretended not to notice when he swiped the blood from his eyebrow, but I internally cursed myself for making it happen. With less than twenty-four hours left before we met Layla, the last thing I wanted was to focus on her all night. From here on out, there was only room for two on this blanket.

The movie started with a scene from the boy's world. It was an inhospitable place, lacking color, joy, and safety. But the boy didn't notice, because it was all he knew. I chewed on my lip, thinking about the Baylor phenomenon. I couldn't compare myself to the boy in the movie because I *had* known better. And surely, my life before this wasn't so far away that I had forgotten what a predictable environment felt like. I wasn't choosing to stay in Baylor because I couldn't remember life was better somewhere else. I was choosing to stay here because I was in love. Because this was where my heart had found its home. Still, I couldn't help relating the entire movie to my situation, comparing my realm to his planet and my relationship to his.

The movie did very little to quiet my mind. If anything, it made me think about my situation even more. I couldn't help but feel like time was of the essence. Gran had said that I would be going home soon. I didn't know how long *soon* would be, but I felt the need to prepare for the war. I knew an army would try to take me home, and more than ever, I needed to know if it was worth fighting for. I needed to know where Walker stood. Would he stand faithfully by my side? Or would he stand across the battlefield?

I couldn't just ask him. If I did, I knew he would tell me to go home. He would be chivalrous. His way of showing me he cared. He would sacrifice my company and live a lonely life because of his love for me. Whether it was a friendship kind of love or something more, it didn't really matter. But if I just stayed quiet, I might be able to stay as long as . . . forever. He'd said so himself. He'd said he would train me *forever*. Whether he admitted it or not, I knew he didn't want me to leave. And I wasn't sure he could survive another heartbreak.

But he'd also said he would stop the accident from ever happening if he had the gift of magic. Even if that meant leaving Layla. Maybe it meant that all he wanted was her safety, not her heart. Maybe he would pick Layla's safety and *my* heart? And that would be our forever. Forever with Walker in Baylor would truly be an infinity of time and space. I would have endless days by his side, and one of those days, he would have to admit that he'd fallen in love with me somewhere along the way. The excitement swirled in my stomach like the wings of butterflies lightly stirring.

On the big screen, the boy reached out and touched the girl's cheek. Without moving my head, I tried to peek at Walker. My hand twitched slightly in his direction, and I tried my hardest to not make it obvious. But as I tried to steal tiny glances at him, I caught sight of something else. Something red. A girl in a red cloak standing near the steamy truck.

Disappointment washed over me. *Not now . . .*

"I forgot something in the golf cart. I'll be right back," I said, eyes trained on the red target. She wasn't supposed to come so early. I had until tomorrow before she ended this for me.

"I can get it. What do you need?" Walker asked.

"It's okay. I'm just going to grab a water," I said, patting his shoulder as I left.

I walked straight back to the row of parked vehicles. I weaved in and out of the cars before approaching the truck, staying in the shadows. I didn't have a plan and was suddenly afraid that Walker would see us together. What would he think then?

The edge of the cloak peeked out from the bed of the truck, and I stilled when I saw it. Did I really want to talk to her? Make a scene? What would I say? Something flipped inside of me, and I no longer wanted to confront her. This was a terrible idea. I looked down at her black boots and saw a flash of her face peeking around the truck bed. But by the time my eyes flicked up, she was gone. Slowly, her shoes took a step back.

I made the decision to let it be. She didn't want to talk to me. She was here to spy and nothing else. I turned around and headed for the golf cart. I didn't even know if I had a water bottle to retrieve, but I had to look. I couldn't come back empty-handed—that would be weird. I glanced at the blanket and was pleased to see that Walker was still there, watching the movie. I rummaged through the golf cart and managed to find little more than an empty crumpled soda can. I supposed I would have to tell him I couldn't find my water. I was just about to head back to the blanket when I heard a swipe of gravel behind me. A flash of red disappeared one car over. *Dammit.*

Layla made it difficult to know if I was being spied on or chased down. Was she trying to get closer or keep her distance? I felt foolish for fearing her, but I couldn't help how my heart rate doubled with her proximity.

I saw her shadow clear as day when the big screen lit up. She was crouched behind the car like a child playing hide and seek. I felt bad for her, but also incredibly threatened. It was an odd mix. My body told me I was in danger, but my mind said she was harmless and needed help. And it was my gran who had conveyed she was a job. A task I must complete. *Find the girl . . . Help the girl . . .*

Maybe she was lost and couldn't find her way to a more restful afterlife? Could I really send her on her way when I knew that Walker had been looking for her? Would it make me a terrible person if I did? I bit my lip and made the split-second decision to try to talk to her. What's the worst that could happen? I was growing sick and tired of wondering where I belonged. I crouched, like her shadow, and snuck around the back of the car.

"Wilde?"

I jumped. My heart hammered in my chest, and I let out a shudder. "Walker?" I asked, extending to my full height.

"What are you doing? You're missing the movie."

"Oh, I can't find my water." I raised my empty hands.

The movie screen lit up, revealing three shadows instead of two. I swallowed a lump in my throat waiting for him to notice, but he never did.

"Do we need to make a run to the store?"

"No, no. That's all right. I can wait." I closed the distance between us, and we turned and headed back for the blanket. Walker slipped his arm around my shoulder as we made our way to our spot in the clearing, and I peeked over his arm to see if Layla was watching. She was no longer hiding in the shadows. She stood, openly visible, in front of the golf cart, arms crossed. Black boots and a red cloak. Long tresses of dark hair cascaded over her shoulders. Her brows were furrowed, and her lips were pursed. Her head tilted ever so slightly to the side, as if she didn't know what to make of us. I felt sick to my stomach.

We sat down on the blanket. Walker lay back, immediately comfortable, while I sat up nervously shredding a single blade of grass into thin strips.

"Are you okay?" Walker asked.

"Yeah. I'm all right." I lifted my gaze from him to Layla.

It was my job to reunite them. But was that my only purpose here? To help them find each other through the veil? Layla had told me I didn't belong here, and that echoed everything my gran had said in her cryptic visits. But I didn't believe it.

But at the same time, I couldn't bear the thought of letting my gran down. I had to find a way to stay with Walker and help Layla. *Separately*. It was an impossible feat, especially since I couldn't even help my friends escape. I didn't know what to do. My friends needed me, Walker needed me, Layla needed me, everybody needed something from me! But what did I need?

I stole a glance back, and Layla was no longer there. Frantically, I searched the darkness between the cars and across the blankets. Nowhere could I find a red cloak and a lonely girl.

An epic space battle began on the big screen. The boy's family was trying to get him back to the safety of his planet, but the government had intercepted them. I couldn't focus on the movie because I refused to believe that Layla was gone. And an invisible threat was far worse than one I could track with my eyes, no matter how uncomfortable her glare. I looked back, searching once more, and this time Walker took notice.

A stream of light blazed past us at lightning speed, knocking Walker onto his back.

"Whoa!" I said, breathlessly.

"What the hell!?" Walker exclaimed, looking for answers.

Another laser shot through the crowd. And then another. A high-pitched squeal whizzed by with each streak of light. The small crowd screamed and ran for cover, leaving their blankets and belongings behind. Car doors slammed shut. Somebody's alarm went off.

"They're missiles!" I yelled.

The missiles being fired in the movie were coming straight through the screen, unleashing their firepower into the crowd.

Another one shot overhead, and I ducked, wrapping my arms around my head. The cars peeled out and sped off, kicking up a cloud of dirt and dust. Even the couple in the truck with steamed-up windows took notice, starting their ignition, and speeding away.

Five more shots fired off. One landed in the forest behind us with an explosion. The ground rumbled as orange flames ignited into the sky.

The last of the cars disappeared from sight, leaving only a cloud of dust in their wake. Walker and I were alone as the fire grew in the distance.

If Layla was hanging around the cars before, she certainly wasn't there now. Breathlessly, I searched the movie screen and tried to recall when the battle scene ended. Walker was the only one who was unafraid— probably because he was already in his afterlife—but it surprised me when I thought I saw a pass of amusement cross his face. He wasn't just entertained, he was . . . *proud?*

He was actually proud of all the hard work I had put into manifestation, and he couldn't care less that it came out in twisted ways. What could have been an embarrassing, tragic night was nothing but excitement for him. He had been trapped in what probably felt like Groundhog Day for the past twenty-some years, and what I suddenly understood was that unpredictability was his friend. Which made it a friend of mine.

A missile shot by, missing us by several feet. The heat blew past us, nearly singeing my brows. The gust kicked up my hair, leaving half of it toppled over my face. Walker broke out in laughter as I swiped my hair back. I couldn't believe he was laughing at a time like this. He reached over me, and my eyes grew wide as he grabbed the edge of the blanket. *What was he doing?*

He pulled the excess blanket over us, and we hid there listening to missiles fire off. I couldn't see the golden amber of his eyes or the dimples in his cheeks, but I could hear his smile through the darkness, and I could feel his energy through waves of heat. He covered me with his body, a human shield, protecting me from my own imagination. His forearms pressed into the ground on either side of my head as the blanket pitched over his shoulders. Missiles whizzed by, and the light from the lasers flashed underneath the blanket, momentarily lighting his face.

I couldn't leave this realm even if I wanted to. I was *incapable* of leaving Walker. He had become my existence. He was my only reality.

Every time I thought he might see the desire written

across my face, another life-threatening missile would graze by. Another explosion would sound in the distance, causing Walker's body to tense on top of me. I licked my lips and waited. I fought every desire to turn my gifts on him. *Make* him want me. *Make* him kiss me. But it wasn't right. And I knew that it would never taste as sweet if I did.

I was so into him, I didn't even notice when the battle scene stopped. I only noticed when Walker relaxed, and his energy turned from heated to curious. That's when I heard the roaring fire gaining momentum in the distance and the soft sounds of a piano playing a sad melody.

Walker threw the blanket off, and we took in the surrounding destruction. We got to our feet, amazed by all the smoke and embers glimmering in the sparse tufts of grass. The blankets and trash had blown all about the field in a whirlwind. It was nothing short of mass destruction, and I had caused it with my typical indecisiveness.

But that's not what stuck with me long after the night ended. The thing that really stopped my heart was the main character, brought to her knees in the middle of the field. The girl was tucked into a ball amid the smoke, crying quietly. The movie continued to play in the background, but she had come to life before our very eyes. Her heartbreak was palpable, and the music leaked from the movie screen and floated all around us in a heart-wrenching melody of a love that could never be.

The Baylor Balloon Festival was alive with sightseers, townspeople, and travelers alike. Everyone within a sixty-mile radius of Baylor Lake had come to see the balloon festival, including Walker and me. My thoughts lingered on Emma, Scarlett May, and Noah back at the cabin. None of them had wanted to see the balloon festival. They really hadn't been the same since Kai left.

I thought it had more to do with failing to find the red door than Kai's absence. We'd lost many of our friends along the way, and everybody had seemed to bounce back —quite unnaturally. This was different. This had affected them in a way I hadn't yet seen this summer. Their hopes of going home were waning.

I scanned the crowd, looking for Layla. I had been on pins and needles the entire afternoon. Just because I didn't see her didn't mean she wasn't there, watching and waiting. I knew she was around us. She was *always* around us. I couldn't understand why she would make herself visible to me when she hadn't done it for Walker all these years. Perhaps it was her way of intimidating me. I imagined she had a laundry list of reasons why she thought I was unworthy to be by Walker's side. I glanced up at him and saw his eyes flickering through the crowd. If I was feeling nervous, I couldn't imagine what he was feeling.

My uncertainty had shot missiles through the woods last night. I'd caused a forest fire just by weighing my options. And I was incredibly thankful that Walker didn't possess the same power. Because I couldn't fathom the trepidation racking through his mind as he looked for Layla, his long-lost love, in the crowd.

"I still can't get over last night. I mean, did you think about the movie coming to life? Did you have to physically pull the light show out of the screen? How did it happen?" Walker's face was alive with possibilities as we swerved around a family with lingering small children.

"Light show? That's a little generous don't you think?" I looked up at him. His eyes were sunken, and light purple shadows lurked below his lashes. Neither of us had slept much last night.

Walker chuckled and shot me a sleepy smile. "I know you were scared, but I quite liked it."

"I wasn't scared!"

He laughed louder, bringing an unwilling smile to my face. "I wasn't!" *Maybe I was, a little.*

"You were so scared, you know it."

"I think you were scared when the movie ended and you realized the entire forest was going up in flames," I exaggerated.

"Well, how was I supposed to know that you could turn it off just as easily as you started it?"

I smiled crookedly, shaking my head. I hadn't known I could do it either. But after last night, after seeing the actress in a heap of tears and her heart broken into a million pieces, I'd just wanted the night to end. I'd wanted the whole thing to shut down. I got lucky is all.

"It was just a flick of your wrist. You clenched your fist, and the entire fire went out." Walker reached his hand out in front of us, snatching at thin air. I felt my cheeks warm.

"Stop it . . ."

"It was nothing short of amazing," Walker said. I rolled my eyes, completely embarrassed, but the truth was, my heart was singing. He was proud of me, and I was too.

"What do you think happened to the actress?" I asked, my heart still hurting for her.

"What do you mean? She got sucked back into the movie."

"You think she was just part of the movie?"

"Well yeah. Why? What did you think?"

"She just seemed so real." I said in little more than a whisper.

Walker chuckled like I was a total sap. But I couldn't tell the difference between the actress from the movie who had come to life in the clearing and the girl in my mirror. She was just as real as any of us, and that frightened me.

Walker tugged my arm and steered me to a small cotton candy booth. His face lit up like a little boy, and it quickly pulled my mind away from last night's movie. "Good call. Cotton candy is always a good call." My mouth watered at the thought of spun sugar.

I pinched the pink cotton candy and pulled a clump off. The web of candy melted instantly into tiny granules of sugar in my mouth, and I wanted more. Walker pulled off a piece far too big for his mouth, and I laughed at him as he tried to fit it in one bite. We walked aimlessly around the festival eating candy and people watching. I knew we were supposed to be looking for Layla, but it didn't feel that urgent. Neither one of us was on the hunt for a change. We were simply enjoying each other's time in a slow and lazy manner. When we became too relaxed, Walker would pull out the photo from his back pocket. It was his way of reminding us to stay focused on the mission. Still, his actions seemed forced, like he was driven by guilt.

The photograph was of a yellow balloon with green stripes and the most beautiful couple there ever was. A tinge of jealousy crept through me every time I saw the picture, but as soon as it was folded away in his back pocket, I did my best to enjoy myself. I didn't need to actively look for yellow hot air balloons with green stripes; I was pretty sure it would be obvious when we saw it. That meant we just had to cover as much ground as possible, and our job would be complete.

But our steps were slow and our eyes nearsighted. It wasn't a stretch to say we were having fun. In fact, it was the first time I felt Walker ease into contentment. And I felt like I might be enough for him to be happy. If this had anything to do with last night, I would have fired off missiles a long time ago.

We strolled through the crowd, passing families with little kids, seniors who still held hands—my favorite—and a wide variety of couples. I spotted a young boy, maybe three years old, peeing behind his parents' backs as they purchased food from a vendor. The little boy's pants were around his ankles, and he leaned back in a practiced and proud stance.

I grabbed the crook of Walker's arm and pointed as the crowd parted around the child, looking at his parents with furrowed brows. We laughed, collapsing into each other. When a random little white dog came up beside the boy and peed with him, my knees grew weak, and I grabbed hold of Walker's shoulder for support.

The hours passed seamlessly. We tried ridiculous treats that you could only buy at a festival, and we laughed

. . . *a lot.* It was far different from the last hunt we'd gone on. The stakes were high at the Fourth of July Baylor Parade, and Walker's heart had been crushed.

We rested on a bench under a sparse sapling of a tree, picking apart funnel cake and cracking jokes. Nearly the whole day had passed, and dusk was fast upon us. Walker had finally stopped pulling out the photo of Layla, which told me his guilt was waning. I kept a careful eye on his brow, which remained a healed scar the entire day. I didn't know why I'd been so worried about coming to the festival.

"Look, aren't they so cute?" I said pointing to an elderly couple sitting at a nearby table. They wore matching purple shirts, and they were incredibly into each other.

"What makes them so cute?" Walker asked, eyeing the couple. I frowned at him, and he laughed at me. "What?"

I swiped powdered sugar from his cheek. "What makes them so darn cute is the fact that they've probably been together for sixty years and they are *still* very much into each other. Probably as much as they ever have been. Most people get sick of one another. They get complacent and grumpy. But they're the opposite. They even dress alike. They love each other so much. You know, I bet they still hold hands." I smiled up at Walker. *Maybe I was a sap.*

He dipped a strip of funnel cake into caramel sauce and handed it to me. I cupped my hand underneath the hot caramel, catching a single drip of sauce.

"I guess that *is* kind of cute, but don't tell anybody I said so," he said with a boyish smile. I laughed, bumping my shoulder into his.

"Do you think that will be us one day?" I asked. It tumbled out of my mouth before I could even think about it. The look on Walker's face made me wish I hadn't grown so comfortable after all.

Had I ruined it? Had I just ruined the entire day? Was this the part where he told me we were nothing more than friends, and this wasn't going to last forever? Was this the part where he chose which side of the war he was on? My throat tightened as I waited for him to say something. Anything.

"Us?" he asked. I stared at him, unblinking.

There was no way to remedy it. I'd said it because I looked at him as the love of my short life. It was very clear that he didn't see me that way.

"Wilde . . ." he drew out my name.

"I know. I'm sorry." I scrunched my eyes closed and hid behind my hand.

"I'm *never* going to grow old," he said, breaking the silence.

He's never going to grow old? That's what he was worried about? Not whether we'd be together, or if we loved each other, just that he wasn't going to grow old like the couple at the table? Maybe I hadn't spoiled the day. Maybe the idea of him and me wasn't so far-fetched.

"I know. I'm sorry," I said, still hiding my eyes. Now, I was afraid he might see my confusion.

He pulled my hand from my face and peered into my eyes. "*I'm* never going to grow old, but you will. I'm going to find a way to get you out of here. I promise."

It was the saddest thing I'd ever heard. Walker never growing old, me leaving him behind, and the sight of two elderly people in love—something neither one of us would ever have. Especially not together.

"But I don't want to leave you behind," I said, dipping my toe in to the conversation I really wanted to have.

"I know you don't. It's okay. I'll be okay."

My eyes burned as tears threatened to spill. Walker seemed to grow more nervous as he looked into my worried eyes, and he turned away as if searching the crowd for answers. "Hey, have you ever gone up in a hot air balloon?"

That caught me off guard. "Me? No."

"Let's go."

"I can't do that. You know I'm afraid of heights, right?"

"You'll be fine."

"I can't even jump off the rocks at the lake, and that's with a rope swing and forgiving water below. What makes you think I'm going to be *fine* in a hot air balloon?"

"Wilde, trust me, I'll be there the whole time. It's about the experience, right? Let's do this together. We might not have another chance."

My jaw hardened as I thought about all the ways it

could go so terribly wrong. The second I began to think was the second the balloon ride would turn into a tragic event. "You understand that when I become afraid terrible things happen, right?" I asked, slowly, putting emphasis on each word. "Walker, I'm already afraid just looking at the thing!"

A flush crept into his cheeks, and his dimples flashed beneath his unshaven face. I couldn't quite read the look, but I thought it might be embarrassment. "Yes. I understand. And I will have to try *very* hard to keep your mind occupied."

My eyes widened. I didn't know what that meant, but it sounded like an invitation that I couldn't turn down. I jumped to my feet, suddenly eager for the hot air balloon ride. Walker's lips pursed together, creating a thin straight line. He held my hand as we walked to the nearest unoccupied balloon. It was then, at the worst imaginable time, that I spotted the yellow and green stripes we were looking for. My heart skipped a beat as I considered not telling him. Or maybe I could tell him afterward? But when I looked up to his bright eyes, I knew I couldn't deceive him, even for an hour.

I squeezed Walker's hand, and he turned around to look at me. "Um, I think I found it," I said meekly.

"Found what?"

"The balloon. It's over there." I pointed with a shaky finger. It was a sacrifice I wasn't ready for, but I made the choice, regardless. I would rather Walker's happiness before my own, and I suppose I would rather his heart be full for an hour longer than for me to get my balloon ride. It had *nothing* to do with the fact that I was petrified of heights . . .

Walker froze, staring at the yellow hot air balloon. I turned my body slightly in its direction, anticipating the change of course, but Walker's hand tightened around mine. "It's okay. We'll head over afterward?" His eyes were fixed in the distance.

"Are you sure? I know you've been waiting . . ."

"I'm sure." He turned away determinedly, and I jumped to keep up with him. I couldn't believe he was choosing a hot air balloon ride with me over his chance at finding Layla. Who's to say she would wait? He didn't say much else about her or the balloon waiting for us across the field, but he was quietly ruminating to himself. My eyes flickered to the scar running through his eyebrow, and I noticed it had turned pink but wasn't bleeding.

We stepped into the basket, and I quickly became anxious. The wicker was sharp against my palms as I grabbed at the edge, looking for anything I could use to secure myself. Why was the basket so old and rickety? The other balloons had leather-wrapped baskets that were newer and stronger looking. Our balloon was a sun-bleached navy blue. The skirt blended into a merlot red and then bloomed into a bright orange on the top pole. The basket was smaller than I would have liked, only large enough for three people: the pilot and one lucky couple.

Our pilot was a tall, thin man with scrawny arms and a long handlebar mustache. His eyes were droopy and glassed over. I was pretty sure he was stoned. I wasn't comfortable in a hot air balloon as it was, but having our pilot be under the influence made me even more nervous.

"My name is Chad, and I will be your aeronaut today. Please keep all hands and feet inside the basket. Do not lean over the edge. Do not crawl over the edge. And if you must use the restroom, please go now. There will be no opportunity to relieve yourself in the sky."

I peeked at Walker, slightly concerned, but his thoughts were elsewhere. I took a deep breath. "What's that thing?" I asked, stalling.

"That's the burner. This is the vent line. That is the envelope. The hot air is released into the envelope, trapping it inside and lifting the balloon into the air. I'll pull this line when we ascend too quickly. Ready for takeoff?" Chad's voice was monotone. I looked at Walker with gigantic eyes.

Were we ready for takeoff? Should we maybe rethink this? Maybe chasing after Layla wasn't such a bad idea after all?

"Great. Ready for takeoff," Chad said when nobody answered.

I squeezed Walker's arm as the burner started and I

heard a loud rumble as flames ignited. The basket tilted sideways, and I let out a yelp. It skipped and jumped before lifting smoothly into the air, and I felt immediately sick to my stomach. Walker seemed to be in a trance, and I couldn't snap him out of it. It was a recipe for disaster.

"Walker?" I asked. But he didn't hear me. His wound had turned from pink to purple, and I could tell that his heart was hurting.

"Walker!" I yelled. He snapped out of it. His eyes tried desperately to focus on mine, but he seemed to be having trouble. "I'm scared."

The purple bruise immediately receded, and his golden eyes turned warm and compassionate. "I'm here. I'm here."

I steadied my breathing and found comfort in his eyes. We lifted into the air far quicker than I would have liked. The crowd below shrank the higher we lifted. I watched everybody pointing at our balloon as the orange flame glowed into the nylon, and the colors lit like a stained-glass window from within. Walker turned me around facing outward and wrapped his arms around my waist. I felt secure in his hold, but the height did weird things to my stomach, and I felt slightly dizzy, like I could collapse at any moment.

"See? It's not that bad, right?" he asked, his mouth pressed behind my ear.

"How high are we going?" I asked.

"We're on a tether. We're not going very high at all. These balloons are meant for the crowds. They go up and down all day but stay right here in the fields." The other balloons were all tethered by thick ropes attached to the bottom of the baskets. I immediately felt better, and the adventurous part of me wondered if I could enjoy it with time.

"Is it okay that I'm holding you like this?" It felt more right than anything had all summer long. And it reminded me of the night I'd slept in his arms.

"Yeah. It's okay. It actually helps. Don't let go, okay?"

"I won't." His voice was riddled with trepidation. I was glad I couldn't see his scar, because I didn't want to know how badly it hurt him to have his arms around me. Especially knowing that Layla was so close.

The basket hitched as the rope caught and the ascent had reached its limit. "This is as high as we're going today folks. Enjoy the view," Chad said.

Walker and I inched forward, his arm still wrapped tightly around me. I grabbed hold of the basket and dared to peer down at the ground. We could see everything from up here. *Everything . . .*

The yellow balloon with green stripes sat anchored on the festival grounds. A splash of red painted the bench by its side, sticking out like a sore thumb. I knew it was Layla, and I knew she was waiting for him.

All this time I had been told to find the girl. Now that

I'd found her, I wanted to keep her hidden. I wanted nothing more than to stay in Walker's arms for the rest of eternity, but seeing the girl in the red cloak waiting for her soulmate to appear pulled at my heartstrings. I really did want to help her, but I didn't want it to be at my own expense.

If Walker told me today that all he really wanted was her, I'd turn away. I'd dust my hands and walk straight through that red door. The problem was—I didn't really believe that's what he wanted. And I was too afraid to ask.

"Time's running out . . ." Chad said.

What?

Walker rubbed my arms in the cool air.

"Time's running out," Chad said again. I stretched my neck to look at the pilot.

"What did you say?" I asked.

He looked perplexed. "Excuse me?"

"Did you say something?" I asked.

"Me?" he said pointing to his chest.

"Never mind," I said, looking back at the remarkable view. I was hearing things again. I let my eyes fall over the horizon. The dense topography met the sky in an artistic smudge of color.

"Time's running out, Kinsley!" Chad exclaimed. I spun around, causing Walker to let go of me. Chad pulled the vent line with a crooked smile. His handlebar mustache turned lopsided. Was time running out? Was I being a coward?

Layla was on the bench waiting for Walker, and as soon as this balloon landed, we were going to meet her face to face. The only thing stopping Walker from leaving with her and not me might be my confession. Maybe I *was* running out of time. Maybe Chad was right. I took in a rattled breath and peered at him one last time for confirmation, but I was shocked to find he wasn't there at all.

I went rigid, afraid Walker might see that our pilot had vanished. On the one hand, it was more private, more romantic this way. But on the other hand, if my feelings were to get hurt, there was nobody to land this thing.

Regardless of risk, the flame in my belly was back. Only this time, I wasn't going to let it fizzle out. I was going to speak my piece, and if this balloon crashed down to the ground, then so be it. At least I would have my answer.

I watched Layla on the bench checking her watch and growing impatient. Time was of the essence. I'd found the girl, but I had something to say first. I turned to face Walker and he kept his arms wrapped around the small of my back. His eyes were a warm mix of spun honey and compassion. I placed my open hands on his chest.

My time was running out . . .

"Walker, I want to stay . . ."

CHAPTER 25

H is eyes squinted ever so slightly, and his mouth twitched nervously. The basket began to rumble, but my eyes were glued to his.

"I want to stay here, in Baylor, with you. *Forever*." I grabbed hold of his arms as the basket lurched forward. My worry escalated. The tether suddenly snapped, sending the balloon racing into the sky.

Walker was immediately alarmed, but he tried to hide it. We braced each other through locked arms as he whipped his head around looking for the pilot.

It was happening . . .

My fear was getting the best of me. He either had to accept it as part of who I was, or he didn't truly love me. His face paled as he realized we were climbing out of control with no pilot. Despite the burner not turning on, the balloon continued to rise. But that was the least of my worries.

"What about your family, Wilde? You can't do that to them!" His voice was rushed as his eyes flickered to the disappearing festival grounds. And perhaps to Layla below.

"My gran is here. Either way, I'm losing family."

"I don't think you belong here. I think you are meant to go home and live a long, happy life." His eyes deepened with sadness as he seemed to finally admit the truth to himself. But I wouldn't accept it.

"I belong wherever I choose!" I was so tired of people telling me where I did and didn't belong. It wasn't anybody's choice but my own. And I had the right to be whoever. Wherever. Always.

"I don't think you understand the gravity of the decision."

"I understand plenty!" I snapped. The basket whipped back and forth as the winds became violent. My hair lashed at my face, and the air became thinner and more difficult to breathe.

"You would be choosing death! If you stay here, you will *die* back home. I don't want that for you." His voice broke up as he yelled into the brewing storm.

"I am more me here than I ever was back home! The Baylor phenomenon has shown me my deepest fears, but it has also shown me my strengths and desires. I may not always know how to control it, but I know what I want. I want *you*, Walker. I want *us*."

"I want you too. Just . . . Just not like this," he said, his eyes searching mine. It was everything I was afraid to hear, and it struck me like a knife.

I reached for the vent line, wrapping my hand around the cord. I pulled down as hard as I could, letting the heat vent from the balloon. It was supposed to let the hot air escape from the envelope so the ascent would slow, but that's not what happened. I didn't have control of my emotions after being rejected by the only person I'd truly fallen for.

All the hot air escaped in one heaping whoosh. The balloon turned flaccid, whipping back and forth as it dropped through the sky. The basket turned sideways, rocking like a pendulum. Walker and I held on for dear life. I grabbed hold of the supporting ties as we flipped entirely upside down.

A scream pierced my ears. As my throat grew sore, I realized it was my own. I wasn't even sure if it was fear, shock, or the pure frustration I'd felt. Dangling upside down from a falling hot air balloon, when I was terribly afraid of heights, could do that to a girl.

The fear of heights seemed so insignificant now that I faced a life without Walker. I had convinced myself that going home was the worst thing imaginable. I couldn't just lie in a hospital bed, beaten and battered, heartbroken and alone. No magic to perfect and no missions to complete. What would be the point? This was my home. *He* was my home.

I clung to the outside of the basket, my hand wrapped fiercely around a dangling line. The basket finally flipped right side up, and Walker crawled inside. He grabbed my arms and pulled me in. The old, rickety basket scraped my forearms and legs as I clambered in. We collapsed together at the bottom of the basket sprawled out and panting. I jammed my feet into one corner and wedged my hands into another.

"Wilde, you have to control this! We can talk when we're on the ground, just bring us down safely!"

"What if I do it, anyway? What if I stay? Would there ever be a chance for us?" I yelled through the wind tunnel.

It was an impossible question for him to answer. And I could see the torture it put him through. A single drop of blood ran down the side of his face.

"I don't know what to tell you! My heart . . . It's broken!" he yelled, slamming his hand into his chest.

"You're not broken! You're perfect to me. I love you just the way you are. You're not cursed. You're *not* cursed!"

"I am!" His voice strained.

"Do you love me?" My voice splintered as I wrestled to my feet. The ground was coming up fast, and we were going to crash. But I wasn't afraid of crashing. I was afraid of the next words to come out of his mouth.

"I do! I do! But . . . You're not the only one," he said, right before he looked over the edge of the basket.

Screams split through the turbulent air as the families below turned to run. I was running out of time. My world was ending.

The basket spun and crashed down into picnic tables and several retail booths with a loud racket.

I landed square on my feet. Like a meteor strike, I shook the ground, completely unfazed. The basket broke into pieces beneath my feet, and the balloon fluttered down, eclipsing our sight. Sun-bleached navy and merlot enveloped the broken tables like a sea of nylon.

I had no idea where Walker was. I pushed at the balloon until I found a way out. Panicked, I slid it off my shoulders and began to rifle through the heavy fabric.

"Walker!?" I yelled.

No answer.

I searched the grounds. Almost everybody had fled, except for a few stragglers who had stayed to watch. They stared in disbelief.

"Walker!?"

"You don't belong here, Kinsley!" Layla called out from the distance. Her red cloak fluttered behind her as my worry for Walker caused the brewing storm to worsen. What was she still doing here?

"You can't tell me where I belong! You don't even

know me!" I yelled, lifting the navy scraps of the hot air balloon.

"Stop fighting it!" she demanded.

"Walker!?" I called out. He was the only thing that mattered now. I needed to know he was safe.

"Go home, Kinsley!" she said forcefully. The threat blew across my face in a fierce wind, and it was clear I wasn't the only one with a mind for magic.

"He loves me! He said he loves *me!*" *I wasn't afraid of her.*

"He loves me more!" Layla said in an all-powerful voice that enveloped me from all directions.

"No!" I yelled. Electricity lit the gray clouds a neon blue. A crack of thunder growled overhead.

"Don't do this!" Walker pled. He stood unscathed. His arms were spread wide as he crouched down ever so slightly.

The three of us were at a standoff, three points of a triangle. The remains of the hot air balloon lay splattered like navy and merlot paint between us.

I watched as Walker's eyes flickered between her and me. He loved me, *but I wasn't the only one.*

It was the first time he had seen Layla since the parade. But he was no longer the guilt-stricken boyfriend. Now, he was neutral. Caught between two, as if his heart had been torn down the middle and each of us had been given half to keep. Neither Layla nor I would ever have his full heart.

And Walker would never experience the marvel of true love. He was right after all; he really was cursed.

I took a step toward Walker, and he inched toward Layla. She took a small, calculated step away from him and closer to me, as we circled around the fallen balloon. Two of us were incredibly dangerous, and Walker was caught in the middle. It was probably a good thing he couldn't die twice.

"Who do you love more Walker?!" I yelled, my eyes fixed on the threat. I had everything to lose, but I was going to lose either way. If he chose me, I'd die. I'd lose my life at only eighteen years old. That was the cost of being with him. But if he chose her, I'd lose my heart, my strength, and my opportunity to live a life I'd only dreamed of.

I inched closer to him, and he took a step further away. *Was he afraid of me?*

"Both! My heart is split down the middle. I love you both," he yelled, no longer amused by my wicked sense of manifestation.

"Don't tell her that!" Layla hissed, and the air grew thicker with humidity. Dark clouds full of angry rain cast a haunting shadow upon us.

"Don't listen to her! She's crazy!" I said, trying to make him understand. He hadn't been there all the times she'd approached me. He simply hadn't been able to see her, and the one time he could, she'd wanted nothing to do with him.

"Be careful what you say, Wilde. We're not in training anymore!"

He knew something. Something he'd never told me. How else would he know that I should be careful? I took another step toward him, and he sidestepped toward Layla, not letting me get close to him. Why didn't he want to be close to me? I was clearly upset, but I would never hurt him.

Layla moved toward me again, arms spread wide. I couldn't quite tell if she was keeping her distance from Walker or trying to keep close to me. What was she going to do? Would she hurt me? Would *I* hurt *her*?

"Walker! Listen to me. Do. You. Love. Me?" I demanded. My sight narrowed in on him, willing him to answer.

"Yes!" he exclaimed sharply.

"Nooo!" A guttural cry came from Layla, and lightning split the sky in half. Thunder broke above, and the clouds unleashed heavy, pelting rain.

I'd had enough of her. I took a step toward her, and she moved away. The three of us turned counterclockwise for the first time, still skirting the remains of the broken balloon.

I didn't know why she was standing in our way when she didn't want Walker for herself. When she had been hiding from him for two decades. I was done with her and her games. But whichever direction I turned, the two of them kept an equal distance, like we repelled each other.

The anger inside of me boiled as the rain pelted my head and streamed down my face, narrowly missing my eyes, and sputtering across my lips.

I felt protective of Walker, and Layla's storm was a threat to him. The fire in my belly had grown to new levels. Total mayhem was on the rise. I seethed with power and anger. My heart drummed in my chest like a hungry predator.

My vision stretched and distorted, turning everything a shade of red. From bright and alarming to deep and alluring and everything in between. There was something so freeing about giving in to my power, and I let myself surrender to it fully.

At first, I thought Layla was shrinking into a powerless form, but I soon realized that I was growing taller. My skin was uncomfortably tight. It felt like it was tearing. A shiver trailed down my back and ripped through my spine. My head pulsed with pain as my jaw extended. Something sharp grazed the skin of my lips and chin.

Walker was terrified. He stumbled backward with enormous eyes.

"Stop it!" Layla screamed.

The few remaining onlookers fled the field, screaming in terror.

I stepped toward Walker and the ground shook

beneath my feet. I caught glimpses of myself in the shards of the smashed glass from the tiny broken boutiques. I must've been ten feet tall, covered in dark brown, shaggy hair. It was jarring to see myself as a grotesque monster, but it matched the greed and jealousy I felt on the inside.

"Kinsley, stop it! Stop it! Don't do this! You're going to ruin everything!" Layla's voice came from every direction. It penetrated my head and drove deep into my mind. She had no right to be there.

I shot her a silencing glare. Her mouth sealed shut as she tried to scrape the spell off her lips with her fingernails. She writhed back and forth, moaning within, but she couldn't get a single word out.

With Layla finally silenced, I turned my sights on Walker and stalked toward him. I cut through the center of the balloon wreckage, no longer edging around it. The nylon caught on my foot, and I knocked several benches over trying to free myself. With a single swipe of my paw, the remaining pieces of the basket flew through the air. Layla ducked as the debris narrowly missed her.

Walker startled and tripped, falling backward. He never took his eyes off me. They were the size of saucers and gleamed with adrenaline and terror. He hadn't blinked once since I'd given in to my power. I was only vaguely aware that I had morphed into some ungodly figure, because I could only focus on one thing at a time. And right now, it was him.

He crab-walked backward as I inched toward him. I was done being weak. I was done hiding my true self. My *twisted* mind. My feelings for him. I knew what I wanted, and I wasn't afraid to take it. I was a predator with a one-track mind. I licked my lips in anticipation of my marked prey. All I felt were teeth, long and serrated, as my tongue slinked over the wet bone.

Layla let out a muffled scream, breaking my focus. A clap of thunder rumbled in the remote forest, and with a silencing glare, I drew a lightning bolt down upon her. I used the storm we had both created to end her. She lit up in a magnificent blue light. Her eyes filled with fright as she turned to a fine black smoke. A patch of singed grass smoldered where she'd once stood, and tiny golden embers fought for survival against the rain.

As the thunder waned, so did my blood lust. I stared at the patch of wet, black grass as I slowly came back to myself. Layers of greed sloughed off me, and color seeped back into my vision. I sucked in a sharp breath. My power was greater than I'd realized.

Walker was on the ground, confused and afraid. I'd never intended to harm him. Either of them. What had I done? This wasn't who I wanted to be. I scanned the deserted grounds. If Layla wore the mysterious red cloak, then she couldn't be the wolf. And possibly, wasn't my enemy either. My creepy neighbor certainly hadn't been the wolf. Neither was Mason . . .

I caught the reflection of a hairy monstrosity in what was left of a mirror hanging from a collapsed jewelry booth. Two yellow eyes peered back at me. Scrutinizing me. *I was the malicious wolf.*

I was the killer we'd been hunting for the past month. I had embodied the very fear I'd felt all summer long. I was angry, jealous, greedy, and so very powerful. I was dangerous. And the only thing I wanted was for Walker to want me as badly as I did him. I wanted to be loved.

I couldn't stop what I'd set in motion, because only half of me wanted to. The better half of me wanted to save Walker from myself. But the darker half wanted to devour him. My claws sharpened and my fangs grew like blades against what little will I had to control myself.

"You should leave!" I somehow managed to heed a warning. There were two sides of me now, and I didn't know which was more powerful.

He scampered backward. The terrified look in his eyes made me sad.

"You should run!" I hissed, still stalking toward him.

He uttered something inaudible, and I kneeled down, grabbing his shirt at the collar. My eyes glowered into his like I was hypnotized. I lifted him with ease, my strength immense. His feet dangled six feet from the ground. He squirmed, fighting me every step of the way as I pulled him in for a deep, ferocious kiss.

My mouth claimed his as my heart hammered in my

chest. My fangs were deadly, and my strength was unmatchable. I gave in to the pure instinct to take what I wanted, and I had all the power in the world to do it. I kissed him ravenously. My tongue exploring every inch of his mouth as I tasted him for the first time.

I pulled away, breathless. A small voice screamed inside my head, just like Layla had. *You're going to ruin everything!*

I felt my sight narrow, and I was shocked to see my wolf's paw was made of human flesh. We were both on the ground. At some point during our kiss, I had reverted to my natural size and form. Though I didn't think I'd ever be completely normal again. I knew the wolf's blood still coursed through my veins, because the anger and strength remained.

Walker's eyes were terrified, and the wound across his eyebrow was gaping. The blood was diluted from the rain, and a sea of red ran down half his face. His dark, wet hair was plastered to his forehead and cheeks, and his golden eyes popped like the fierce summer sun.

Kissing me had hurt him, and I knew why. It wasn't because of my ferocious fangs, but because he loved both of us at the same time. He knew being with me hurt Layla and vice versa.

"Go! Run!" I blurted out. Fighting my own drive and now-twisted genetics.

Walker turned, and I let go of his collar. He got several

strides away but then stopped unexpectedly. Thunder cracked ahead and rumbled the ground. It felt like the world might split in two, and I was standing on the fault line.

I closed my eyes and tilted my head up to the heavens and the angry storm. I begged for forgiveness. Though I wasn't sure who from. The rain washed over my face, and I felt the wolf's anger disperse through my fingertips. I opened my eyes to see black smoke emanating from my hands and pluming up around me in a massive dark cloud.

I was relieved to see it go. No matter how badly I wanted Walker, I never wanted to be filled with that poison again. And it scared me that, deep in my bones, a part of me liked it. I didn't know who that girl was. But I'd been fighting her all summer long. The strength of the wolf drained out of me, and the fire in my belly dissipated. Watching Walker leave was heartbreaking, but knowing I'd hurt him was even worse.

He turned to face me, as if reconsidering, and then slowly he took a step closer.

"Walker, don't come any closer!" I held my hand out in warning.

He took another step. His face half bloodied and etched with sorrow. Still, there was something else. Curiosity? Trust?

"I can't control myself! I'm a beast! A monster!" I spat into the rain.

He suddenly closed the distance between us and crashed into me. His hands tangled in the back of my wet hair as his lips met mine. He kissed me so deeply and passionately my heart melted into a puddle at his feet, and I could have sworn it sent us floating into the air.

The kiss was everything I'd wanted our first to be and more. It felt like the death of me and the birth of something stronger. Something better. Something addicting.

His mouth was warm on mine, erasing the chill from the rain. His eyes were a blaze of golden amber and danced like flames of a fire. They were set deep with desire and framed with crimson blood. He smiled mischievously, a look I'd never seen on him before. He wiped the blood from his mouth with the backside of his hand.

"We're more alike than you realize."

"What?" *I didn't understand.* I'd been through a lot in the last hour, and the pieces weren't adding up.

"You didn't think you were the only one fighting our draw, did you?" he asked.

"What do you mean?" I touched my mouth and stared at the diluted red rain on my fingers.

"Wilde, I've wanted you from the moment I first saw you. But it wasn't right. *This* isn't right."

"You have?" All this time, I'd tortured myself? And for what? *What was I missing?*

"You! Don't! Belong! Here!" His shout was as clear as day in the cascading thunderstorm.

"Then why did you kiss me like that?" I snapped back. The taste of copper spread across my tongue.

"You started it!" He flailed his arms in the air.

"I was taken over by a wild beast! I grew ten feet tall! I couldn't stop that thing, even if I wanted to!" My voice was shrill.

"Did you want to?" he asked.

I opened my mouth but couldn't make the words come out.

"You didn't want to stop the animal inside. And *I* didn't want to stop *this* . . . Wilde. I've been fighting my feelings for you for a long time. I've tried to do what's best for you. But when you kissed me like that, I couldn't see straight! And I lost the strength to fight it. I want what's best for you, but it's *so* hard when you're standing right in front of me looking like that."

He motioned to my body, and I glanced down. I was drenched in rain and covered in blood. Long scrapes covered my legs, and my shorts were ripped, leaving the front pocket dangling by threads. I didn't understand.

"I haven't felt this alive in a very long time. You do something to me, and I think I need you—more than you need me." His eyes lowered to my lips, and he sucked in a shuddering breath.

"Then let's stop fighting each other. Let's stop pretending. We can have it all. We have the power to create it and forever to build it."

"But it's so wrong . . ."

"I'm okay with that . . . if you are?" I could hear the thread of hope in my voice.

He stared into my eyes, weighing his thoughts for what seemed like an eternity. My heart fluttered in my chest as he finally leaned down and kissed me with all the urgency in the world. As if time was slipping by and this was all we had left. Our worlds couldn't be further apart, and yet, somehow, our souls fought to be next to one another. I was going to stay here forever. And I knew now, undeniably, I belonged here.

But as I held Walker tight, kissing him like my life depended on it, I couldn't help but see the bright lights of the Ferris wheel spinning in my mind's eye. Images of the red door screamed for my attention. They were the visions I had when I'd drowned the first night in Baylor, and they were still haunting me.

I'd had the power to silence Layla, but I knew she wasn't gone forever. If I wanted to finally be rid of her in my new life, I'd have to listen to the wise words of my gran. Find the girl, and help her. I needed to help her cross over, and I needed to sever my ties to the realm I once knew and loved. And, somehow, I had to save my friends from the darkness that sometimes crept into my mind and distorted my reality, placing them in unspeakable danger. I had only weeks left to do it. Maybe less.

Now that I knew which side Walker was on, I was

ready to fight for my place at his side. The haunting Ferris wheel in my visions told me the battle would find me at the Summerfield State Fair. It was going to be a knockdown, drag-out fight, and I was nearly ready. Now that I wasn't afraid of losing Walker, I had no reason to shy away, shrink, or cower.

I was ready to get what I wanted, and there was a monster inside me that knew just how to get it. All I had to do . . . was give in to the poison.

THANK YOU

Thank you for taking the time to read Haunted Waters.

Please take a moment to write a review. It's _so_ important for a book to have social proof, and I'd love your help getting this series out there.

Do you want to know how the series ends? Read **Beautiful Poison.**

For more information, subscribe here:
https://www.subscribepage.com/redenbooks

Xoxo,
Laura

ABOUT THE AUTHOR

Laura C. Reden is an emerging paranormal and fantasy author.

Overcoming the struggles of dyslexia, Laura found that creative passion and hard work triumphs over her disadvantage.

Laura is a Southern Californian native, wife, and mother of two daughters. Her pastimes include video production, pottery, and horseback riding. While she received an education in social and behavioral science, she currently works as the chief financial officer for her family-owned law firm in San Diego.

If you are interested in staying updated on new releases, subscribe to my monthly email list. It's short and sweet with opportunities to help name characters, get advanced review copies, and even have your pet featured in upcoming scenes.

https://www.subscribepage.com/redenbooks

Xoxo,

Laura

bookbub.com/authors/laura-c-reden

amazon.com/kindle-dbs/entity/author/B08L1KH3LM

ALSO BY

YOU'VE HEARD THE TERM «OLD SOUL» BEFORE,
BUT WHAT IF SOME SOULS NEVER REALLY DIE?

THE TETHERED SOUL SERIES

FOLLOW THE TRAGIC TALE OF A DYING GIRL,
AND BOY WITH AN IMMORTAL SOUL.

LAURA C. REDEN

DREAMS ARE FICKLE, EMOTIONS ARE BOLD.

THE
PHANTOM SERIES

CAUGHT BETWEEN WORLDS,
KINSLEY WILDE CAN SEE THE DEAD,
MANIFEST HER DREAMS, AND CONJURE HER FEARS.

NOTES FOR BOOK CLUB:

NOTES FOR BOOK CLUB:

www.ingramcontent.com/pod-product-compliance
Lightning Source LLC
Chambersburg PA
CBHW061042190726
48286CB00006B/1567